HERE
I STAND

Other books endorsed by
Amnesty International UK

Max
by Sarah Cohen-Scali

The River and the Book
by Alison Croggon

Daughter of the Wind
Under the Persimmon Tree
Under the Same Stars
by Suzanne Fisher Staples

Buffalo Soldier
by Tanya Landman

The Extra
by Kathryn Lasky

War Brothers: A Graphic Novel
by Sharon McKay and Daniel Lafrance

The World Beneath
by Janice Warman

Sold
by Patricia McCormick

EXPLOITATION

FREEDOMS

IDENTITY

GENDER

BULLYING

TRAFFICKING

RACE

RIGHTS

PROTEST

RTIES

HERE
I STAND

edited by Amnesty International UK

**WALKER
BOOKS**

This collection first published 2016 by Walker Books Ltd
87 Vauxhall Walk, London SE11 5HJ

2 4 6 8 10 9 7 5 3

Compilation © 2016 Amnesty International UK
"Harmless Joe" © 2016 Tony Birch; "Harvester Road" © 2016 John Boyne
"Stay Home" © 2016 Sita Brahmachari; "Barley Wine" © 2016 Kevin Brooks
"Deeds Not Words" © 2016 Bryan Talbot, Mary Talbot, Kate Charlesworth
"Sludge" © 2016 Sarah Crossan; "I Believe…" © 2015 Neil Gaiman, Chris Riddell
"A Suicide Bomber Sits in the Library" © 2016 Jack Gantos
"Redemption" © 2016 Ryan Gattis; "The Invention of Peanut Butter (And Why It
Caused Problems)" © 2016 Matt Haig; "Bystander" © 2016 Frances Hardinge
"Glasgow Snow", "Push the Week", "Constant" © 2015 Jackie Kay
"What I Remember About Her" © 2016 A.L. Kennedy; "Love Is a Word, Not a
Sentence" © 2016 Liz Kessler; "School of Life" © 2016 Elizabeth Laird
"Darling", "Black/White" © 2016 Amy Leon; "When the Corridors
Echo" © 2016 Sabrina Mahfouz; "Speaking Out for Freedom" © 2016 Chelsea Manning
"Dulce et Decorum Est" © 2016 Chibundu Onuzo; "The Colour of
Humanity" © 2016 Bali Rai; "The Importance of Screams" © 2016 Christie Watson
"Robot Killers" © 2016 Tim Wynne-Jones
Cover art and interior typography © 2016 Chris Riddell

The right of the above listed to be identified as authors of this work has
been asserted by them in accordance with the Copyright, Designs and Patents Act 1988

This book has been typeset in Bembo

Printed and bound in Great Britain by Clays Ltd, St Ives plc

British Library Cataloguing in Publication Data:
a catalogue record for this book is available from the British Library

ISBN 978-1-4063-5838-4 (hardback)
ISBN 978-1-4063-7483-4 (trade paperback)

www.walker.co.uk

CONTENTS

Join the conversation online:

#HereIStand
@AmnestyUK
@WalkerBooksUK

INTRODUCTION

As the vastly outnumbered Scottish forces looked out over the looming ranks of the English army on a September morning in 1297, William Wallace, the Scottish knight and leader, roared: *They may take our lives, but they will never take our freedom!*

In that moment, Wallace – or rather Mel Gibson playing Wallace in the screen version *Braveheart* – was tapping into the deep truth that the freedoms we enjoy today are worth dying for; and have in fact been paid for, in blood, many times over.

Today our freedoms and liberties include the right to vote for our leaders, the prohibition on the use of torture, the right not to be arbitrarily detained, the right to speak freely and the right to protest.

Freedoms do not spontaneously arrive, and they are not handed to citizens by benevolent rulers. Our freedoms in the UK were gained through a long and often bloody history of slowly establishing limits on the powers of mighty monarchs and tyrannical rulers.

The history of Western freedoms has many important milestones, including King John signing Magna Carta in 1215; the Bill of Rights in 1689; the US Bill of Rights in 1791; the 1833 Slavery Abolition Act; the 1948 Universal Declaration of Human Rights, to name but a few. Campaigns, demonstrations, protests and legal battles have resulted in many people now being able to vote in their leaders, enjoy greater protections at work and have the right not to be discriminated against.

But we need to be ever vigilant, because the freedoms that have been hard won for us can be lost in a moment by the stroke of a politician's pen — as they were in the UK during the World Wars, when the army was given control over almost every aspect of civilian life and many injustices were suffered by ordinary people.

The greatest threats to liberty today come not from terrorism but from the fear of terrorism and our politicians' misguided quest for absolute security. Unlike Wallace, the cry of the modern government at the first whiff of a terrorist threat is: *They can take our freedoms, but they cannot take our lives.*

We should not go along with governments' counter-terrorism strategies that attempt to criminalize thought, limit free speech, restrict access to courts, ban protests and put society under continuous CCTV and internet surveillance. We must all be jealous guardians of our freedoms, and appreciate that many of the liberties that we enjoy in the West are still being fought for by citizens in other parts of the world who are ruled by dictators and tyrannical regimes.

To protect our freedoms and ensure that they are not diluted or removed, we need to:

- CARE about rights and freedoms, want them for society and speak up for them when they are under attack;
- QUESTION politicians and leaders when they say it is necessary to remove freedoms to create a safer society: ask them where their actions will lead;
- ACT – there are many small actions we can all take to safeguard our freedoms: write letters (see page 313), speak out against injustice, vote, join campaigns and attend demonstrations.

Every gain for human rights and those freedoms we enjoy began with one or two people recognizing that something was worth fighting for, and joining with other like-minded people to make a difference. I hope you will all be inspired to do the same.

Jules Carey, Partner, Bindmans LLP

HARVESTER ROAD
John Boyne

Damien, age 8

I still miss my dad. I don't remember him very well because
I was only four when he got cancer and died. Mum said
that he hadn't been feeling well so he went in for tests but
by then it was already too late and he was gone within a
few weeks. Mark says that I'm the only one who can stop
Mum from getting cancer and dying too. So far, I must be
doing a good job because she's really healthy and last week
she won a badminton tournament and took home a trophy
that she put on the mantelpiece next to my music prizes.
I can tell she's really proud of it. She doesn't know that if

it weren't for me, she wouldn't have won anything. She probably wouldn't even be alive.

I used to call Mark "Dr Richardson", but when he moved into our house on Harvester Road he said that I should call him Mark. After he and Mum got married he asked me if I wanted to call him Dad, but I said no and he seemed a bit disappointed. He wasn't trying to take my real dad's place, he told me, no one could ever do that, but I should know that he would always be there for me just like my real dad would have been if he hadn't got cancer and died.

On Tuesdays and Thursdays Mum plays badminton and then she goes for a drink with the girls and doesn't get home till I'm asleep. She calls it her Me Time. When I go up to bed, Mark comes with me. First he reads me a story and then we play the game that stops Mum getting cancer and dying.

I wish I'd known Mark when I was four because then we could have started playing it earlier and maybe Dad wouldn't have got cancer and died. He was the one who explained to me the way medicine works and told me that I couldn't tell anyone or it wouldn't work and then Mum would get cancer and die and it would just be him and me, and I didn't want that to happen.

Months ago, Mum started to get sick and I asked Mark if we should play the game more often, but he said no, twice a week was enough. Mum was throwing up every morning and I got really worried. After a few months, though, she stopped getting sick and got fat instead and last week my baby brother was born. Mark said we should call him Edward after my real dad, and Mum cried and said that was the most thoughtful thing she had ever heard in her life and she was so lucky to have found a man like him, a second chance of happiness when lots of people don't even get one. All babies look the same to me but Mark says that Edward is something special and will be very handsome one day. Just give him a few years, he tells me, just give him till he's your age, Damien, and you'll see how beautiful he is.

Rachel, age 14

Julia Sheers used to be my best friend but she's not any more. I hate her: she smells and she's got spots. She hates me too because I'm prettier than her and she knows it. She used to like Steven Hailey and she sent him a note in class one day saying, *Do you like me?* with two boxes underneath that said *Yes* and *No*. It was so embarrassing. Steven sent it back with a third box saying, *I'm out of your league,* and put a big *X* inside it. I took a photo of the note and sent it to Donna Wilton, who I really want to be friends with because she's the prettiest girl in our class. When I showed it to Justin, he said that was mean and I felt a bit ashamed of myself. I didn't want him to stop liking me so I deleted the photo and told him that I was going to punch Steven in the face for what he'd done but Justin said that violence doesn't solve anything and I should just let things be.

I knew that I was in love with Justin on the first day of Mrs Richardson's maternity leave, when he came in and told us that he would be our substitute teacher for the rest of the year. He was wearing blue jeans, a white shirt and a really cool tie that he kept loosened in front of an open collar. He had sexy stubble and glasses but he only put them on when he was reading. When he asked my name I could tell that he liked me. And, *no*, it's not some silly schoolgirl crush, *actually*, because he's *told* me that he loves me and that we're going to spend the rest of our lives together and buy a house and go to concerts and have dinner parties where our friends come over and we try out recipes from Jamie Oliver's books.

Every time we do it, Justin cries afterwards and says that we can't do it ever again but then he texts me the next day and asks if I want to come over after choir practice, which actually just proves how much he loves me. When we first did it, it really hurt and it still does sometimes because he goes so quickly. It's like he just wants to get it over with but I've read in magazines that if you do it slowly it's even better. I've told him this but he says that we'll do it slowly in a few years' time when I'm out of school and we can tell people that we're in love and going to live together for the rest of our lives. Until then I'm supposed to keep *shtum*, which is a word from when he was my age that means *quiet*.

We've seen the house that we want to live in, too. It's on Harvester Road, a few doors down from where Mrs Richardson lives. It has three bedrooms and a granny flat that Justin says he could use as his studio because he's really artistic actually. The people who live there need to just sell it and move to a village somewhere with a pub and a garden centre like those posh twats you always see on *Relocation, Relocation*.

Melissa, age 26

I don't care what anyone says; I know for a fact that the boys *love* it. It's not like I force them to do anything they don't want to do, after all. They're the ones who look like they'll explode if I don't let them. They're so sweet, actually, and so grateful. I honestly think that I'm doing a really kind thing. Years from now, when they're grown up and having proper adult relationships, they'll think of me and probably want to thank me.

Anyway, it's not like I do it that often. Four times a year at most, when my company holds its quarterly sales conference in London. I stay in a hotel and make sure to give myself a free day after work is over to do a bit of shopping and have some time away from James. I love James, of course I do, but everyone needs a little space, don't they? And then, once I've had a little drink or two, I go into one of the chat rooms and see who's around.

Eric was the first but he was a little older than I usually go for. He was sixteen, and when he turned his webcam on he reminded me a little of a young Adam Sandler. Kind of goofy looking but kind of cute too. He was only two tube stops away, Harvester Road, and he was in my room in less than thirty minutes. I learnt a lesson after that, though. It was obvious that it wasn't his first time, and that's not what I'm into. I prefer it when the boy is completely innocent. Even a little frightened.

So the second time, the boy – I think his name was Jack – was fourteen. He was incredibly nervous but when I said he could leave if he wanted, he shook his head and looked so confused that it was totally adorable and I told him that we would take things very slow. Afterwards he asked, could we meet again? And I didn't want to disappoint him so I gave him my phone number. Well, it wasn't my real number, of course, just a set of random digits that I scribbled on a piece of hotel stationery, but he seemed pleased.

Since then I've probably met about fifteen to twenty boys. All types: I don't discriminate. Black, white, tall, short. Spots, no spots. Sometimes I take pity on some fat kid and let him come over so he'll have a story to tell his friends, even though there's no chance that they'll believe him. One boy tried to take a photo once, for proof, but I made him delete it. I thought that was incredibly disrespectful of him.

I've stopped using my preferred hotel, though, because a maid walked in on me one time and went pale before running out again. Then I got a call from the manager asking me to leave. Now I always put the *Do Not Disturb* sign on and latch the door so there can be no surprises. The new hotel is nice but the towels in the other one were fluffier. Still, you can't have everything.

Anyway, I don't care what anyone says. There's nothing wrong with it, there's nothing dirty about it and no boy has ever left my room without a smile on his face. You could say that I'm providing a public service. Not that anyone will ever find out. I wouldn't let that happen. I'm too careful. But I'm a good person, really I am.

Justin, age 34

I didn't want to be a teacher. I wanted to be an actor. I applied to RADA when I left school but I failed my audition. Then I tried my hand at playwriting but I could never get one finished. Then I thought about novels but it was even harder to get one of those started. I just feel that inside me, at my core, I'm an artist, you know? A creative person. Perhaps I'm still too young and I simply haven't found my voice yet. I mean, I'm only thirty-four. Practically still in my twenties.

Anyway, I know one thing for sure: I'm never going to be a real teacher, only a substitute. That way I can leave a place pretty quickly when whoever I'm replacing comes back. School isn't like it was when I was a boy. The kids all know so much and they seem to despise me, which doesn't make any sense as I'm not that much older than they are. The boys try to act hard by taking the piss out of me, but the girls are worse, with all their flirting. Don't take this the wrong way, but even at fourteen you can tell whether or not a girl is going to be hot in the future. Julia, for example: no. Rachel: absolutely. Carla: no. Donna: well, she already is.

Of course the thing about Donna is that she's not really fourteen at all. I mean, yes, she's fourteen in terms of her *actual* age, but at heart she's at least nineteen or twenty. Which is only a few years younger than me. A woman trapped in a child's body. She's so knowing and always dresses to impress. I can see her working in a solicitor's office in the future, maybe. Or managing a commercial radio station. Something like that.

Rachel was a mistake that should never have happened. Samantha and Karen: well, if I could go back in time, no, I wouldn't have asked them, though they seemed pleased to be chosen. But Donna? Donna is something different. The truth is *she* seduced *me*, not the other way around. I know that sounds crazy, a kid that age seducing a grown man, but it's what happened. I actually had no say in the matter, none at all. If I told you the things she said to me you would absolutely agree that no healthy man could have said no to her. It's her fault, when you think of it, although I'm not really keen on apportioning blame. I wonder what her family background is like? She must have had a troubled childhood. Well, maybe I've taken her out of herself a bit. I hope so. She's a nice kid really. But such a *flirt*!

Joseph, age 92

There's not many of us left alive who remember the Blitz. Historians write about it and I've seen it portrayed in films but they never get it right. They don't understand how frightening it was, the terror that would descend on us every evening when the sun went down and we knew it wouldn't be long before the sirens sounded, the skies were full of Luftwaffe bombers and it was a race to the bomb shelters. I had a rotten time of it because I was nineteen and everyone looked at me as if to say, *What's the matter with you, Sunshine? Why aren't you out there doing your bit like the rest of them?* Sometimes I'd explain about my heart condition but I could see they didn't believe me and thought I was a coward. I wished I had an ailment that was more obvious: a patch on one eye or a set of crutches.

It was dark down there in the tunnels and people got

lost easily. Children became separated from their parents. I tried to help them. I'd take hold of one, a little girl usually, and tell her there was nothing to worry about. I'd wrap my arms around her when the lights went out and the bombs fell over Eastman Street and Harvester Road and none of us knew whether or not our houses would still be standing when we got out again. *If* we got out again. There was always the chance that the roof of the shelter would cave in and crush us all.

The little girls liked it when I held them. I know they did, because they always stopped crying and snuggled in like kittens. They couldn't see me in the darkness and I thought I was doing the right thing, holding them close like that. But the other things I did, when I look back I can see that perhaps they weren't quite right. And if any of those little girls were here beside me now perhaps I'd even apologize to them. But they've probably forgotten all about it anyway, so no harm done. Children are very resilient; everyone says so. If they think of me at all, they might think fondly of the man who took good care of them when they were frightened.

Sometimes when I watch the television news and see a woman in her seventies, someone in the public eye like a politician or an actress, I look at her and wonder where she grew up and does she remember the Blitz and, if she does, can she recall the underground bunkers and the man who took care of her and showed her a little tenderness when she most needed it? And then I think, well look at her now! She's made a real go of her life. Which sets my mind at ease because then I know that I didn't do any harm, not really.

Stephen, age 32

Today was a good day. Some of the kids, when they first start to talk, are embarrassed or ashamed or frightened. They're worried what their friends will think of them, if people will blame them or say they're just making it up. But Damien? I've never met a fourteen-year-old like him. Smart. Brave. And angry too, of course, but able to control that anger. Able to use it.

He wasn't intimidated by the courtroom, the press gallery or the judge. When the defence counsel accused him of being a liar, he looked her right in the eye and said, "Of course I'm a liar. I'm a teenager. I tell lies every day to get me out of trouble or detention or to rent an 18 game. But I'm not lying about this. Every word I've said here today is true. Every single one. You can twist them; you can call me names; you can choose to believe me or not. It's up to you. But I'm telling the truth."

When he talked about his little brother, I knew that we were going to get a conviction. "Edward is really annoying most of the time," he said. "He comes into my room without knocking. He steals my Xbox. He jumps on top of me on a Saturday morning when I'm trying to sleep. He drives me nuts. But that night, when I saw Mark looking at him the way he had looked at me when he first moved in, I knew I had to say something. Now that it's come out, all the lads in my year are calling me gay. They can call me whatever they want: I don't care. So can you. But this is what happened. And it will happen to Edward too if you don't stop him."

Moments like this make my job worthwhile. My mates ask me, how can I do it? Does it not affect me? And of course it does. Sometimes when I go down the pub after a case has gone badly, it's all I can do not to scream out loud in frustration. But when Damien stood tall in the witness box and didn't flinch as he recounted every detail, I looked across at Dr Richardson, saw the complete lack of emotion on his face and knew that I was doing something worthwhile. The man just didn't care. Unlike that teacher we caught last year who blamed it all on the girls in his class. That guy broke down and cried like a baby when they sentenced him and I felt even more disgusted by him than I had before.

Anyway, the case is closed. And it's an early night for me. But I won't forget Damien in a hurry. That boy is going to do something important with his life: I can just tell.

What am I talking about? He already has.

DULCE ET DECORUM EST

Chibundu Onuzo

"Good morning, Matthew. I'm Derebo Pepple and I'll be representing you in court."

"No disrespect, miss, but aren't you a bit young? I want a real lawyer, fam. Man ain't going to prison cos of no rookie."

I stared through the glass at the juvenile delinquent – black, of course, as most of the young men I represent are. The statistics do not lie. These brown males, whether bearded or shaven, dreadlocked or clean cut, tattooed or unblemished, are more likely to end up in prison than their white counterparts. In law school I thought these were the cases I would gain most satisfaction from. I, Derebo

Pepple, would prise my clients from the jaws of a criminal justice system trained to snap shut on dark ankles, to hold fast and never let go.

"Right," I said. I opened up Matthew Adebọwale's file. "Let's get started before we're called up."

"Derebo? Are you, like, African?"

"I'm Nigerian," I said.

"Me too. I'm British, yeah, but I identify with my roots. Adebọwale is a Yoruba name. It means 'the crown has entered'. So I'm, like, a prince. That's what they call me in the south east: Prince."

"You've been charged with aggravated burglary. That means burglary committed with firearms."

"Lies, man."

"If you decide to plead not guilty, you will need a convincing explanation for why you and three other men were parked outside a house in Lewisham that had just been burgled, with two guns between the four of you."

"I don't know about no guns or no burglary. They're my mates, yeah. I just got in the car ten minutes before the police stopped us. They were giving me a lift home."

"Plausible enough, but I must warn you that the other men involved might try to give a similar explanation."

"Why is it me you don't believe? Fuck this."

My client was thickset, built like a man but with round cheeks and a hairless chin spotted with blackheads. He was only fourteen. No previous convictions but a warning for antisocial behaviour. I stared at him as my mother had stared at me countless times, eyelids rigid, corneas drying, a look that could still arrest me in my tracks at thirty.

"I do not appreciate your language," I said, finally.

"I'm sorry, miss."

"As I was saying, you're a minor with a reasonably clean record. The judge is very likely to be lenient. The victim has already stated that there were four men. Four balaclavas were found in the car. The victim's diamond engagement ring was in the glove compartment."

"I don't know what everyone else is going to say," he said, looking down.

I had seen this unswerving loyalty to the gang before: out of fear or love or the sheer bloody-mindedness of teenage boys. They run in packs, with hierarchies and structures that show a perverse love of order, a shadow army of adolescents running amuck on the streets of London.

"This isn't about anyone but you, Matthew. The others in the car were over eighteen. They're adults, facing adult prison, and they're not my clients. You need to finish school and get your GCSEs and move on with your life."

The warder rapped on the door to signal that it was time. This would be Matthew's first appearance at the magistrate's court. He would be formally charged and the case transferred to the Crown Court, which dealt with more serious crimes.

We met in the hallway. His growth spurt must have

been recent. He was ungainly in his movements, like a foal testing out its legs. He smiled shyly at me.

"Here we go, miss."

We walked into the courtroom. Dark wood panelling ran up the walls, solid, patrician beams that gleamed with decades of polish. A coat of arms, etched in gold leaf, hung above the magistrate's head: lion rampant, unicorn rearing, motto in a dead language that a privileged few could understand.

"That's my mum," he whispered to me.

Matthew's mother was seated in the front row. Her hair was hidden under a scarf so tatty it might as well have been a hairnet. Her body was middle-aged – bulging stomach, hefty arms, neck as thick as a tyre – but her face was still beautiful, all smooth angles and straight planes. She waved at her son and he waved back. There was no one beside her.

Matthew's alleged accomplices were also in court, dressed in identikit Nike trainers, sagging jeans and oversized jumpers. It was the first time they had seen Matthew since their arrest. They flashed him a hand signal: thumb and index finger pressed together, the remaining digits raised stiff and straight. Matthew returned the salute.

The magistrate, Quentin Fowler, was an experienced hand. I had stood many times before him with his head of thick silver hair, centre parted and combed in sweeping eaves to his ears. He spoke in a clear Etonian accent that matched his Old Etonian striped tie. The charge was read out and a date fixed for the first Crown Court hearing. My bail application was denied on the grounds that Matthew's home address was unsuitable.

"In the light of Mr Adebọwale's possible involvement with gangs in the area, it would be unwise to permit a return to his home," Quentin concluded.

"I'm sorry we couldn't get bail," I said to Matthew as the warder came to take him back to prison.

"Not your fault, miss. My mum don't know anybody outside my postcode and if I go home, I might get in trouble."

"Let's be positive. Think about what I said. The best thing to do is tell the truth. I'll see you soon."

"Thanks, miss."

I wanted Matthew to get as light a sentence as possible. It was the first verdict I had cared about in months. It still surprised me how much I disliked the majority of my clients. When they had been dark brown statistics read out of textbooks, I had raged at the injustice of their incarceration, the harshness of their sentencing, the institutional bias that rose like bile when a judge saw a black man in the dock.

But once these statistics were transformed into flesh-and-blood criminals who stabbed and raped and stole, I discovered how shallow my empathy was. In recent years, I had become as much a profiler as the Metropolitan Police.

The sight of a group of black teenagers was enough to alter my behaviour as I travelled around the capital. I changed carriage; I crossed the street; I never sat upstairs on the bus.

Still, I liked Matthew. He had called me *miss*.

I caught the 91 to my Islington home, where I knew my husband would be waiting. Ladi was a second-generation Nigerian, UCL graduate and one of the youngest consultant gynaecologists at Guy's and St Thomas' Hospital. His father was dead, his mother a cleaner and he had grown up on a council estate famous for gang violence. I had been attracted to the determination that encompassed his studies, his career and me. It had been flattering to be so single-mindedly wanted by someone who had never taken no for an answer. I was what Ladi Ogusanwo wanted and I was what he got.

"I'm home," I announced as I walked into the hallway.

"Was it a murder?"

"Not yet. Still hoping."

We kissed – a sterile, dry-lipped peck – before he hurried back to the kitchen. Ladi rarely let me cook. He associated Nigerian food with the cramped council flat he had grown up in, food that left smells in your hair and your clothes and on your breath, announcing your African origins to the world.

"What are we having tonight?" I asked.

"Tranche of turbot with bearnaise sauce."

Ladi knew which vegetables should go with which cut of lamb, which fish went with which sauce, which wines were fruity and which were dry, which parts of a scallop should be eaten and which should be thrown in the bin.

"So, how was your day?" Ladi asked, as we sat opposite each other at our empty dining table. He was not a handsome man – his face was too square and his eyes too closely set together – but many of the other girls at our university had wanted him. He was so obviously "going somewhere" with his life.

"It was fine," I said. "I'm representing a fourteen-year-old charged with aggravated assault. It's scary when they're that young. I don't want to mess up anybody's life because I gave a poor defence."

"You're not the one who'll mess up his life. He messed up by running with the wrong crowd," Ladi stated as he spooned some buttered potatoes onto his plate.

"You're too hard," I said.

"And you're too soft. I grew up with boys like this. While I was washing cars for a bit of extra change, they were selling drugs, walking around like they owned the place. And now, half of them are probably in jail, still walking around like they own the place."

There was an unattractive smugness that surfaced any time my husband and I spoke of my clients. Usually at this point, I would change topic. But Matthew's face as I had last seen it, eyes puffy with unshed tears, rose before me.

"Even though your mum was a single parent, she pushed you. She was very strict," I reminded him.

"You think these boys didn't have strict mums? Strict teachers, strict uncles, everybody telling them the right thing to do? They did, but they wouldn't listen. People have to learn to be responsible for their actions. They decided to sign up to a foolish postcode war. Child soldiers in Hackney threatening everyone with knives. They made their choices and I made mine."

"They're not soldiers. They're teenage boys. Easily influenced. Easily led astray."

"Poor little drug dealers. You can't understand, Debs. It's all too far from your childhood, innit?"

I hated this pointed use of slang he had long erased from his speech. He placed his hand on mine but I withdrew it. It had seemed an affectionate running joke at first, my bourgeois Nigerian childhood compared with his school-of-hard-knocks life in east London. I don't know how I missed the resentment that underlay the teasing.

Yet I knew how he loved to tell his colleagues that his father-in-law was a big man in Africa. That his wife had gone to Roedean to do her A-levels, a finishing school for an African princess. Would he have married me if I hadn't fitted into his ideas of advancement? I had met his childhood sweetheart once, a woman in her thirties who still wore gel in her hair, the loose strands slicked to her forehead in sickening, glistening curls.

I stacked the crockery and took it to the kitchen: two serving bowls, two dinner plates, two side dishes and a pair of silver tongs, laid out for two people. Ladi did not think we could afford children yet. Private school was expensive.

I slid on yellow rubber washing-up gloves. Matthew would be in his cell now, alone for the first time in his life. His mother would be awake, somewhere in south-east London, wondering where she had gone wrong with her son.

"I'm sorry," Ladi said from the doorway of our kitchen. "I might have let things get a bit heated." He slipped his hands around my waist and pressed himself against my back. I wondered when I should tell him that I had come off the pill and was three months pregnant.

Matthew's plea hearing was two weeks away, and while he waited in the detention centre there was a sudden surge of violence through the capital. A sixteen-year-old boy was stabbed outside a JD Sports store in Oxford Street while a crowd of shoppers and tourists looked on, filming with their slim handheld smartphones. With his death, an invasion of yobs was launched, flowing up the tube escalators and spilling out into the streets of central London, staging their battles in once sacrosanct public spaces. The Royal Albert Hall, the National Theatre and the Barbican became the sites of conflicts that news commentators now scrambled to understand. North west versus south east. Kill City Massive vs Brick Lane Bloods. The barbarians were at the gates and no one could speak their language.

I was glad Matthew had not been granted bail. Had he been let out, he would most likely have been part of the uprising. When I next saw him, on the day of the trial, he was animated.

"Morning, miss."

"Morning, Matthew. Glad to see you looking so cheerful. You don't have to call me miss, you know. Derebo is fine."

"But you're old, miss. Not old like ancient, but I reckon you're the same age as my mum. She's thirty-two. She had me when she was bare young."

"So, have you decided what you'll be pleading today?"

"I spoke to my youth worker and my mum came in as well. I've decided to tell the truth."

"Which is?"

"I was there for the burglary. But, like, I didn't even do nothing. I just stood by the door looking out, but yeah, I was there. I don't know nothing about no guns though. I just turned up and the guns were there. I'm fourteen, man. This ain't America. Where am I going to get a gun?"

"Thank you, Matthew. I will write a statement with what you've just said, and if you read it over and agree, we'll both sign it. If you don't understand anything, please ask me."

I drafted his confession.

"*I, Matthew Adebọwale, was present at the burglary on 25*

July 2015. I had no prior knowledge of the guns used to carry out the robbery and affirm that they were not mine," he read out. "What's *affirm*, miss?"

"Swear."

"My mum doesn't like me to swear."

"It's more like a promise. A deep promise."

We both signed the piece of paper and I slid it into his file.

"So, what next?" he asked.

"You wait to be called."

"What do you think I'll get?"

"With your confession I'm hoping no more than four years, and it's likely you'll only have to serve two of those."

"Can you do exams in prison? Like GCSEs and stuff? Cos I want to take my GCSEs."

"Yes, you can. What's your favourite subject?" I asked him.

"I like English. We had this book, *Oliver Twist*. Bare fat book, yeah. I didn't read all of it. Went on SparkNotes cos that shit was too long. But I could relate to the story, you know. Like these poor young kids stealing cos, like, everybody got stuff but them. It hasn't changed, has it, miss?"

"No, it hasn't."

The warder came and rapped on the door. It was time.

"I'll see you inside court, Matthew."

It was a triumph of sorts. Two years in juvenile prison

would hopefully straighten Matthew out. It wasn't like adult prison, where the state had mostly given up on you, leaving you to fester for the length of your sentence before returning you to a life of crime. I walked through the courts looking for Sarah Hall, the prosecuting lawyer. She was young, already making a name for herself, not with the number of cases she'd won but because of her thick Geordie accent, which she flatly refused to refine.

"Sarah, I have a signed confession from my client," I said, finding her by the water cooler.

"This the aggravated burglary?"

"Yes. He was there but he knew nothing about the guns. He's only fourteen."

"Well, that'll make my life a lot easier. The other three are pleading not guilty. Can you feckin' believe it? They know absolutely nothing about a robbery. They all got into the car a few minutes before the police stopped them. Even the driver. Are you sure your client won't change his mind?"

"He can't. He doesn't know what the others are pleading. He hasn't seen them since their first appearance in court."

"Well, if I were you, I'd keep it that way. I'll see you inside."

My case was due to be heard in ten minutes. I didn't have enough time to eat the sandwich Ladi had prepared for me: venison, horseradish mayonnaise and rocket plucked from his windowsill garden that morning. The rocket would be wilted by the time the hearing was over. Another reason to bin the sandwich and go to KFC.

I stood by the court entrance with the other defence barristers waiting for our clients to arrive. Left to right: Priscilla Darlington (Benenden and Oxford), Claudius Coleridge (Harrow and Cambridge), Anish Thakur (St Paul's and Oxford) and me. We were dressed in our identikit uniforms, formless black robes, white starched cravats and ridiculous horsehair wigs that still made me feel like I was in a pantomime.

I wondered if I should have mentioned to the warder that Matthew should be kept separate from the other gang members. Even if it meant bringing him in just before the judge arrived. Sarah's words had troubled me. He couldn't change his mind. He wouldn't.

There he was, approaching the stairs with his gangly, ungainly motions. His foot on the first step, now on the second, like a toddler taking a climb. I had worried for nothing. I looked behind me and saw the other members of Matthew's gang also approaching the steps. How had I missed them? They began to ascend more swiftly than Matthew.

"Excuse me," I said. I hurried, my robes spreading like wings, my black heels clicking on the stone floor.

My hand had just touched the banister when they caught up with Matthew. The salutes were flashed. And then Matthew recoiled as if struck.

My case was over.

I turned back, walked into the courtroom and waited for Matthew to be brought in.

They placed him in the dock, a wooden box with high walls. His mother was already seated, better dressed this time in an ill-fitting grey suit that struggled to button over her bosom. Matthew beckoned to me.

"Miss. I need to speak to you, miss. They said I could speak to you quickly before it begins, miss."

I walked over to him.

"Yes, Matthew."

"I can't plead guilty, miss."

"What do you mean? You signed a confession saying you were guilty of burglary. You can't just change your mind."

"I can't plead guilty."

"Don't throw your life away. You could get up to twelve years. Think of your mother. Think of all the people believing in you. If you change your plea, I have to resign from this case."

"I don't want that, miss. But you and I both have to do what we have to do."

"You don't have to do this."

"I ain't no snitch."

"No, you're not. You're a fool."

"Aww that's harsh, miss." He smiled, the pimply smile of a teenager. "It's not so bad. I'll still take my GCSEs."

"Make sure you do. Goodbye, Matthew."

"Bye, miss. Thank you."

I handed my resignation to the clerk and walked out of the court, past the three senior gangsters, past Matthew's mother, who watched in confusion as her son's defence lawyer abandoned him. I made my way to the barristers' common room almost in tears. It was empty except for Alistair Cunnington, legs stretched out and crossed at the ankle, broadsheet covering his face. On paper, Alistair represented all the reasons to hate the bar: old, white, male, faintly aristocratic. But he was well liked, a lay preacher with a mild, kindly manner that invited confidences.

"Out so soon?" he asked, folding his paper.

"I had to resign. My client changed his plea after signing a confession."

"Oh dear, I haven't had one of those in years. Would you like to talk about it?"

And so I did, in a rambling rant, the words *stupid* and *honour* and *code* coming up repeatedly as I got angrier at Matthew and those three men who had ruined his life.

"Poor boy," Alistair said. "I suppose he thought he was being honourable. My gang, right or wrong. If he had been in the army, we'd have given him a medal for courage."

"You sound like my husband. He calls my clients child soldiers. Maybe he has a point."

"He does. To see them so young and so violent. It

brings to mind Liberia or Sierra Leone. Don't be so hard on yourself. You did your best. Shall we have lunch so I can properly commiserate?"

"That's very kind, Alistair. Thank you, but I think I'll just eat my sandwich and go home."

I bit into the mixed-grain bread that I loathed and the dry venison that I was indifferent to. The horseradish in the mayonnaise went straight to my nose and drew tears to my eyes. Ladi's sandwich gave me an excuse to cry.

"I was asked to write a story on the theme of child soldiers and I wanted to turn a familiar trope on its head. Many young people all over the world are coerced, pressured or manipulated into violence. The setting may change but the human effect remains the same." Chibundu Onuzo

GLASGOW SNOW
Jackie Kay

You were found in the snow in Glasgow
Outside the entrance to Central Station.
Your journey took you from an Ethiopian prison
To the forests in France where luck and chance
Showed you not all white men are like the men
In *Roots* – a film you watched once.
The people-smugglers didn't treat you like Kizzy
Or Kunta Kinte, brought you food and water by day,
Offered you shelter in a tent, and it was sanctuary.
And you breathed deep the forest air, freely.

But when you were sent here, Glasgow,
In the dead winter – below zero, no place to go,

You rode the buses to keep warm: *X4M, Toryglen,*
Castlemilk, Croftfoot, Carbrain, Easterhouse,
Moodiesburn, Red Road Flats, Springburn,
No public fund, no benefit, no home, no sanctum,
No haven, no safe port, no support,
No safety net, no sanctuary, no nothing.
Until a girl found you in the snow, frozen,
And took you under her wing, singing.

Oh … would that the Home Office show
The kindness of that stranger in the winter snow!
Would they grant you asylum, sanctum,
For your twenty-seventh birthday?
On March 8th, two thousand and thirteen,
You could become not another figure, sum, unseen,
Another woman sent home to danger, dumb, afraid,
At the mercy of strangers, no crib, no bed,
All worry: next meal, getting fed, fetching up dead.
And at last, this winter, you might lay down your sweet head.

THE INVENTION OF PEANUT BUTTER
(AND WHY IT CAUSED PROBLEMS)

Matt Haig

In the beginning everyone was happy.

There was only one village in the whole world as far as the villagers were concerned, and because there was only one village they didn't need to give it a big fancy name or anything, so they just called it *Village*.

Everyone in the village felt safe from outsiders because of where the village was located. There was a thick forest of jamba trees all around, and to the north there was a mountain. The village was hidden. Everyone felt free to be themselves without any fear.

Everyone cared for each other but didn't pry too much into other people's business. If people wanted to talk to people, they left their front doors open. It was a simple system. There was no crime; no robberies, no violence; and generally most people died in their sleep at a very good age. No one was the leader, because everybody made the big decisions together. No one was in the army, because there was no war. No one worried about death, because they saw that they were part of the whole, like a leaf on the tree, and if the tree still survived they didn't worry too much when leaves had to fall.

Everyone ate just pineapples and peanuts. But no one complained.

The economy was also very simple. People bought things with peanuts. People never worried about eating their currency because there were lots of peanut trees so there were always enough peanuts to go around.

People had no names at first. They were known simply for what they enjoyed. The Woman Who Swims in the Lake. The Boy Who Likes Frogs. The Man Who Likes the Smell of the Air Just After it Has Rained. And so on.

But after a while, when the sixty-sixth baby in the village was born, they – well, her parents – decided to give the baby a name.

The baby was a girl and the name they gave to the baby was Charlotte. After that, everybody gave their children names.

Then a boy was born. His name was Solomon.

But people called him Sol, because his bright open face reminded them of the sun.

He was a clever boy, who liked to make people laugh with his impressions of animals. He was also very fond of food.

Well, he was fond of peanuts.

You see, the only unusual thing about Sol was that he didn't like pineapples. Not at all. He complained that they made his mouth feel sore and that they gave him stomach aches, so after the age of seven he never ate a pineapple again. It was an exclusive diet of peanuts. He didn't mind, because he liked peanuts. Even though his mother joked, "Now, Sol, come on, if you carry on eating so many peanuts you will probably turn into one!"

Of course, Sol never did turn into a peanut.

But then, when he was ten years old, he woke in the middle of the night with a terrifying thought. What if I become bored of peanuts? Food is my only joy in life, and peanuts are the only food I enjoy, but earlier today I ate a peanut and it didn't feel like anything at all. It was just like breathing air. If peanuts stop being interesting to me, then maybe life will lose its interest too.

Sol was so petrified by this idea that the very next day he started to work on making something *different from* peanuts that was made *out of* peanuts.

No one in the village had ever thought to do this before. People made things, yes. They made chairs and tables and wooden bowls. They made friends and they made promises, and sometimes, when they were old enough, they made love. But they never made food. Food may need to be peeled or shelled, but it was, essentially, eaten with the minimum work done to it.

But Sol decided to grab as many peanuts as possible and put them in a large wooden bowl that he found in his parents' kitchen. He then headed towards the mountain just beyond the village, and he found a rock and he crushed the peanuts. He tasted the crushed peanuts. It was an incredible discovery. Crushed peanuts tasted even better than ordinary peanuts.

He returned to the village with his bowl of crushed peanuts and everyone agreed. Crushed peanuts were amazing.

Over the next few days he kept on crushing the peanuts and sharing them around. But soon Sol became dissatisfied. The peanuts, he believed, could be better. They were a bit too dry. They stuck to the mouth too much. They were hard to swallow. So he decided to do an experiment. He took some olives and crushed them down in the same wooden bowl. Oil came out. The oil tasted quite nice, so he put it with the crushed peanuts.

Then he had an idea.

What if he didn't tell people about the oil? Wouldn't that make it more special for them? A mystery ingredient. Then, if they didn't know how to make it, he could get them to pay him *in peanuts*. Peanuts were, after all, the main currency in the village. As it took fifty peanuts to make each jar, and as jars cost five peanuts, he would sell each one for a hundred peanuts, keeping the profit for himself.

He started to sell the peanut butter in jars.

People were happy to pay, because they had never tasted anything as good.

"What is the secret ingredient?" they would ask.

"That would take away the mystery."

"Ah yes," people said, "the mystery! We wouldn't want to lose the mystery, that is true."

Pretty soon, Sol found himself with enough peanuts (47,000) to buy the best house in the village. It was big enough for him to have a little peanut butter factory in his living room. But the trouble was, the biggest house in the village had the biggest windows and people always looked in when they walked by. Sometimes a boy called Luno would sneak along and stare in at the window, trying to discover the secret ingredient.

This is no good, thought Sol. I am becoming too successful. I will need a bigger place, away from the village.

So he decided to build a house on top of the hill, just north of the village, where the pineapple plants grew. He paid ten of the strongest men in the village to make it. They were happy because they got a thousand peanuts each, and a free jar of peanut butter. However, it was a bit unpopular with some of the other villagers, because of all the trees that were needed to make it.

The thing that had always made the villagers feel safe from outsiders was the jamba trees all around, and now, without them, they felt vulnerable.

"The jamba trees scare off the thieving monkeys," the villagers said.

Sol had never heard anything so ridiculous. "Monkeys love trees! Don't be silly! And anyway, this means each one of you will get a free jar of peanut butter."

Everyone loved peanut butter more than they feared monkeys, so even though some people said they would stop buying peanut butter, they never did, because it tasted too good. People began to wonder how they had ever survived without peanut butter. Ordinary peanuts just weren't the same. They were mundane and boring. They tasted cheap.

Everyone loved heading to Sol's peanut butter shop in the centre of town. Selling, as the sign said, SOL'S PEA-NUT BUTTER. This was the first time an apostrophe had been used anywhere. You see, as well as inventing peanut butter, Sol invented the apostrophe. Without apostrophes it would have been impossible to know who owned what. Apostrophes put that straight. This was Sol's peanut butter. No one else's. There was even a peanut butter day now, and that was called Sol's Peanut Butter Day. And a peanut butter festival called Sol's Peanut Butter Festival. Sol was in charge of all of it.

These things took a lot of organizing, so Sol gave

himself the title Head of Village Organizing, and everyone was fine with this because they were too busy fantasizing about peanut butter.

Sol was happy. Or he had a lot of peanuts. Which probably amounted to the same thing. Who needed friends when you could have so many peanuts? He was now twenty years old.

But late at night he would worry. He'd imagine he could hear noises.

People are trying to break in and find the secret to my peanut butter! he thought. When he went to get the olives, he started to look over his shoulder, imagining someone was following him. He now decided to change his title from Head of Village Organizing to Head of Village, as it was easier to say and it might make people a bit more scared of him.

"I am now Head of Village!" he told the villagers at a meeting in the square. "And I will make this village great."

"This village already is great," said one of the villagers.

"But I will provide more peanut butter festivals," said Sol, and there were no more complaints.

Then one morning when he opened up his shop he was horrified to find the front window had been smashed and all the peanut butter had been stolen.

He was angry.

"Who is the thief?" he shouted out loud, right there in the main square.

He then began knocking on all the doors.

"Who stole my peanut butter?" he asked over and over again.

"I don't know," Charlotte said when he asked her. "But it certainly wasn't me." The others said the same.

Sol grew angrier and angrier. And then he reached the last house. The house that belonged to an old woman who was born before the era of names.

"It wasn't me," she said. "But I don't blame those who did it. Your peanut butter is the source of all our problems."

Sol felt an anger grow inside him. "What are you talking about?"

"We are running out of peanuts. You have taken all the peanut trees and used them for your own purposes. You have put a very high fence around them." (This was true.) "And yes, there are other peanut trees, but not many – and now there are not enough to go around. By the time the villagers have paid for their peanut butter they are broke. No one ever used to be broke."

Sol was hardly listening by this point. He was too busy losing faith in humankind.

What if there is a way, he wondered, of watching everyone all the time?

So here is what he did. He built a watchtower. He stayed up all day and night, forcing his eyes open. When he could take it no longer, when his eyelids couldn't be kept open any more, he started to interview for guards.

With the promise of a free jar of peanut butter for every nightshift there was a ready stream of guards. Things worked for a few weeks. But then, one morning, Sol saw that the peanut butter shop had again been raided, after the guard had fallen asleep. So Sol walked through the land that used to be the forest and thought about how to make the village understand. The first part of making them understand would involve stealing something from each of the villagers.

So that night, at three in the morning, he and a few of his most trusty guards went out and stole items from every single house – simple items such as bowls or spoons or chairs or paintings of the lost forest.

Then the next day Sol's plan really got going. He held a meeting in the village square.

"Villagers, there is a thief in our midst. We must be vigilant at all times. We have been naive for too long. We must all watch our neighbours. We must never stop watching each other. No one can be trusted. Whoever catches the thief will be given a lifetime supply of peanut butter."

And so everyone left the meeting and went back to their homes vowing to watch each other and stay suspicious of everyone.

"Can't you see what is happening?" asked the old woman. "Can't you remember how it used to be? There was none of this."

But no one could see anything any more, because they

were too busy watching. And the village changed for ever that day. Everyone watched each other for ever more. And the thief was never found.

Well, that is not quite true.

One night, Sol accidentally fell asleep in Sol's Peanut Butter Shop. He heard a sound. And woke up to see the place full of monkeys, each holding jars of peanut butter.

"The villagers were right. You really were scared of the jamba trees. Shoo! Get out!"

And the monkeys did get out, but the truth never did.

Because what good could that possibly do?

LOVE IS A WORD, NOT A SENTENCE
Liz Kessler

Dear Gabby,

I've been trying to remember the day we met. When was it? Nursery school? Before that, even? I've been obsessing about it, forcing my mind to keep going back, and back, reeling in reverse like an old film until I can find the exact point when you came into my life.

I can't locate the moment and it panics me. I need the beginning so that when I come to the end, I can join the ends together and tie them in a knot.

Then I can slip inside the loop and take it with me.

It'll come to me.

Or maybe it won't. Maybe it doesn't matter. I have plenty of memories without it, and enough of them are clear and sharp.

Sharp enough to cut myself on. Sharp enough to make me bleed. Deep, thick, red blood running out of me, taking you out of me, taking it all away.

Do you remember the day it started? I do.

Year Six. Autumn term. We thought we were so big. Top of the school. We felt so old, so confident. We had it all: the best of best friends.

Remember?

We were walking home from school. You were quiet and I asked why. It wasn't like you; we were never quiet. The teachers used to have to separate us in order to get any work done. Every waking moment we could spend together, we did – and yet we never ran out of things to say.

But you weren't speaking that day.

Eventually I pushed hard enough and you came out with it.

"Jess, d'you ever think it would be fun to try kissing?" you asked in a rush. "Like, with me? We could see it as practice, so that when we're ready to kiss boys, we'll know how to do it."

I was taken aback. I had never thought about it, not once. Now it was my turn to be struck dumb.

You saw the shock on my face and recovered in less than a second.

Maybe that was my first clue.

Do you remember what you did?

You punched my arm. It didn't hurt. Not that time.

"Just kidding!" you yelled. And then you ran home and wouldn't let me talk about it any more.

But you'd planted a seed on fertile ground in my mind and I couldn't stop thinking about it.

A few days later, we were in my room doing our history project together. The Victorians. My parents were out; we had the house to ourselves. Something was itching inside me, pressing on my heart, making it beat so hard it was hurting my chest.

I leant towards you and whispered, "I want to."

You looked up and I saw it in your eyes. You knew what I meant. How long did we hold each other there with our eyes? Who was going to blink first?

It was you.

You leant closer to me. Just a tiny bit. Enough to pull back and pretend you hadn't moved at all if you needed to. Enough to tell me you hadn't stopped thinking about it either.

I shuffled forwards so our faces were so close our noses almost touched. I closed my eyes. A moment later, I felt your lips on mine.

My bedroom spun around me.

We were both breathless when we pulled apart.

I wanted to do it again. I knew you did too; I knew it better than you did.

Remember what you did then?

You ran away. You always ran away. Packed up your school bag, made up some rubbish about remembering your mum had booked you a haircut. No more words. You left; you always left.

But you always came back.

We did it again a few days later. I wanted to do it all the time. I didn't want to do anything else. I wanted to scream it out, wanted to run down the road dancing around people at bus stops, tell them all.

I terrified you.

All too quickly, we started secondary school and we stopped, for a while. We'd been put into different forms and we moved apart. We never mentioned it to anyone – not even to each other. It was as if it had never happened. It was as if *we* had never happened.

Our lives moved in separate orbits for a couple of years. And then it was Year Nine and we were both in drama club. We started getting the bus home together on Tuesdays, and soon fell into a pattern of spending the rest of the evening at one or other of our houses.

It was at your house this time. We were talking about boys, about who we fancied. You told me all these names. Reeled them off.

I didn't have any names.

I remember waiting till you'd got to the end of the list.

Then I asked if you wanted to kiss any of them. You shrugged.

I asked if you thought you'd be any good at it. I asked if you needed to remember how to do it.

"Remember what we used to say?" I asked. "That we could see it as practice, so that when we were ready to kiss boys, we'd know how to do it."

As soon as the words were out, I knew it was all still there. For both of us.

That was the first time it became more than kissing.

After that, we were inseparable again. Outside of school, anyway. In school, we had our own paths, and mostly we followed them.

I sometimes wonder what might have happened if that had been enough for me. But it wasn't. *You* might have been happy living a double life, but I wasn't.

You were my lover. I loved you. Why should I have to hide it?

And so I tried to jump lanes, tried to join your gang. Hovered around the edges of it.

I made you uncomfortable; I cramped your style; I was blind to your discomfort.

I had no shame.

You had enough for us both.

The first hints were subtle. The slightest turning of your back. Just enough to show them you were with them, that you chose them over me.

You'd still talk to me at that point.

I remember the day that stopped. Do you? Is it burned into you as though with a branding iron, as it is imprinted on me?

I could see that Janie was talking, but I needed you. Drama club was starting and I wanted to know if you were coming. You hadn't been for three weeks.

Janie was the leader of your pack and she didn't like people interrupting her. She stopped her monologue and stared at me. "Gabby," she said, without taking her eyes off me. "Please can you tell your *girlfriend* I'm talking."

I'd never seen someone crumple before. I saw it happen behind your eyes, the internal collapse. You recovered in about two seconds.

"Fuck off – she's not my girlfriend. Don't be so disgusting," you said.

Then you turned your back to me, completely. You were in the circle and I was firmly out.

You didn't speak to me in public again.

Actually, that's not strictly accurate, is it? Perhaps I should clarify.

You didn't have a conversation with me. You didn't engage with me. You didn't meet my eyes. But you spoke to me. Oh yes, you spoke. You said lots of things to me in front of your precious friends.

You said, "Fuck off, dyke."

You said, "Stop trying to get off with me, you filthy lezzer."

You said, "Touch me again and I'll touch you right back – with my fist."

The laughter grew every time you said something. And your status grew with it. You fast-tracked through the ranks and before long you were Janie's second in command.

Even then, I was blind; I wanted to be blind.

I was jealous of Janie. Why couldn't *I* be the one you wanted to please? Why wasn't *I* the one you sent notes to, the one you hatched plans with? I would still have done anything for you, anything to swap places with Janie.

You knew that.

That was how you got me to do it.

I can still barely believe you did it.

We hadn't spoken for months, not even in private. But you sought me out at school. You came to me. I should have known it was a trap, but I was too full of desperate, naive hope, even then.

You told me to meet you at the toilets after school. Said we had to talk. I got there first, and when you joined me, you told me to go into a cubicle. We went in together.

You said you wanted to start again.

Remember what you did then? I've asked myself so many times if you meant this part. It felt like you did.

You kissed me so hard I couldn't breathe. But I didn't care about breathing if it meant you were kissing me. I mistook it for passion.

I think it was hate.

You told me to take off my clothes.

"What, here? Why don't you just come back to mine?" I asked. I should have known. I should have fucking known.

You shook your head. "I want you now," you said. "I can't wait." You wouldn't look at me.

So I did it. Even after what you'd put me through. I did it for you. I told you – I would have done anything for you.

I took my clothes off and stood there for you.

I remember smiling at you. If I close my eyes now, I can still remember that feeling. It takes the breath out of me, even now. The last moment of innocence.

And then the door was open and you leapt away from me.

The phones in my face. Cameras on. *Click click, snap snap.*

The laughter. The girls. The laughter still echoes inside me. It follows me everywhere, even now, even here.

I dressed hurriedly and ran from the laughter as if it could propel me home. I arrived sweating, breathless. Told Mum I was sick and went straight to bed.

And then that evening. My phone, pinging with notifications. One after another after another. Eventually, I dragged myself out of bed and looked at it. There was an invitation to join a new Facebook page.

The page was called: *This is what a dyke looks like.*

I should have deleted the notifications, switched off my phone, thrown it in a river – done anything but look at it.

Instead, I clicked on the link.

The banner photo: my naked body. My eyes wide with terror and shock.

The page already had over three hundred likes.

I refused to get out of bed the next morning. And the morning after. How could I ever face anyone again?

Eventually, Mum suspected it was more than a stomach bug. I told her a fraction of the truth. That some of the girls had been calling me names.

She sat on the side of my bed and stroked my hair. "Sticks and stones can break my bones, but words can never hurt me," she said.

The well of pain inside me was too deep for me to clamber down and bring it up to show her she was wrong. If I reached the bottom, I would never get out again.

I wanted to tell her that at least broken bones mend.

Though I found that out the hard way too, didn't I?

You were on first lookout. I sometimes wondered how the roles were divvied up between you. Did you draw straws, or were the jobs all assigned by your leader?

I'll never know.

Doesn't matter now.

Here's what I do know.

After nearly a week of refusing food, company, daylight or conversation, I couldn't hold Mum off any longer. She took a few days off work and wouldn't leave my side. She made me talk to her. Not about … it. I couldn't do that.

But I think she found out. And I think she did something

about it. I heard hushed phone calls. The notifications died down. Eventually, I forced myself to look at my phone.

The page had been removed.

So, after nearly two weeks, I went back to school. I even got through the first few days. I lasted as far as the journey home on day four. Much of that journey is a blank. Not enough of it, though.

I remember being on my own, someone calling my name, turning round. The fist in my face.

I remember hearing, "Fucking grass us up, did you, bitch?"

I remember being curled in a ball, on the pavement. The cul-de-sac two streets from my house. I remember the kicks. I remember begging.

I remember her voice. Janie. "Go on, Gabby. You can have the last kick." Like she was doing you a favour. Saving the best bit for you.

I remember you saying, 'Take this, you fucking gay bitch," and thinking it was the first time you'd used the word *gay*. I remember thinking you were going to kill me.

I remember it flashing through my mind that there were some countries around the world where it was still illegal to be gay. Some countries where it was punishable with the death sentence. We'd done it in PSHE.

That was the moment I realized there's more than one kind of death sentence.

It was the last time our eyes met. You saw the pleading

in mine; I know you saw it. And then your hatred – of me, of us, of yourself – took over, and you started. Your foot in my stomach. And then again. Again.

Three kicks before Janie stopped you. "OK, come on, let's go."

I was left alone on the pavement, curled up, crying, dead inside. No one saw me.

It was a Thursday evening. Did you plan that? You knew my parents were always out on Thursdays. Did you make sure there would be no one home to question me?

I have so many unanswered questions. I'm going to start throwing them into the river. Soon.

I dried up inside after that. Turned cold. Switched off.

You know why? It's funny, really.

It turns out that if you have three cracked ribs, it really, really hurts to cry. So I didn't.

I told my mum I'd tripped on a towel and fallen down the stairs. I even crumpled up a towel at the bottom of the stairs to convince her.

I was off school for three more weeks. Every cloud and all that.

I didn't have much to do in those weeks. Everything hurt. Everything was always going to hurt.

It came gradually, the thought. The idea. The plan.

At first, I glimpsed it as if at the edge of my mind, a tiny black dot in the distance that I refused to look at. But it came closer, it developed a shape. It took over. I became the blackness. I craved it. It was my way out. My only way out.

I couldn't take another day of it, never mind the remainder of my school years. There would never be another exit.

And so I decided. I planned. I formulated.

And then the day came.

That day is today.

I wait for Mum and Dad to go to work.

I can't think about them. I can't bear it. You have stolen my parents from me. You have stolen everything.

I close the front door behind me, pull my coat around me and make my way to the bridge. The one where we used to play pooh sticks when we were little. Remember?

Remember?

And I get ready to finish writing you this letter. My goodbye letter.

My suicide note.

I have the envelope ready and everything. There's a post box just past the other side of the bridge.

How handy is that?

And then I get to the bridge, and something crazy happens. Something that you'd expect to happen maybe in one of those mushy romantic comedies we used to laugh at and take the piss out of. Not something that happens in real life. Definitely not something that happens in *my* life.

Someone's already there. Throwing a stick into the water.

You turn as I approach. The shock in your eyes gives way to something else. I can't work out what it is at first.

"What are you doing here?" I ask. My voice is metal.

"I..." You drop the stick you're holding. I watch the river carry it away. You shrug, turn to me. "What are *you* doing here?" you reply eventually.

"Wouldn't you like to know," I mumble.

"Well, yes, actually. I would like to know. I—"

"No you wouldn't." The words come out of my mouth like fire. "Anyway, you'll find out soon enough."

There's a moment. A beat. You take a step towards me. "Jess, you're crying," you whisper.

I step instinctively away from you. Swipe my sleeve across my face. I'm almost shocked at the tears. I didn't realize I had any left.

"Oh God," you say, reaching out to me. "You're..."

I shake you off. "Just leave me alone, Gabby."

There's a wriggly wet track running down each of your cheeks. "I'm sorry," you say, so softly I can barely hear you over the rushing of the water below us.

I stare at you. You know. I can tell. I don't care.

You edge closer to me. "Jess. I'm so sorry. Please, please don't do it."

I recoil.

"Please, Jess. I just – I'm ashamed. I'm ashamed of myself, of what I am. I hated you for not being ashamed. I blamed you for all of it. I was wrong."

Your face is streaked with tears now. There's snot hanging out of your nose. You don't even wipe it away. "Please. Please! Forgive me. *Please*, Jess."

I keep staring at you.

"I love you," you say. As if this is enough. As if it can undo anything. As if it can undo me. As if it could unpick the lock inside me, the bolt holding together the metal bars around my heart. The ones you helped me build, the ones with the nails driven in so hard I felt every strike of the hammer.

And maybe it can.

As if in a dream, I let you take my hand. I let you start walking me home. I let you speak. I let you apologize. Over and over and over again.

We nearly make it.

We so nearly make it.

A couple of roads from my house, the bus comes past us. One of the girls is in the window. Not Janie. One of the others. I don't even know her name. I see her, and so do you. And without missing a beat, you flinch and drop my hand.

That's when I know.

So I let you walk me home. I let my mum feed me. I let my dad tell jokes over dinner. And when I go to bed that night, I hug them both extra hard, tell them both how much I love them. I guess I'm grateful to you for that. For that extra night – for the memory that I'm giving them.

I let the dark come.

I creep out of the house like a burglar who operates only in darkness and shadows.

I walk slowly. Might as well. There's no rush.

I have never felt so calm.

Every street is silent and empty. I feel as if the world has laid out a blanket for me to walk on. A path leading me to my destiny.

And yes, there are tears this time. Tears for those two little girls who knew only their own pleasure and desires and weren't tainted by the judgement and rules of the world around them. Who hadn't yet been told it was wrong. Who still had the chance to decide it wasn't.

Tears for my parents.

And tears for you. Because in your sick, warped, fucked-up way, I know you do love me. I don't think you will ever forgive yourself for what I am about to do.

Please do one thing for me, if I'm right, if you really love me.

Take your shame and your fear and your anger and throw them in this river. I'll look after them. I'll take them with me.

The sky is starting to lighten. The river is dark. It's time. I need to post this letter.

The water is swirling and rushing under the bridge. I am almost a part of it already.

I'm sorry it was too late for me. Don't let it be too late for you. Change something. Be brave. Make a difference.

Do something good.

Forgive me, Gabby.

What was it we used to say?

See it as practice, so that when you are ready to forgive yourself, you'll know how to do it.

Jess

"I had recently begun to think about how much progress we've made in the area of LGBT rights in the UK in recent years, as opposed to some other parts of the world where being gay is illegal, dangerous and in some cases punishable by death. Then a friend of mine told me that her nephew was distraught because one of his best friends had committed suicide after homophobic bullying. I suddenly realized that being gay is sometimes punishable by death in this country too – and that this was what I wanted to write about. I hope my story will help some young readers to realize that we all need to support each other, to stand up for each other and to do what we can to help bring about a world where no one is ever made to feel so bad about who they are that they can no longer cope with life." Liz Kessler

DARLING
Amy Leon

Darling,
They will ask of you silence
They will expect of you rage
They will give you no time to make a mistake
They will have no explanation
And every excuse
They will do everything they can
To destroy you
But you
Must. Not. Let. Them.

Darling,
They will tell you about your skin

They will tell you about your bones
They will even tell you about your marrow
But they will never know your name.

Darling,
Give them a good reason
To know your name
You are a miracle
A survivor of yesterday's bloodshed
A reason to believe in change
Stars and planets collide with the thought of you
Time stops to welcome you
You are made of light.

Darling,
They will fear you because of this
And that is OK
Do not be scared
This world will give you anything
If you fight for it
So fight
Fight with your mind
Fight with your words
Fight with everything you've got
They expect nothing of you but surrender
So stun them.

Darling,
Stun them with your intelligence
Shock them with your well of passion and ability to love
Terrify them with your grace and forgiveness
And watch
As they make space for you
At the very table you created.

"'Darling' is a letter to the child I was, growing up in Harlem. It took me a long time to believe that I would one day be 'allowed' to succeed. It wasn't something I could strive for, it was something I had to ask permission for. Through writing and performance I have found that I can command whatever space I choose to occupy, so darling please know you can do the same. Let no one compromise your shine." Amy Leon

STAY HOME

Sita Brahmachari

"You stay home today, isn't it?" Mum calls to me.

It's what she's been asking me to do every day. "Stay home with me, please, Niya. No school just for one day."

"Yes, Mum! We've got your doctor's appointment. Have you forgotten already?" I ask.

I can hear her mumbling to herself in Urdu about interfering people.

I take the letter that's been scrunched up in my bag for weeks now and lob it at the bin. Getting Mum to the last parents' evening was hard enough, but there's no way she'll make it this time, not the state she's in.

She's not been taking her pills again. She says she

doesn't want to be "all evened out", which is what I made the mistake of telling her she is when she remembers to take the pills that Dr Chen gives her. She complains the medication makes her feel like she's watching a reflection of herself floating in a mirror ... that doesn't sound good, but the way she goes downhill when she stops taking her pills isn't good either.

But I know what she's thinking – pills can't stop Dad's deathday coming round again. Dr Chen says stuff like, "Time eases the pain," and, for a while, it did seem to be getting better. But now, as the second anniversary of Dad's death approaches, Mum seems even worse than she was on the first. At least back then she was still so in shock she let people give us some help. Sometimes I wonder how she's managed to push everyone away. In the space of two years our whole world has shrunk to just me and Mum and the dreaded three-monthly review with Dr Chen. I check the home diary I keep for Mum. *15 November, 2 p.m. with Dr Dread.* That's what I've written. I know, it's not even funny, but it keeps me sane.

Mum's hands are shaking as she picks up the phone to call my school. I wish I could do it myself, but parents have to call in if you're going to be off sick – that's the rule. I hear the attendance officer's voice in the background and then watch Mum's shoulders relax and her hands stop shaking.

"Only machine voice," she whispers to me.

She's reading from her notepad ... the words she's

rehearsed in her best English, which I keep telling her has got really good – not that she believes me.

"Niya Sulimani. Her tutor group?" Mum looks panicked. She forgets things all the time these days.

"Miss Rose," I whisper.

"Tutor – Miss Rose," Mum says to the answer machine. "Niya will be absent today, having doctor's appointment." She speaks slowly as if she's afraid that she's going to stumble over the words.

She sighs with relief as she puts down the phone.

It takes me the whole morning to psych Mum up to actually leave the flat. I always make the appointment with Dr Chen for the afternoon if I can. This is the closest me and Mum get to a family outing these days. She even lets me put a bit of blusher on her cheeks, like she used to when we went out with Dad. Going out together reminds me that we really do exist as mother and daughter outside the walls of this flat.

As soon as we get to the lift I forget all about my family outing fantasy because I can feel Mum's panic rising, a million sparks ricocheting off the cold white walls. She's clinging on to me so tight my arm hurts.

As the lift passes floor six I make my wishes like I always do – six is my lucky number. When I was six the world was happy and exciting with this whole new country to explore. When I was six I would hold out both hands and Mum would take one and Dad would take the other as

71

we'd *one, two, three … whee!* our way up the road to school every day.

Today at floor six I wish for Mum not to have one of her panic attacks and for Dr Chen to be off work so we have to see another doctor. It happened once, so it *could* happen again. With a stranger it's easier to pretend that everything's getting better. Miss Rose, my form tutor and English teacher, did a lesson last week about fear, and we had to write down what we're really afraid of, no matter how odd it might sound to anyone else. I wrote something obvious about snakes, even though Mum's the one who was terrified of snakes when we lived in Pakistan, not me. The point is, I could *never* tell Miss Rose what I'm really afraid of – that someone will try to separate what's left of my family, Mum and me.

We watch the red lights count down each floor … 5, 4, 3 … and with every number that leads us closer to the ground, Mum gets more and more breathless.

I check that I've brought the paper bag for her to blow into, the way Dr Chen showed me, in case she starts doing that weird hyper– What did Dr Chen call it? Hyper-something breathing thing that makes Mum go all faint and tingly.

As soon as she steps outside she gasps as the icy air enters her lungs. She stops short for a moment as if she's walked into an invisible iceberg. I take Mum's hand to remind her to keep moving. She looks down at her feet, taking tiny steps as if the pavement's a tightrope she's going to fall off. I notice the wisps of ice-breath we make together on the air as we walk.

When we finally get to the surgery I log us in on the computer and tell Mum to go and sit down. Her breath's coming out shallow and fast.

We sit in the waiting room for a while. A woman smiles at Mum, but she doesn't smile back, so I do instead. Then Dr Chen opens her door.

"Mrs Sulimani and Niya," she calls out, as if this is *my* appointment too.

There are two chairs next to Dr Chen's desk. Mum places her coat on the one furthest away and sits down, so that doesn't leave me with much choice but to sit right next to the doctor. She smiles at me and runs her fingers through her black, shiny bob, then peers at Mum.

"So how are you feeling now, Mrs Sulimani?"

Mum just nods.

"And how are you getting on with the new anti-depressants?" Dr Chen slightly raises her voice, as if that will help Mum understand more.

"Better, better," Mum lies as she rolls up her sleeve to have her blood pressure taken.

"Hmm, we'll have to keep an eye on that. Quite high," the doctor says as she helps Mum roll her sleeve back down. "But maybe it's just the white coat effect!" Dr Chen smiles.

"What's that?" I ask.

"As soon as people see a doctor their blood pressure goes up. Explain to your mum," Dr Chen says. I do and her reaction makes me laugh.

"What's so funny?" Dr Chen asks as she records Mum's blood pressure in her notes.

"Mum says you're not wearing a white coat."

"True! But you understand what I mean, Mrs Sulimani?"

"Understand," Mum says.

Dr Chen looks up some notes on the screen then casts her eyes back over me before carrying on her questioning. I can tell she's trying to be subtle. She's not like that doctor who actually asked *me* once if I thought my mum was depressed. I mean, how was I supposed to know?

Dr Chen seems to be ticking boxes on some kind of questionnaire.

"So, would you say your depression has eased? Do you feel happier in yourself?" she asks without looking away from the screen. I feel like she's asking *me*, too.

"In myself?" Mum repeats. Her guard has gone up.

Dr Chen raises her eyes to me and I translate. She has no idea how much Mum actually *does* understand, which is just about everything. It's just that when Dad was alive he always did the talking, especially at official things like doctor's appointments and parents' evenings. This is how it would always go. Someone would speak to Dad and he would translate to Mum. Then she would speak to Dad in

Urdu and he would translate back into English. I suppose he was kind of her full-time interpreter, now that I think about it. He was her voice. He used to get so annoyed with her – even when we knew she could understand every single thing being said, she still got Dad to translate. Now it's up to me. I used to think it was because she was shy, but I know now that it's her way of not really being in the room.

Mum tells me in Urdu to say that she's feeling much better, coping well, and that the medication is working.

So I do what I'm told and lie.

"And have you found any side effects with the new pills?" Dr Chen is looking to me for an answer.

"Sometimes little forgetful," Mum mumbles under her breath.

"What kind of things?" Dr Chen asks.

"Just dates and things like that," I jump in. It's better to look as if you're telling the truth.

"That can be a side effect, but then again I have the same problem," Dr Chen jokes. "Always losing my keys!" I know she's only trying to make us feel comfortable. "If you can just pop on the scales here, Mrs Sulimani." Mum sighs and stands up slowly. I swear she always makes out her hip is worse than it actually is to distract Dr Chen from talking about her state of mind. I suppose she thinks her hip is something that can be fixed.

"You've managed to keep all that weight off. That's

good. It'll be less pressure on your sore hip," says the doctor, tapping her own leg.

"Yes, yes, but still walking is pain here." Mum points to her side.

"We'll need to keep an eye on it and see if your mobility gets worse, but I don't think it's critical enough yet for an operation. You won't need that kind of stress at the moment."

I start to translate, but Mum puts her hand up to stop me.

"No operation. OK. I understand."

Dr Chen nods as she writes up her notes on Mum, then turns her attention to me.

"Looks like you've lost a bit of weight, Niya. Are you eating well?"

This is what I mean about Dr Chen. You have to work hard to fly under her radar.

"The offer of more counselling is always open to both of you." Dr Chen has pulled her chair up so she's in touching distance of me, as if she's really saying this for my benefit. She's almost whispering now. "Anniversaries can bring up some raw emotions. It's only been two years…"

"We're OK," I assure her.

"That's good." Dr Chen wheels her chair back to her desk and goes about the business of printing out a repeat prescription. Mum's already putting on her coat, readying herself to leave.

"And school still going well?" Dr Chen asks me.

I can't tell if she's just making small talk or if the words she's tapping out on her screen are logging any suspicions she might have that things are *not* going well.

"All fine, thanks," I tell her.

Dr Chen hands the prescription to Mum, who folds it neatly in half, places it in her handbag and heads for the door. I follow her then realize I've left my gloves on the table and go back for them.

Dr Chen picks them up for me and as she hands them over she whispers, "Are you sure you don't need me to arrange some help for you both, just temporarily?"

Now Mum's back in the doorway staring at me and Dr Chen as if we're in on some conspiracy.

"Got them!" I wave the gloves in the air and hurry out.

I can feel the doctor's eyes burning into the space between my shoulder blades. Well, whatever she's written in her notes, at least the appointment is over.

Mum's always calmer going back up in the lift.

"Lift me up!" she says and I imagine that she's shrunk to the size of a child with her arms outstretched towards me. *One, two, three ... whee! Lift me up! Lift me up.*

It must be my turn to look glum, because Mum starts playing Dad's "passing time" game as we climb up, up, up to the fourteenth floor. I used to love the three of us in the lift together. We'd imagine that every floor was a different place we wanted to visit. Floor one – Buckingham

Palace, floor two – Edinburgh Castle (that was one of Dad's favourites, but we never made it there), floor three – Kew Gardens (one of Mum's that we *did* manage to get to once)... Mine would change every time, but nowadays the place on our wish list that I always picture on floor six is Hyde Park, because that's the first place we actually went to. I'll always remember us laughing together as we ate our way through Mum's stacked-up tiffin-tin towers stuffed full of paratha, dhal, puri, samosas and every kind of curry. She looked around at other people eating sandwiches and felt sorry for them.

"Mum, why don't we go to Hyde Park together for a picnic?" I let the thought out.

Her back tenses and she curls into herself again.

"Too cold," she mutters.

"In the spring, then?" I persist.

She looks at me like she doesn't trust me. "What did Dr Chen say to you?"

"Nothing, Mum! She just asked if we needed help."

She holds my arm tight. "No help! No interference," she says in English.

I watch her mouth forming these perfectly pronounced words and pull away from her, more roughly than I intended. The red lights flash on and off: 13, 14. Fourteen floors for fourteen years of my life. What's beyond fourteen? I don't even want to think about the future, about what comes next. I give myself a talking to, like I always do when I know I have to toughen up. "Don't ask questions. Don't think about stuff like that. Just get through today." But Mum's words keep racing through my head. "No help, no interference ... no help ... no interference..." and suddenly the metal walls are closing in on me.

The doors open and I run out and gulp the air. I think maybe this is how it's always going to be for us. We're frozen in time and nothing's getting better. The only thing we're getting better at is pretending. I rummage in my bag for my keys. Mum just stands next to me, arms flattened against her sides. I want to shake her as we walk into the hall. Tomorrow will be two whole years since Dad died and it doesn't feel like time has healed anything.

Mum's ahead of me when these words burst from my mouth: "I don't want to translate any more, Mum. You have to start speaking up for yourself."

She turns to me, her eyes glassy with tears. "Sorry, *beta!*" she says, walks into her bedroom and closes the door.

The sink's full of dishes. The washbasket's overflowing and the floor's starting to look grime-grey. From our kitchen window I can see over the low rise flats below. Sarah's block is on the corner. My old best friend, Sarah, seems so far away from me now. A stream of sunlight catches the icy roof of her flat and glints at me. I feel like running down to her and telling her everything, trying to explain why I can't let her come over any more. Why I've got no time to see her after school. Why I'm always avoiding her. But I can't risk her talking to her parents about me, can't risk the interference. I see her looking at me some days and I know she really wants to understand why I've stopped spending time with her, and I'd so like to tell her that I miss her. But how can I do that without her worrying about me? Instead I fill the mop bucket and make a start on the floor. There are no ugly sisters here keeping me from going to the ball, it's just poor Mum and her sadness.

Today is Dad's deathday. That's what I call it. Tomorrow will be parents' evening. Or, in my case, no-parents evening. I wonder what Dad would think of his "princess" if he could see me now? I leave a note by Mum's bed. Since Dad died I've stopped practising writing in Urdu, but somehow it seems important to try to do it now. I've almost forgotten how.

> *Sorry I got angry with you. Thinking of Dad today. Thinking of you, too.*
> *Love you, Mum.*
> *Niya XXX*

Sometimes there just aren't the words in either language to say the things I need to.

Mum's wrapped herself tightly in a shawl like a baby. A photo of her and Dad on their wedding day is resting on her chest. I've got that panicky feeling I had in the lift again, like a thousand moths are gathering in my stomach and rising up to my throat. I can't be ill. I'm never ill. I look on Mum's bedside table to check if she's taken her tablets. The seals of two of the little silver compartments are broken. At least she'll sleep peacefully now.

As I leave I check the front door is properly closed. I just wish the chain was on; sometimes I think if Mum was really sound asleep she wouldn't hear if someone tried to break in. My hands hover over the keyhole. Would it be safer to lock her in? But what if there was a fire? Maybe I could call in to Mrs Asir and ask her to pop by, but then Mum would only get angry with me.

Inside the lift I look up at the numbers. 14, 13, 12, 11, 10, 9, 8, 7, 6 ... I wish that Dad was still alive ... 5, 4, 3, 2, 1.

My breath's a tight fist in my chest. I'm going to have to toughen up to get through today.

Two lessons gone, four to go.

I'm sitting in English and Miss Rose is going on about some poem, but I just stare out of the window. A robin lands on the sill. It hops along and then peers in as if it has a message for me. I wonder if it's hungry. *Friendliest sweet-songed birds.* Sometimes Dad's voice just comes to me like that, as if he's in the room with me.

The robin flies away in the direction of our flat, its little red breast brightening the wintery sky. If only I had a pair of binoculars I'd almost be able to see Mum from here. Our flat is only a few streets away. The block's in a dip and school's on a hill, so it feels like there's not that much space between Mum and me. I often imagine that *I* could just fly out of the window, check in on Mum and then soar back into the classroom and no one would even notice I'd left the room.

I slip my phone under the table to check that she hasn't texted.

"So, Niya. What do you think the refrain means?" Miss Rose asks.

My head jolts as I scan over the lines of the poem.

"It's about missing someone," Sarah whispers.

"Missing someone," I echo.

Miss Rose nods, but looks from Sarah to me as if she's not convinced it's my answer. But she should be because if anyone here knows how it feels to miss someone, to wish and dream every minute of every day that their heart had never stopped beating, today of all days, it's me.

"Thanks!" I whisper to Sarah.

She shrugs. When she helps me like this I know that I'd only have to say the word and Sarah and I would be best friends again. I don't blame her for going and joining Zena, Rachel and Jodie in a cosy little foursome, even though we used to laugh at the way they strutted around like they owned the place. Maybe, if you find yourself alone, it's better to be *with* them than against them.

We're supposed to be writing a poem about missing someone, but my page is empty.

I yawn all gape-mouthed and Miss Rose frowns at me and the pen that's still lying on my desk. I think about at least pretending to write, but I can't even be bothered to do that. It's not like I would write anything true anyway. I have never felt this tired before. When Mum sleeps all morning she's awake half of the night wandering around, mumbling phrases from her Learn English tape ... and then I can't sleep for listening to her voice through the wall. Last night was even worse than usual because she was talking to Dad's photo and crying.

"You can finish the poems off for homework. Can I have a word, Niya?" Miss Rose interrupts my thoughts. She waits for everyone to file out of class and I know what's coming. "You were off sick again yesterday. Are you feeling all right?"

I nod. "I had to go to the doctor's." Well, it's not a lie, is it?

I throw in something about stomach ache and period pains, hoping she won't ask any more questions. That's not really a lie either because my stomach feels tight and all coiled up most of the time.

"Can I see your work from today?" Miss Rose asks, ignoring my various excuses.

I just stare at her.

"Your poem, Niya?" she prompts.

I feel around in my bag a bit lamely, stalling for time.

She sighs and seems to give up. "Just make sure it's completed for next lesson." She bites her lip as if wondering how best to deal with me. "Actually, I've been wanting to talk to you about your work. Your homework's late again and I know I'm not the only one chasing you. I did give you a final warning last time, Niya, to catch up on everything before parents' evening. I'm afraid I'll have to give you a detention this time."

"I can't today!" I look down at my hands. They are shaking uncontrollably and I clasp them together behind my back.

Miss Rose tucks her fine hair behind her ear, turns away from me and finishes tidying away her things.

"No buts! It's not personal, Niya. I can't make exceptions. Perhaps next time you'll heed my warning and get work in on time. It'll be GCSE year before you know it and you can't afford to let your grades slip any further. I'll see you here after school."

I'm glad I threw the parents' evening letter away. Seeing me in trouble at school would send Mum right over the edge.

In the lunch hall I get my tray as quickly as possible, trying not to draw attention to myself, and sit down. Further up the bench, Sarah's with Zena, Rachel and Jodie. They're all being really loud, apart from Sarah. This is how they are. Wherever they go they make sure everyone knows they've arrived. Sarah looks a bit embarrassed by all the noise they're making and glances at me sideways as if she wishes that I would call out and ask her to sit next to me, but I've already surrounded myself with a wall of books.

I have too much work to catch up on, homework and classwork. I feel like a hamster going round and round on a wheel and never really getting anywhere. Sarah has a hamster. She called her Mango because I said she was sweet and just the same size as the fruit. I remember the day I went with Sarah's mum and dad to get her. It was exactly two weeks before Dad died. So Mango must be two years and two weeks old. I wonder if Mango's still alive. How long do hamsters live, anyway?

I check my phone again. No messages. I don't want to call Mum just in case she's still sleeping peacefully. I take out the blank piece of card that I'm supposed to write the poem for Miss Rose on, pick up my pen and these words pour out:

Today is my dad's deathday
My dad,
with his big laugh,
with his round belly ... too round.
My dad,
who used to smooth my hair and call me his princess,
pick me up and twirl me even when I was too tall to be twirled.

My dad,
who two years ago today
walked up the stairs
because the lift was broken
climbed up and up and up
heart racing too fast until it
stopped.
My dad,
falling,
falling,
falling
down cold concrete steps.
My dad,
whose deathday's today.
Only the lift is mended.

Zena and Rachel pass where I'm sitting, so I hunch forward and cover up my poem with a list of French vocab. I have no idea what half the words mean. To think I used to be the best in the class at French. I look up a word in my dictionary.

dehors (pronounced *day ore*) = outside

That's how I feel – on the outside of everything.

When the bell rings I slip the poem and vocab into my pocket, pack my bag and go to clear away my tray. Sarah,

Zena, Rachel and Jodie are ahead of me so I hang back a little.

Mrs Alim steps in between us to collect some trays.

"Hurry up! On your way now, girls!" she says to the others, ushering them out.

"What?" Zena bristles. "I thought we were supposed to clear away our rubbish!"

Sarah hovers in the doorway, looking uncomfortable. Mrs Alim takes my tray and starts telling me in Urdu about a vacancy for a lunchtime assistant she thinks my mum could apply for. Mr Alim was a good friend of my dad's, and Mrs Alim's always looking out for me and Mum. Perhaps she knows what today is, although maybe not because she doesn't say anything. I wish she would stop talking to me in Urdu. It makes me feel like everyone's listening. I wish she would stop asking about my mum and being nice to me. I feel like my chest is about to explode. I just want to disappear.

Outside the lunch hall Sarah hangs back from the others, waiting for me.

"How's Mango?" I ask, because it's the first thing that pops into my head.

She looks a bit taken aback, but then smiles. "Fine. Why don't you come over and see her?"

I can't think of what to say to that, but I find my hand plunging into my pocket and two pieces of paper fly out ... a poem and a list of French words. The words that mean nothing to me flutter to the floor and Sarah picks them up;

the words I realize now I want her to read are carried across the courtyard on an icy breeze. Zena reaches down to pick up my poem. I shove past Sarah, run at Zena and push her so hard that she falls sideways and lands awkwardly, scraping her hands and arm. A tiny smudge of blood smears my words. I grab my poem and rip it into shreds. What was I even thinking of?

I can hear Zena and the others screaming at me, but it's as if there's a screen between us and their voices can't get to me. Maybe this is why Mum pretends not to understand English – to shield herself from what's going on. I stare at Zena's grazed hand and bruised arm. That's how I feel – like one angry purple bruise. Miss Rose appears and I watch her mouth moving for a long time before I can tune in to her words.

"Well, Niya, don't you have anything to say for yourself? I'm calling home about your detention later anyway, so I'm afraid this is just another thing to add."

Good luck with that, I think, because I know Mum won't answer the phone to a teacher.

"I can't do the detention today," I tell her, and walk away as if I don't care one way or the other what she does.

"Right, you've pushed things too far now. You leave me no choice. Tomorrow you'll be spending the whole day in internal exclusion. Come on, Zena, let's get this hand cleaned up." Miss Rose casts me a look as if she can't quite believe that it's me who's caused all this trouble.

Sarah bends down and starts picking up the pieces of my poem.

"Don't bother. It's too late," I tell her.

She stops and stares at me as if she doesn't know who I am any more.

Tomorrow, that's a whole day away. For now all I can think of is getting through the afternoon and then running home to Mum.

I sit as quietly as I can all afternoon, trying to slip under everyone's radar. In maths I get this weird thought that maybe I have actually disappeared and become a great big nothing. It's hard to imagine nothing – zero – but it's what I try to make myself into when I walk straight past Miss Rose's room and feel her watching me.

On my way home Mr Asir is standing outside his shop, waiting for me as I walk up the road. He holds a gift box in his hand, decorated in golden swirly patterns.

"Some little sweets," he says, handing them to me. "We haven't forgotten. Please accept our respects, from your community."

My eyes fill up. I quickly take the box from him, mumble my thank yous and head for the entrance to Tower View. I wonder what it would be like now if Mum had accepted everyone's friendship and offers of help after Dad died. I wonder what would have happened today if Sarah could have read my poem.

LIFT TEMPORARILY OUT OF ORDER. MAIN-
TENANCE WORK IN PROGRESS, a sign says.
APOLOGIES FOR ANY INCONVENIENCE.

What is this, some kind of sick joke?

I start the long walk up to the fourteenth floor and
with every step my legs and chest feel heavier and heavier
… 115, 116, 117… On which step did my dad's heart falter,
on which of these hard concrete steps did he fall?

As I reach our floor the rich scent of spices wafts down
the corridor – the smell that used to greet me every day
after school.

I open the door to find Mum fully dressed with her hair
in a neat ponytail. The table is covered with pots and pans.
I place the box of sweets beside them.

"From Mr and Mrs Asir … they say that the community is thinking of us today. Mrs Alim, too, at school, sent
her best wishes. She says there might be work for you."

Mum nods and places her hand on my cheek.

"Hungry?" she asks.

I shake my head then run through to my bedroom so
she doesn't see me welling up.

Mum follows me. She has tidied my room and emptied
my bin and I see it straight away – the letter about parents'
evening has been smoothed out and placed on my bedside
table.

"I find this." She holds it up to show me.

I shrug. "It's not that important…"

Mum nods slowly as if she's trying to take in what I'm saying. "I have been thinking to come. You are right. It's time that you stop translating for me." She speaks this slowly in English.

What am I supposed to say to that? Now, when I'm in all this trouble for the first time! I glance out into the hallway, where the message light is flashing on the phone. "Any messages?" I ask, trying to sound as innocent as I can.

"I haven't listened, too busy cooking."

"It's fine, Mum, about parents' evening. I don't need you to come. Anyway, it's icy outside and I don't want you to fall. I'll explain about your hip to the teachers and bring back the reports myself," I say, walking back through to the kitchen to escape the look on her face.

"No, *beta*. I want to go!"

Great, I think. She's going to love hearing about the fight and the internal exclusion. How's that going to make her feel?

"Niya, *bayttoe*." I do as she says and sit down. She picks up the box of sweets, takes out a creamy triangle with pistachio nuts on the top, holds my chin and places the sweet in my mouth. I have no choice but to eat.

Then she takes another, places it in her own mouth and stands up. She hardly ever speaks more than a few random words in English to me, so I'm not expecting what she says next.

"I am so proud of you. The best thing I can do for you,

for your father, is try to be stronger." She takes another sweet and places it in her mouth. "Best thing I can do for me, too." She savours the sweet before swallowing. "There are very kind people." She nods at the gift box.

I feel like screaming, crying and punching something all at the same time … and like hugging Mum because she's got this look on her face as if she's on a mission and I just feel so proud of *her* for making this mammoth effort for me. Any other parents' evening it would have been fine, but now, just as she's trying to get herself together, I'm going to let her down.

It's two o'clock in the morning. I'm lying in bed listening to Mum rehearsing her pronunciation, and instead of annoying me it makes my heart swell with love… I know she's trying to do what I asked her and not rely on me to be her voice. It takes her a long while to get her mouth around the word "curriculum", but eventually she manages it without stumbling.

How is Niya doing with the maths curriculum?

How is she doing in history curriculum?

How is she doing in the English curriculum?

Internal exclusion is a plain white room where you have to go to do your work on your own. There is a folder on the desk, of worksheets from all the lessons I am missing. In internal exclusion you're supposed to use the time to be quiet and think about the behaviour that's caused you to be separated from other people in the first place. It could be not doing your work, disrupting a class or getting into a fight. There is a glass window so that the secretary can keep an eye on me. I feel like a fish in a bowl – but not moving. A dead fish.

At lunchtime the secretary brings me a sandwich and a drink. I don't think she's supposed to be chatty, but she stays and talks to me for a few minutes. She asks me what I did to be here. I tell her I got into an argument.

"Next time take a deep breath before you react," she advises.

After I've finished, she picks up the tray and winks at me in a way that makes me think that, if it was up to her, she'd let me off and send me back to class. There is a toilet attached to the room so you don't need to leave. Through the glass screen I can see the hours tick by as the digits on the clock change and change, and now I know how Mum must feel every day ... just waiting for me. I try not to think about going home to pick Mum up for parents' evening tonight. With a bit of luck the lift will still be out of order. There is no way Mum could make it down all those stairs, even without her bad hip. But what if there was a fire?

I can't concentrate on my work. For a few moments I let myself think about nothing at all. Some people might feel claustrophobic being in internal exclusion, but in a way it's kind of relaxing.

★   ★   ★

Typical! The lift's been fixed.

I can hear music through our front door. There hasn't been any of this kind of music in our flat for two years. This was Mum and Dad's favourite – Abida Parveen singing one of her ghazals. What is the matter with me? I should be happy that Mum is listening to this song, but hearing it again makes me feel dizzy. I stand for a while and watch her body sway as she closes her eyes and feels the music – it's as if it's charging her up. Why do I feel the exact opposite?

All the grey is gone from Mum's hair and she's had the straighteners on so it's lost its fuzziness. I haven't seen her dressed up and with her hair done since she lost so much weight; she looks like a different person, all smoothed out and thin. And she's done all this without me.

"*Bohat payree lag re hay!* You're beautiful," I tell her.

Mum checks herself out in the mirror as if she's not sure, as if she doesn't really recognize herself.

I wish it could be the three of us heading off to parents' evening. If Dad was here I wouldn't be in this state. I wouldn't be in all this trouble and they could both be proud.

Mum covers her head and puts on her coat and shoes. She hardly ever wears them and they look brand new. Last of all she puts on her leather gloves.

"I am ready!" she says and holds her hand out to me.

Floor six. Let it get stuck right here… But I should have learned by now. The lift carries on

down

down

down

and I feel my breathing sharp and unsteady in my chest. I glance over to Mum and see that her hands are shaking, but I don't reach out to her because I feel so unsteady myself. I can't stand the thought that she will be disappointed with me. That she'll find out I'm so behind with everything … that she might even blame herself. But worse than that, I'm too scared to tell her about this pressure in my chest that's making me feel like the air is being squeezed out of me. What will Dr Chen write in her notes if we're both ill? What will happen to us then?

I don't remember the walk across the three roads between home and school. I feel floaty, as if I'm hardly here. I think Mum stops and talks to Mrs Asir and thanks her for the sweets. I think Mrs Asir walks with us for a while. I slip on the ice and I think she and Mum pick me up. It's all gone hazy.

Then we're inside the school and Mum's asking me where we should go first. I look at my planner and my head starts to spin. We're standing outside the lift when Sarah and her parents appear. I don't meet their eyes, but I hear Sarah's mum say something to my mum about how nice it is to see her and how well she looks. Mum says she'll never make all those stairs with her sore hip and we get into the lift while Sarah and her mum and dad go off in another direction.

As soon as the lift begins to move, Mum starts humming a tune that she and Dad always used to sing to me at bedtime. It's probably to calm herself down, but suddenly I can't stand it any more. I see the whole thing play out right in front of me: Mum making a super-human effort to speak English, to be brave, not to show her pain and not to make me translate for her. Mum's face crumpling as she realizes that her clever girl's grades are slipping and that she's spent the day in internal exclusion for pushing another girl over and walking out on a detention. The shame of it.

"Please stop humming," I want to say, but the words that slip from my mouth are, "Lift me up, Mum. Please lift me up." I raise my arms as I slump to the floor. "Please, Mum, lift me up." My face tingles and my whole body goes numb. Mum is holding a bag to my mouth and I'm breathing into it, and slowly my head stops reeling.

I feel the lift lurch, the doors open and Mum's arms around me as she struggles to help me up. Someone guides me along a corridor to a room. I am gently eased into a seat.

After that I have only a faint memory of someone offering me sips of water and hearing what Mum's voice sounds like when she's really in charge. Her words waft over my head like in a dream. Now here's Miss Rose's voice. She's saying, "I understand. It has been too much pressure."

"Mrs Sulimani..." Miss Rose's words are as soft as feathers as they float through my mind. I feel tears wash my cheeks. Mum reaches out her hand to me and we sit together in Miss Rose's office. I have the strangest thought that Miss Rose has turned into the robin flying busily in and out with twigs and feathers and words to build us a safe nest. I only catch a few of her words.

"Always willing to give support... My door is open... You are never alone... But of course, I know for myself, Mrs Sulimani, grief has a long fuse."

"I think Mango really did recognize you. The way she climbed into the palm of your hand!"

Sarah and I are chatting about Mango mostly and jumping up and down to try and keep warm. My feet, hands and nose are ice blocks and the lift is a fridge-freezer.

1, 2, 3, 4, 5, 6. I wish...

The lift door opens and Mum steps in carrying a tiffin-tin tower.

I can't get used to seeing her out and about without me. It's strange sometimes how words you didn't even know you'd learned pop into your head. "My mum is *dehors, dehors, dehors* the flat without any help from me!" I want to shout out to the world.

"Sarah! Good to see you." Mum smiles at my friend.

"You too, Mrs Sulimani." Sarah peers at Mum around the tiffin tins.

"Mrs Asir has a terrible cold so I took her some food," Mum explains. Then she shivers.

"It has been sooooo cold this year, but spring is just around a corner. I can feel it here." Mum taps her chest. "Maybe soon we can go together on picnic in Hyde Park? Here! Warm hands, girls."

Sarah giggles and places her frozen fingers below mine so our arms and hands are all intertwined.

Mum presses the lift button and the three of us carry on up.

I feel so stupid sitting in the waiting room with a box of Alphonso mangoes on my knee, but Mum insisted I bring them for Dr Chen. The old woman next to me keeps sniffing the air and licking her lips. I didn't realize till now how honey-sweet they smell.

Dr Chen comes out of her room. "Niya, come on in," she says, greeting me with a big smile.

I actually feel happy to see her.

"Mum made me bring you these," I say, handing the mangoes over.

Dr Chen picks one out of the box and smells it. "Ooh, delicious. I always think if sunshine had a smell it would be like that!" she says and places the box on the side. "That's too kind. Thank her for me, won't you?" Then she looks down at her notes. "Actually I can thank her myself. I'm seeing her tomorrow anyway."

We begin our review of all the "joined up help" we've been getting at school and at home.

I know why Mum's given Dr Chen a box of her favourite mangoes — because for the first year since Dad died it finally feels like we're going to have a summer.

"I sat in a school reception one day while waiting to give a talk, and a young girl of around thirteen arrived late. She said she had been taking her mum for a medical appointment. The receptionist replied that she would call home and check. The girl explained that her mother never answers the phone because she's not confident with her English. 'She needs me to translate.' The receptionist made a note of this and the girl carried on in to school. All through my talk I thought of the exhausted-looking girl and wondered how her day was going." Sita Brahmachari

A SUICIDE BOMBER SITS IN THE LIBRARY

Jack Gantos

He is a boy and he is bored. He is wearing a lovely new red jacket which conceals an explosive vest which has been cleverly sewn into the jacket's lining. He is a little warm but his commander has instructed him not to undo the jacket, and to sit still with a peaceful face, and to wait for orders. He has been told to fear nothing and that he will be perfectly safe in the library. Not even the secret police will think to look for him there, since he cannot read. The boy is obedient, and so he waits. It is hard to sit still, because of the excitement of the day and the honour he has of being chosen to blow up an enemy of his people. With his hand in his pocket he is holding a mobile phone. When it rings he is to answer it and listen. A voice will inform him of his target, where, God willing, he will detonate the bomb and step into paradise.

To pass the time, the boy imagines his target. He is hoping it is the leader of the people he hates because he has been taught to hate him and all his people. They are impure. God willing, he will find a place to stand by the side of the road, and when the leader's car passes in front of him he will whisper his final prayer and trigger the bomb. Perhaps the voice on the mobile phone will send him into a place of worship where the people praying are praying to the wrong god, and he will cleanse the world of them while he soars upwards like a bird into an eternal paradise beyond the sky. Or perhaps he will be sent to a checkpoint where enemy soldiers wait to inspect his people for weapons, and the moment they pat down his red jacket he will whisper his final prayer and look them in the eye as they vanish into a red mist of nothingness. Or he could be sent into a market where many enemy women and children and farmers and merchants gather. He will stand in the middle of them and courageously whisper his final prayer.

Now the heavy door to the library opens and another boy enters. He walks to a shelf of books. He carefully inspects them. After choosing one he sits down at a small desk. He opens the book and begins to read. He is smiling. He laughs out loud. Now he covers his mouth with his hand and laughs silently to himself. The suicide bomber wonders what it is about reading a book that makes the boy smile so widely. Then a girl enters the library. She too chooses a book to read and sits down. Soon she is sighing. Then she squints at a page and cries out as if someone has sneaked up and touched her shoulder. She closes her eyes and presses the open book against her face as if it were a mask. The suicide bomber wonders how a book can cast a spell and turn the reader into its puppet. Then a young man comes in with a very small boy. He sits the small boy at a desk, then, taking his time, chooses several books from a shelf. When the young man sits down he begins to read out loud to the small boy, who listens. It is a story about a lost pet that is hungry and lonely and missing its home and good food and a hot bath and the warm lap of its owner. The small boy points at the pictures in the book. The young man points at them too. They both look a little sad. Where could the pet be? How did it get lost? Did it take a wrong turn? Will some nice person find it and give it shelter and food? Will it ever find its way home again? The small boy looks under his desk for the pet. He wants to give it a new home. The suicide bomber glances under his own desk. He wants to ask what happens next in the story but he has been instructed to remain silent because books will master him just as they have mastered his enemies. He has been taught that books create a false life in a godless world that should not exist. Books cannot be trusted when only God has the key to paradise. And so the suicide bomber turns his face away from the readers and does not see the young man turn the final page in the story, nor does he see the small boy's joyous relief that all ends well.

Soon even more people arrive and choose books, and before long the library is crowded. The boy sits in the middle of the room. He is the only one without a book. He feels uncomfortable. He prays he can soon blow up, when abruptly his mobile phone rings. At that exact moment everyone in the room stops reading. They raise their eyes above the pages and stare fearfully at him. He lowers his face and listens to the voice of a man instructing him where to go, and then he stands. He weaves around tables and chairs and the people whose eyes have been dragged back to their books by a dark chain of words. He wonders, have the books captured the people? Or perhaps the people have captured the books? He wishes he had the answer, but there is no time to waste on questions that God does not care to answer.

The little suicide bomber walks out of the library as instructed. He walks for a long time down a crumbling road. He does not see the man following him. He passes blown-up houses. He passes burnt-out trucks. The man keeps an eye on the red jacket. The boy passes crying children. He passes angry men. He passes ruined families on their knees, sobbing in anguish. He stops for a moment and looks at a starving dog. It has suffered enough. Everything has. And when everything is broken, he wonders, are you winning or losing? Only God knows.

He walks away, thinking of the faces of the readers in the library. They were not ruined. They were happy. They were safe. Whatever power lived within those books did not hurt them. He keeps walking. The man keeps walking. The boy is walking faster now. He is thinking faster. He is thinking that he must prepare himself for a new life. He raises his eyes towards paradise. He whispers a hopeful prayer he knows by heart. He watches the words rise from his mouth. He cannot read them, but in his heart he wishes words could make him laugh and cry and sigh and give him the courage to do what he must. The man behind him is also thinking about what final words he will tell the boy.

Now the boy stops. It is time. He gathers up a deep breath and turns down a path. It is the wrong path and it is rugged and the boy jumps over hard ruts and ridges of mud. The man is alarmed and quickly follows, but at a distance. The boy comes to an orchard and walks between shattered trees full of singing birds. He steps into a shallow stream and cools his feet as he moves on. Finally, he arrives at a smooth black rock. He turns his head but sees no one. But the man has followed him quietly, like a shadow, and he hides behind a larger black rock. He thinks that maybe the boy is lost. The boy keeps looking up into the sky. Clouds pass overhead like waves on an ocean. Nothing can stop them. Nothing can stop the boy from thinking.

Something inside of him has changed. Now his thoughts have become a book only he can read. He picks a stone up from the loose earth. He holds it tightly in his fist. He thinks that if he blows the stone into a hundred pieces, each piece might be smaller but it will be just as hard. The next suicide bomber could blow up the smaller rocks a second time and the pieces would be even smaller but still just as hard. It is the same with life, he thinks. He could blow it up a hundred times and it would become a hundred times smaller, and yet remain just as hard. From a safe distance the man watches the boy. He is troubled. He thinks this boy may be too young because he is still thinking like a boy. Only a grown man can will himself not to think. The man looks into the sky. He prays. What should he do next? He listens to the harsh command and now it is time for him to act. He picks up his phone.

The boy answers. The man speaks. He says it is now time for the boy to return to the path that will lead to infinite pleasure. The boy says nothing. He closes his eyes so hard that his mind becomes an infinite pool of black ink. From that pool every pen could be filled, and any thought could be written, and any question could be asked. The book inside of him writes a question in his mind. What were those people doing in the library? he asks himself. He knows there is only one way to answer that question.

The man closes his eyes. He prays the boy will return to the correct path and fulfil his destiny. He prays that he will not have to press a special number on his mobile phone that will detonate the bomb. The boy drops the rock from his hand and stands up. He is hot, and very cautiously he slips out of his red jacket. He looks around. In the distance he sees the man. The boy turns and runs. He does not stop.

At the library they heard the explosion. Some readers ran out into the street and looked up into the air. They gasped. They cried out. They pointed towards a dark blossom of smoke. Then, from the uncurling petals of ash, a red jacket floated upwards. It floated above the tallest trees and beyond the naked mountains and their snowy peaks and then it was never seen again.

Until years later a man sits alone in a library. He is reading a powerful book. Every time he turns a page, the page turns up inside the man. First, he laughs. Then he sighs. He moans. He cries. He sets the book down and wipes his eyes. He looks out of the window and remembers where he came from. He says a prayer for those left behind.

Suddenly his mobile phone rings. His breath quickens. It is his young son. He tells the boy exactly where to meet. The man stands up. He holds the book in his hand as he heads towards the door. The librarian waves to him. He smiles and waves in return and then hurries out of the library and down the sidewalk. He walks quickly. He looks left and right. The boy is not at the meeting spot. Where is he? He calls him on his mobile phone. He doesn't answer. Perhaps he has been captured, the man thinks. He panics and dashes around a corner.

There is the boy. He is wearing a red jacket and walking very, very slowly. His face is pressed into a book. He is reading the last page. When he finishes he sighs and lifts his eyes. He sees his father standing on the corner. He is smiling. The boy smiles too as he raises the book over his head. "This is a good one!" he shouts.

A page turns.

"I was reading up on Denis Diderot, who wrote a good bit on religious fanaticism – a subject which is presently fuelling international terrorism. There were several quotes by Diderot, which I wrote in my journal. 'People stop thinking when they cease to read,' and 'From fanaticism to barbarism is only one step.' The one that started me to write this story, however, was: 'But who shall be the master, the writer or the reader?' (Denis Diderot, 1796)." Jack Gantos

SCHOOL OF LIFE
Elizabeth Laird

Everything was boring. Pointless, stupid and boring. School was driving me crazy. I hated the teachers, and the teachers hated me. As if that wasn't bad enough, my best friend, Maria, had walked out without a word to me. She was there one day and gone the next. No explanation, no goodbye, and no answer when I called her phone. As for home, what can I say? It was as bad as it had ever been, my mum shouting at me and my stepdad laying into me with his fists. I couldn't wait to get away.

There was only one person who listened to me and seemed to know how I felt, and that was Andrei, my stepdad's cousin. He used to come round to our place all the time.

"Ignore them, little Katya," he would say when my mum and stepdad drank too much and began fighting. "Look, I've got something for you. This'll cheer you up."

He bought me all kinds of things. The best was a pair of red shoes with mile-high heels.

"Wow!" he said when I put them on. "You look eighteen! Fabulous! Give me a hug, my Katya."

And I threw myself into his arms.

It took my mum a while to notice my new clothes and make-up, but when she did she went crazy.

"Look at you!" she screeched. "Dressed up like a tart! You're fourteen years old! Where did you get all that stuff? You've been stealing, haven't you?"

"How dare you?" I shouted back. "Andrei gives me things. He – he's my boyfriend."

I'd never used the word "boyfriend" before, not even to myself. It made me feel wonderful.

Mum slapped me across the face.

"Andrei? Your dad's cousin? Liar. Think he'd look at a skinny little rat like you? If you steal any more stuff I'll throw you out. I mean it."

I ran outside, crying. Andrei was right there, leaning on his moped under a street light. He looked gorgeous, lean and cool in his tight jeans with a lick of dark hair falling over his forehead.

"Hey, hey, what's with you?" he said, catching me in his arms.

He took me into town on his moped. We went to a grown-up bar. He was right. I could and did pass for eighteen. I felt almost dizzy with excitement that night.

"You're too good for this place," he told me the next day when he met me outside school. "You deserve better. I can get you a job, you know, in the fashion business. In London. Think of it, Katya. London! Pretty girl like you, you'll go places there. Money, clothes – whatever you want."

"I don't want to go anywhere without you," I whispered back.

"Think I'd let you go alone?" He looked shocked. "My little Katya? I'll be going with you, of course."

I suddenly realized that he was serious and my heart thumped with excitement.

"Do you – are you…?" I stammered.

"I mean it, my darling. Let's go and get your photo taken. I'll need it to sort out a passport. Don't say a word at home. They'll only stand in your way. We'll be gone by the end of November."

I suddenly felt a bit panicky.

"What about school?"

He snorted.

"School? The school of life's what I'm offering you, Katya. Grown-up stuff. The real thing. Trust me. You'll never look back."

He was waiting there for me again the next day. He smiled when he saw me running towards him. He pulled a letter out of his pocket and dangled it tantalizingly in front of my face.

"What is it?" I said, reaching for it.

He flicked it teasingly out of reach.

"Wouldn't you like to know?"

I lunged forwards and snatched it out of his hand, then stared down at the envelope in utter amazement.

"But this is Maria's writing! How did *you* get it?" A horrible suspicion hit me. "She's not – you haven't been – she's not your girlfriend, is she?"

Andrei laughed.

"Silly Katya! I've only got one girlfriend, and you know who she is."

"Then why...?"

He held up both his hands as if he were fending me off.

"I'll explain if you'll give me a chance. Maria got herself a wonderful job in London. She had to leave straight away. No time for goodbyes. A friend of mine organized the whole thing. He came back yesterday. It's the first I'd heard of it or I'd have told you, of course."

I couldn't believe it. Maria! In London!

"What sort of job?" I said.

"She's a receptionist in a five-star hotel," said Andrei. "Film stars, musicians – they all stay there."

"Why didn't she write to me at home? She knows my address."

He pinched my chin.

"She didn't have any stamps, I suppose. Anyway, she knew my friend would bring it back with him and give it to me by hand."

I tore the envelope open and read the letter. It was very short.

Dear Katya,
No time to write much. You wouldn't believe what life in London is like. I miss you SOOOOO much! Wish you were here!
Love
Maria

PS I hope your cat's better.

I frowned. I hadn't got a cat. We'd never had a cat. Surely Maria knew that?

"You see?" Andrei was saying. "Your friend Maria's in London and she loves it. Trust me, she's having the time of her life. What do you say now?"

So I did trust him. I trusted him while I packed the cheap suitcase he bought me. I trusted him as I crept out of the house in the middle of the night, my heart pounding in case my stepdad heard the creak of the floorboards. I trusted him as we rolled west along the motorways of Europe, even though he frowned more than he smiled and spoke to me less and less. I trusted him all the way to Brussels.

I didn't realize at first that he'd abandoned me. He had sat me down in a cafe and told me sharply to stay where I was. I'd been so strung up with excitement, love for Andrei and the beginnings of a nagging sense of anxiety, and I was so tired, what with sitting up night after night on buses, that everything caught up with me and all I wanted to do was sleep. I could barely keep my eyes open.

The last time I saw Andrei was when he was standing outside in the street, talking to a couple of men. I couldn't hear what they were saying. Through bleary eyes I saw one of them peel some notes off a fat wad of money and hand them to Andrei. It was warm and fuggy in the cafe. I'd dozed off before he'd finished counting them.

Someone shook me awake. It was the bigger of the two men.

"Come on, you. Get your skinny butt off that chair."

I stared up at him, dazed.

"Where's Andrei?"

"Gone."

"What do you mean, gone? Where? I've got to find him!"

I could see from the look in his eyes that he'd have slapped me if he could, but the barman was watching. Instead, his big, meaty hand closed so tight around my arm that it began to throb.

Cold fear was making me shiver. Nothing made sense. I couldn't believe what was happening.

"Get your hands off me!" I hissed. "Leave me alone!

I'm going to wait here for Andrei."

He pushed his face right into mine. I caught the waft of stale alcohol. My stomach lurched with fright.

"I'll take you to him. No fuss, do you hear?"

The barman's hand was sliding towards his phone.

Why didn't I scream then, when I had the chance? Why was I such a little fool? The barman might have helped me. He might have called for help.

But I didn't scream. I picked up my suitcase and stumbled outside, looking frantically up and down the street. Andrei wasn't there.

The big man was right behind me.

"Give it up, little fool. You won't see your precious Andrei again. He's sold you to me. You're mine now. You'll do what I say or you'll suffer for it."

I stared at him as his words slowly sank in.

"No!" I whispered, violently shaking my head. "No!"

But I knew he was telling the truth. Andrei had sold me for money, like a dog, or a piece of meat. He'd never been my boyfriend. Everything he'd ever told me had been lies.

The nightmare began then. A little hotel in Brussels. The big man first, then others. It hurt so badly I screamed, and they beat me till I stopped. I felt dirty, after that first time, but then there were others, many, many others. Punches. Kicks. Never on my face, where bruises would have shown.

As the bus rolled out through the dull concrete suburbs of Brussels I felt worthless. A nobody. Nothing.

They gave me pills that made me feel sleepy and a bit sick. There was another bus, and another. More men. More angry conversations outside bus stations in languages I couldn't understand. More stacks of banknotes changing hands. And my passport changing hands too. My passport. Me. My life. Bought and sold.

It was cold the night we arrived in London. My coat was thin and no proof against the November rain. I stood huddled outside the big glass doors of a huge, impersonal bus station, staring at the rows of coaches without seeing them, dully expecting to be shoved into one, craving a soft seat, a chance to sleep and, above all else, food.

But my new "owner" didn't kick me onto a bus. He seemed nervous and was tapping his foot on the pavement impatiently, fingering his phone. It rang suddenly. He listened for a moment, then jerked his head to indicate that I should follow him.

I was so beaten down by then that I'd have followed him into the mouth of hell.

I didn't know that that was exactly where he was taking me.

A car drew up. He pushed me into the back seat and climbed in beside me. I hardly bothered to look out of the window as we drove through the dark streets of London. I wouldn't have seen much even if I'd tried. Rain was sluicing down and steam was fogging up the glass. All I saw was the glow of lights and an impression of huge buildings, their unlit windows as blank as blind eyes.

We stopped outside a small house in a row of identical ones that ran the length of a long, dingy street. Number 48 was painted on the door. I didn't have time to notice anything more. Another man, my new "owner", was waiting for me. He was smaller than most of those who had come before, but meaner and uglier. His first blow winded me. The second nearly knocked me out.

"Just to let you know who's boss around here," he growled, speaking in my language but with a strong foreign accent. "You do your work, you live. You eat. Any trouble, you get trouble back."

"What work?" I whispered. "Please, I'm so hungry. Can I…?"

His third blow left me sprawling on the stairs.

I don't want to remember the times that followed. Sometimes they flash back into my mind. Less often now. One day, perhaps, the memories will fade.

Other girls, lots of girls, were living in the house, but we were never allowed to talk to each other. I'd catch glimpses of one of them sometimes, on my way to the toilet or the shower, but we didn't even dare to exchange looks.

It must have been several weeks after I arrived in that hell (it can't have been much more, though it seemed like for ever) that I saw Maria. I had just come back from the bathroom and she was hurrying past me on her way there. Our eyes met for the briefest moment, then she scurried on. I was filled with a blinding rage. She had been my friend! How could she have written that letter to me? How could she have betrayed me?

The weather was foul that night, with rain lashing against the windows and a howling wind making the rickety old casements shake. There were fewer customers than usual. I suppose the rain put them off. By about three in the morning the whole house seemed asleep. I was very tired, and was just dropping off when there was a faint knock on my door. I dragged myself wearily out of bed, dreading yet another visit. But the person standing outside was Maria.

I lunged forwards, wanting to hit her. She pushed me back into my room, her finger to her lips, and closed the door behind us.

"Why did you write that letter? *Why?*" I hissed. "You knew it would make me come. We were *friends*!"

There were tears on her cheeks.

"I'm so, so sorry, Katya. They made me do it. They beat me and beat me until I agreed. They said they'd break my little brother's legs and set fire to our house. I didn't say anything in the letter about being happy in London, just that I was here and missing you. You read into it what you wanted to believe. And I put in the bit about a cat because I hoped it would make you suspicious. Didn't it? I was taking a risk, actually."

Now she was the one to look reproachful.

I stared at her. Was she right? Had I just believed what I'd wanted to believe? Why hadn't I thought harder about the cat?

"I didn't – I don't know," I said grudgingly. "I only read it once, and…"

"And you were too thrilled and excited to think about it properly. I know." She nodded. "Just like I was. Who groomed you?"

"Groomed? Oh. My stepdad's cousin. Andrei."

"Him. He's good. He's done lots of girls." My fiery old friend Maria would have spat out a curse. This new Maria just looked sad. She came closer to me and I flinched. I was afraid she would put her arm around me, and I couldn't bear the thought of being touched, not even in friendship. She understood.

"Listen," she said in a low, urgent whisper. "You've got to listen. You're not in deep yet. You've still got – your spirit. I can see it in your face. Your eyes. They haven't crushed your soul. Not yet. You have to get away."

I snorted.

"How can I? They'll come after me. You know what the boss always says. Any attempt to escape and they kill you."

She shook her head.

"They don't kill us. They've paid too much to get us. They'd beat you bad if they caught you, but they won't.

I can tell you what to do. I've thought and thought about it. I've worked out a way."

A creak on the stair outside made us both freeze. We sat side by side on my bed, our hands over our mouths, but whoever it was carried on past my door.

"Why don't *you* escape if you've worked it all out?" I whispered accusingly. "Are you trying to get me into trouble? Haven't you done enough already?"

"I can't, Katya. I've been here too long. I've lost – I don't know – *I'm* lost." She was silent for a moment. "And anyway," she went on, "I daren't risk it. I told you. They'd tell their friends at home and they'd cripple my little brother and burn our house."

"They said things like that to me, too," I said bitterly, "and do you know what? I wouldn't care. My stepdad is my trafficker's cousin. Mum doesn't love me anyway. She only wants her booze."

"Then go! Go!" urged Maria.

"You say that, but how? The outside doors are always locked and the windows are all nailed up. Don't think I haven't checked."

She gave a little smile.

"You haven't checked all of them. The window in the toilet on the lower landing's come loose. Someone must have made a stink in there and wrenched it open. I found it like that and shut it quickly. No one else has noticed, I'm sure. You can open it easily now. And there's a drainpipe

119

outside. It's not a big drop to the ground."

I was listening intently now.

"But the yard has a fence around it."

"A fence!" she scoffed. "It's nothing. You can climb over that easily. And there's a lane beyond. I can't see where it goes, but it's sure to take you out to a road."

"And then what? They've got my passport. Where would I go? Who'd believe me? I can hardly speak a word of English."

She did touch me then. She took my hand, and the caress of her fingers was so gentle, so different from the brutal maulings of the hundred other hands that had been on my body, that I felt a softening weakness before a rush of strength passed through me.

"Go to the police, Katya," she whispered urgently. "They're good here. They'll listen to you. Bring them to this house to rescue me. To rescue all of us."

"I don't even know where we are!" I said. "Only the number. Forty-eight."

She nodded.

"It's called Bridgend Road. Forty-eight Bridgend Road. Say it."

"Forty-eight Bridgend Road," I repeated, then said it again under my breath, as if it were a spell. I looked back at her. "I'll think about it," I said. "I'll…"

"No." She had spoken too loudly, and stopped herself, shocked at the sound of her voice. "It's got to be tonight. Think about it, Katya. How often is the house this quiet?

And how do we know they won't find the window tomorrow and nail it up again? Do it, Katya. Please. Go now."

The look in her eyes was so desperate it frightened me. I saw how much older she looked, how thin and beaten down and hopeless.

I'll look like that soon, I thought. *Perhaps I do already. She's right. I've got to take my chance.*

She watched me, biting her nails as I put on a jumper and a pair of jeans. The only shoes I had were the red ones with those silly high heels that Andrei had given me. They would have to do. My captors had taken away my other ones, along with my coat.

There are different kinds of fear and I've never been a brave person. I'd been scared half senseless by many of the men who'd beaten and abused me, but as I climbed out of the toilet window and lurched dangerously sideways to reach the drainpipe, I was filled with a new kind of terror. The rain drummed on my back and the wind beat my hair around my face, half blinding me as I slid awkwardly to the ground. But when I stepped out across the rubbish-strewn back yard, with nothing worse than a scratch on my hand where it had snagged against a nail, I felt wildly triumphant. A moment later I was over the fence and out in the lane.

The good feeling only lasted until I reached the road. I peered out anxiously from the shadow of the lane. The street lights were horribly bright. It was about half past three in the morning. Any car coming along would notice a girl walking alone at this time of night, tottering along on high heels without even a coat to protect her from the rain. What if my "owner" was out and came back? Or one of the men who'd used me?

I suppose it was the rain that drove me on. I was already wet and shivering. At least walking would warm me up. I didn't know whether to turn left or right, but the lights were brighter towards the right, so I chose that way. I don't know how far I walked that night. It felt like a long way. I kicked those hateful shoes off after a while and hurled them into someone's front garden. My feet soon felt bruised and numb with cold. I seemed to walk for miles down long streets like Bridgend Road, the windows of the anonymous houses blank, like unseeing eyes, before I came to a broader road where there were shops, all shuttered and dark of course. There was a church on the corner with a clock on its tower. It was quarter past five. The rain had stopped at last, but I was wet through, and so exhausted that I knew I couldn't go on. I saw a bus shelter on the far side of the road. There was a bench in it. I crossed over and slumped down, frozen in mind, my whole body shaking with cold.

I sat there for a long while, unable to even think about what I should do next. Eventually a car pulled up beside me. I leapt to my feet, ready to run. Then I saw the blue light on top of it. A woman was getting out. She was wearing a blue uniform.

"You all right, love?" she said. I'd only learned a few words of English by then and did not understand her.

"Please," was all I could say. "Please."

She came closer. I backed away from her, pressing myself against the glass wall of the bus shelter.

"How old are you?"

I knew what those words meant. I'd been taught the question, and that I was always supposed to answer: *Eighteen.*

"Fourteen," I said.

She had a radio clipped to her shoulder. She bent her head and spoke into it. Then she opened the back door of the police car. I stared at her. I'd trusted Maria. I'd trusted Andrei. I'd thought I'd never trust anyone again. But what choice did I have?

"Come on, love," she said. "Get into the car."

So I did.

"Some years ago, in Pakistan, I met a group of young boys, some as young as five, who had been trafficked to the Gulf States to be camel jockeys in the rich camel racing industry. I was deeply shocked and moved by their experiences, and wrote a novel about them, called Lost Riders. *Slowly, over the years, I have come to realize that there is a widespread and vicious trade in trafficked girls, some very young, into our own country. It's time we stood up and shouted about it."*
Elizabeth Laird

CONSTANT

Jackie Kay

It is following you and you can't escape.
You cannot hold your head up or be happy.
You lose your confidence. You turn a corner: it is there.
You cannot step on it; make it disappear.
You are feeling many complicated things.
Dawn raids strike and you are terrified.
You are imprisoned in your own life.
Every time you go to the Home Office, there it is.
They make you feel inhuman. Every word you speak
A complete lie. An untruth. You cannot begin
To imagine. It is always there. Constant.
It is your only companion. There is no freedom.

There is just this *fear*. You can't really describe it.
It gets everywhere. It gets in your hair.
Under your arms; between your legs.
It gives you a bad taste in your mouth.
You can see it in your eyes; hear it in your voice.
It is hard to describe. It never takes a break.
When you walk away, it follows you. When you
Stay inside, it stays by your side, so quiet.
It is under your skin. It is your heartbeat.
Never leaves you be. *It is you. It is me.*
It will stroke your hand when you die.

"This poem, together with 'Glasgow Snow' and 'Push the Week', was written in response to stories told to me by three different women, who I was put in touch with by the Scottish Refugee Council. Their stories were so very different that I wrote three separate poems, which were read out at an event in the Scottish parliament with many of the refugees present." Jackie Kay

REDEMPTION
Ryan Gattis

On the drive into San Quentin State Prison, the contrast stays strong and strange no matter how many times I see it. I always feel like I'm entering a dystopian novel: on the peninsular tip of Marin County – one of the richest areas on the entire planet, dotted with multimillion-dollar, San Francisco Bay-view homes stacked on hills – stands one of the worst prisons there ever was, chock-full of poor people of every stripe, those who had the worst possible legal representation the first time around, all of them housed inside the thickest of walls, walls that stand between them and a gorgeous view that most will never actually see.

The irony of it all is a rock in my stomach. It's something

I didn't want to swallow but it's there, and I can't digest it. A first-rate science-fiction writer could probably come up with plenty of metaphors and allegories for this, but I get stuck in emotion. To me, it just feels wrong, unfair on so many levels, and – more than anything – sad. Stomach-ache sad. "Don't think about it too much or you'll go crazy" sad.

So I don't.

I focus on pulling up, turning left into the visiting lot – except I can't. The guard at the gate puts his hand up at me because some first-time visitor didn't know any better and missed the turn, so I have to sit and wait while he turns his car around and cuts into the lot ahead of me.

This is a courtesy visit, an "I'm your lawyer and I need to check up on you and see how you're being treated" visit. The paperwork's already filed. The federal courts found difficulties with my client's appeal that they had to kick back to the state level for resolution.

Dawn's done, but it's still early: 7.20 a.m. for an 8 a.m. appointment. There are spaces closer to visitor processing, but I park facing the water because I always park facing the water. Even this early, the parking lot is already half full. I can't see the Golden Gate Bridge, but it's out there on my right, south of Belvedere. The bridge to Richmond is on my left. Gulls on the rocky beach fight over something that looks like a dried banana skin but probably isn't. Seabirds cut loops in the sky in front of me as I check emails on my phone. I leave a message for Janine at the office, reminding her to file the motions we finished last night, and then I get out of the car, empty my pockets, take extra keys off my ring so I only have the car key left and lock the rest in the trunk with my phone.

Inside the processing building that looms over the parking lot is what Janine calls the Sad Corridor. She's not wrong, but it doesn't feel that way to me when I walk in today. Sure, the near side is heavy with quiet gloom. These are the walk-ups: mothers, grandmothers and grandfathers and kids sit pressed together on a long bench, but the far side – the appointments, the jail wives and kids – is alive with chatter, with hugs and hellos, and questions. None of them fake. Nobody talking for talking's sake. All as real as church, because every single person here knows the deepest consequences of the law as the lived experience of ripple effect, as a life changer. The only other people who fully understand it are the families of their husbands' and daddies' victims. Once that web gets you, it never lets you go, no matter which side of the crime you're on.

This is the domain of women, and they know it. Sure, there might be a brother in there on any given visiting day, but this side of the corridor is all the high voices and appraisals of women obeying the dress code. Nothing too tight. Nothing too short. Nothing too sexual. Nothing that matches what inmates or guards wear at this California Department of Corrections and Rehabilitation institution: no jeans, no chambray shirts, no dark green, no khaki, no brown – which basically means there's a lot of black and white here. It being December, a coat is allowed. Beyond that, they've all got plastic baggies or clear little purses holding dollar bills and quarter rolls for the food machines, and their government ID. Nothing else.

I'm standing in the middle of the corridor, waiting to be buzzed through, watching. You can learn more about the human race from ten minutes in this hallway than a whole lifetime anywhere else if you know how and where to look. For me, it's at the little boy sitting up as straight as he can, fiddling the top collar button of his shirt open with one hand, and then back closed, and then open again. It's a button with stakes. Done up is to be formal, strait-laced, armoured. Undone is to be loose enough to let the world in, to be open to undue influence.

His mother sits beside him, holding his other hand in a grip so firm that even from here I can see it's part help and part hurt; I know this because it's how my momma used to hold mine in a hallway just like this, before I knew what it meant. It's a complicated grip. It says: *I will not keep you from your father; you will learn from his mistakes and absolutely not make the same ones; you must understand this shadowed corner of the world most people never see so you can be damn sure you don't end up on the wrong side here. I show you the dark,* it says, *even though we're both afraid, because the stakes are high and this is the most important lesson you'll learn in your life: be good, don't stray, don't ever fuck up like your father fucked up.*

It's a Shakespearean moment about fathers and sons, about burdens, and paths, and costs, crammed into two seconds. All of that in a fussed-with button and a hand squeeze that doesn't let up, even as I get buzzed through to visiting and can't see it any more.

My ID is scrutinized, and they bring my visiting file up, then the list gets checked. My name is on it. I have to open my briefcase, but only so they can see it just has papers, pens and file folders, then I close it. They print out my visiting form. It still has my client's mugshot on it from eighteen years ago: smiling crazily.

Every time I see it, I think, *That's not him any more.*

I have to duck under a string of tinsel to get into the screening room, where I remove my blazer and put it in the tray to go through the X-ray machine. I'm cursing myself for wearing new shoes I haven't broken in yet as I lean down to untie them. It's like I'm at the airport, going on vacation, except on the other side of that exit – after a long walk in the wind – it's pretty much the opposite of that.

"Designer," the guard working the X-ray says as she taps the toecaps of my shoes with her fingernails before resettling them in the tray. "These are real nice."

"Thanks," I say as I shrug my blazer back on.

She watches the monitor as my shoes go through, then slides them out the other side and says, "You're good."

I thank her again when my shoes are back on, and I'm through the door.

Back out on the bay, walking the yellow line and feeling my heels rub with every step, I pass an older couple helping each other. On the water, far off to my left, a crew boat glides by with a coxswain shouting orders to rowers by bullhorn: "Get your butts up!" and "Watch your balance!"

I wonder what these athletes think about the prison, or if they've ever visited, as I cross another parking lot and turn left at the central building that looks like a castle. I hug the red brick wall next to it, my footsteps bouncing off concrete as two men unload a snack food pallet from a nearby truck. There's a big door just past a metal staircase, and next to it a tiny sign: *Visitors Entrance*. No punctuation mark.

I wait to be buzzed in, and then leave my driver's licence with the guard behind the double-plexied window. When a gate behind me shuts, one opens in front of me. Also black. Also heavy. There are two correction officers joking together on the other side.

I'm about to brush past them and turn left to the room used for legal visits, beyond the partitioned visiting area, when the taller one stops me.

"Mr Hill?"

My heart drops in my chest. Bad news is on its way, I know it. I've come all the way out here only for them to deny me, to tell me he's lost privileges, or he's in the infirmary. I'm making my face a mask and getting ready to hear a sorry explanation when the shorter, fatter CO points behind me.

I follow his finger to the cages for contact visits on my

right, the ones that have white bars stretching from floor to ceiling and plexiglass behind them, and there he is – sitting the closest to freedom he's been in eighteen years.

My jaw actually drops.

My eyes hit his and we have a fast, wordless conversation. My high eyebrows ask, *When the hell did* this *happen?* He shrugs and his hands come up, telling me that it's so new he's still trying to figure it out himself.

"Your inmate's up," the CO says behind me, like it isn't obvious.

I'm already walking towards the cell, speaking to him through the vertical crack between panels of plexiglass.

I say, "How long?"

Meaning: *How long have you been out of the hole?*

For eighteen years he was in the solitary housing unit – or SHU – two doors between him and anybody else, even guards. Torture is what it was.

"Last Tuesday," he says. His head is bowed as if his words are heavy, and they are. You can hear it in his voice.

I do the math: a little over a week and a half. Eleven days.

I'm smiling a smile I can't control. I say, "You hungry?"

He nods.

At the humming machines, I get us two burritos and heat them up while I press the buttons for two orange juices, the full cans thumping to the chute bottom. California must make a fortune on these things.

When I'm back and locked in with him, he knows his boundaries. He shakes my hand and lets go first, but I'm aware that this respectful, positive touch is no small thing.

I study his wrists, the hard red lines on them: double parallel lines, one for each side of the shackle. I know how they work. I'll be here two hours. In that time, they won't fade.

Around bites of burrito, he tells me his mother has already visited, that he got to hug her for the first time in way too long.

I'm caught by the thought of that. My mom's been dead three years herself – three years and two months, actually – and the idea of being able to hug her again overwhelms me, so I just nod and say, "How did it feel?"

He's right there with me, half frowning. His nostrils flare a little. He's riding a wave inside, but hiding how complicated it is.

"Pretty good," he finally says, and it's the kind of understatement you hear a lot here. Of course it was better than pretty good, but it's tempered because it happened while locked in a box like this one, and it was only for a few hours, that connection, and then it was gone; she left, and he had to be led away, and he couldn't watch her go. He would've had to leave first, to be strip-searched behind the main door before they even let her out, but having that warmth, even for a moment, and losing it again, would've been about the worst feeling he'd felt in years.

He was a teenager when he did what he did, undeveloped

brain and all. Making bad choices. Doing "gang shit" as it's known around my office. Got sentenced as an adult. Grew up behind bars. His story is the same as a few thousand others. Poor kids. Doesn't matter if they're black, brown or white. They have an overworked public defender, and in shocking numbers, they don't pass go, they go directly to jail.

Still, he's alive in here. Still human. Against all odds, really.

Eighteen years in the hole.

No contact twenty-three hours a day until eleven days ago.

Still waiting to die.

Here's the thing, though: the state of California hasn't executed anyone since 2006. It's got hundreds of condemned prisoners, and more than a few with exhausted appeals, real no-hopers forming an awful long line. The state knows it needs to resume executions. New proposed regulations for doing just that have been released. The public hearing date is already set. We talk about the proposal: the absurdity of it, the insane bureaucracy of how to kill "humanely" and how many people get paid to actually do it.

"What hit me," he says, "is that it's going to cost tax-payers one hundred and eighty-six thousand dollars to kill me."

I give a slow, sad nod. I highlighted that number in my copy too: $186,886.

I also highlighted its breakdown – CDCR Training Staff and Ancillary Costs: $85,200; Cost of Lethal Injection Chemical (based on previous purchase of thiopental – the drug the state of Arizona has been buying, against federal law): $4,193; Contracts with other law enforcement agencies to provide crowd control outside the prison: $97,492. I added it up and was off by a dollar. They rounded somewhere.

He says, "All that for a couple hours?"

It's my turn to shrug. Like no place on earth, prison in America is a business.

"You're a job creator," I say, and he smiles, trying to hide the sour edges of it.

I can see he's got deep smile lines on his face. He's also got listening eyes and brows that tent and react genuinely when I'm talking: signs of empathy and sympathy written all over his body language.

He's still human, I think. *But even more amazing is this: he's a better human than when he got locked up.* It's remarkable that he could grow up so much in a place built to dehumanize. It's what you'd hope prison does, but which it rarely ever achieves.

We talk about how he's doing.

"Fine," he says. Meaning: *Not fine, but surviving.*

He's SHU-sick, he says, like homesick. He misses the quietness of being shut up alone behind a door, of having the space to disappear into a book. He's been relocated to a tier, and given a cell with only bars on it. You hear everything happening on all five tiers, fifty-seven cells per floor, the snorings and the fights. All night. As a result, he's not sleeping much. He's wrapping one of his bedsheets tight around itself, tying it to his desk, and using the other end to anchor the cell door so it's difficult to open.

"People here just call that security," he says.

I change the subject.

We talk about case specifics, because after that it's easier to talk about what we know. We talk simple stuff. Stuff we've covered in the past, but once more now, mostly to build a buffer between the last topic and the next one.

After a little while, we relax again.

We talk books, long books – the longer, and the more epic, the better. He's a Robert Jordan fan. He's starting on Diana Gabaldon soon. He lights up talking about premises and plots. Stories are the only way he can escape. I feel that, and I listen, impressed by his passion.

He ends with a question: "Have you ever wanted to write fiction?"

"I've thought about it," I say. "I think most lawyers do."

His brow wrinkles. "Since they moved me, I got this self-help book that says I should write fiction to turn bad feelings into art. I tried writing fantasy, but halfway through, it just turned into a story about a guy dreaming it from prison." He's looking at me, not hard, but intently. "If you had to write about a prison, how would you make it better? Like, what would you change from this one?"

"Tough questions," I say, and they are. Big questions. So big that I'm scared to think too much about them or I'll slide right into clinical depression.

"I know," he says, "but what do you think you'd write for it? If you had to."

I push the possibility around in my head, get nothing but a blank, and say, "I'll have to think about it."

He looks disappointed by that, but we move on to movies. Of the last three they screened for inmates here, one was good and all of them were censored.

Then we talk TV, skipping right to the episode of *60 Minutes* that aired a couple weeks ago, the one about the guy getting killed in an Arizona death chamber who took two hours to die, gasping all the way. On the programme, a pro-death penalty federal judge called the DP "barbaric", and advocated a guillotine instead, or a bullet – because both are cheaper, quicker, and result in less suffering.

"Didn't that judge say something like –" his eyes go internal as he tries to remember – "*the death penalty already is barbaric, and if we can't accept the cruelty of it, we shouldn't be doing it?*"

"Something like that," I say.

He's nodding, opening his mouth to say something more, but the fatter CO is standing outside our cage and motioning for my client to put his hands through the little lowered door in the plexiglass, so he does. The cuffs go on then, the door comes open and I'm told to step out and away behind a yellow line.

This kind of goodbye – where one person goes to be locked up and the other gets to go free – it's always awkward.

"See you in two weeks," I say.

"You take care driving back," he says before being led through the largest metal door of all.

When he's gone and cleared of having any contraband, I get to go too.

The wind is up when I'm walking out. Even though the sun is higher, there's no heat, and fast breezes come in cold off the bay, meeting me with swiping gusts.

My head is full, and reality is a little too heavy right now. So I walk.

I think about the current system, concerned more with budgets and overtime than humanity, as my client's big questions whirl around inside me. With each step, I wonder how a prison could be better in a story – what it would look like, and be like, and accomplish – and all I can wonder about then is how to make more people like my client; how to make prisoners more human, to make personal growth standard, not just an anomaly.

I shiver. It'd have to be windy, and cold, and maybe on an island, this prison. Maybe it's on a watery moon somewhere, out in space. And there's a single island on that moon. On the island is the prison, a futuristic Alcatraz that can't be escaped because it's the only landmass in an endless salty sea.

Just so nobody misses the utopian point, I'd name it Redemption.

My steps are faster now, my new shoes still chewing my heels, but I can't stop. I see two guards walking in with blank looks, their belts on their shoulders. One nods at me. The other stares straight ahead.

And something clicks.

Add some robot warrior monks to the story, I think, as guardians. It has to be monks, people with some legitimate spiritual training, not just high-school educations and four months at cadet academy like nearly all the COs have. These monks would train the inmates, not in combat, but in self-control, self-awareness, anger management and a craft. This wouldn't allow prisoners to stagnate, but would trigger personal growth by prioritizing purpose and putting them to work. Proceeds from this (whether a daily wage or profits from the sale of the products they make) would go to victims' families, not the state. Training focus would be placed on problem-solving and coping skills, awareness of personal responsibility and interconnectedness with other humans. Empathy rituals would be performed weekly, where the prisoners would have to actively imagine themselves in their victims' places (including the family), and how it felt to be wronged.

What type of job it'd be, though – that's a story problem I haven't worked out yet.

Above me, a gull cuts inland. I follow its flight past a hill outside the walls of the prison compound, to a house crowned with slick black solar panels, catching sun.

Fuel cells then, I think. Something solar punk.

I'm not sure if that's a thing, but if it isn't, it is now.

The robot monks teach their prisoners to create solar fuel cells (or maybe batteries?) that the main society needs to power its underground cities and will pay greatly for. The proceeds are catalogued and the inmates get to send them directly to victims' families via a special tubing system. These inmates will not be free until they have paid off what income an impartial court deems the amount their victims might have earned in the remaining balance of the lives taken from them.

If they pay it off, each prisoner is capable of earning a train ticket back to the underground capital. In this way, they can be free again.

All because of Redemption.

I have to stop there, because I've been walking too fast and my right heel has blistered. A burning feeling works its way up my calf as I fight a pen and a torn planner page out of my briefcase. The paper flutters in the wind and I write awkwardly against my hand, shivering as I try to recapture the broad strokes of the premise – all the while thinking, *What a fantasy world* that *would be.*

"*I travelled to San Quentin Prison to sit down with a man sentenced to death before writing this story. It was only his third visit in over twenty years without a partition separating him from his visitor. Death sentences in the United States overwhelmingly affect the poor, and this was no different. I wrote this story because I cannot understand the state bureaucracy of 'humane' killing and its astronomical costs. I wrote it because, when I locked eyes with a man condemned, I was forced to ask myself if a better system was possible, and how it might function.*"
Ryan Gattis

SLUDGE

Sarah Crossan

The fishing boat dipped to the right, then to the left, slowly and gently. Rax and his father bit into their sandwiches and glugged milk from their flasks. Light glinted off the tight ripples in the river. The sun made them sweat.

Rax pulled the brim of his hat over his eyes and sighed. He imagined himself lying in the shade of the iroko trees, Sula next to him, one smooth, strong arm sticking to his. He imagined her lips and her hips, her braided hair and long eyelashes. He imagined the lacy hem of her dress, the one with the yellow flowers printed on it.

Rax's father stood up and tugged at a rope. "No sleeping, Rax. Help me with the nets. Come on now. Up, up.

You can lie on your back when you're dead."

Rax yawned, got to his knees and dragged in another rope until a small, rusting cage appeared from the water, in it a cluster of nipping crabs. "Papa, when should a man get married?" he asked.

His father cleared his throat. "For pity's sake, Rax, can't you focus on fishing for five minutes? It's always Sula on your mind. Sula, Sula, Sula. She is too young and so are you. Wait until you have more hair on your chest and smarter ideas in your head. Married?" His father laughed, then suddenly stopped and wiped his brow.

"I can't wait too long," Rax grumbled. "Sula will meet someone else. All the boys want her, and she's impatient." Rax hated admitting this about Sula – that her feelings for him could wither away so easily – but a part of him believed it was true. And perversely it was something he liked about her; she wasn't going to waste her life waiting for fate to build her future – she lived as if the future was today and she owned it.

His father dropped a cage into the bottom of the boat. It clanged and a crab scuttled out, making a futile dash for freedom. "Sula is so full of herself. As is her father. What about Keila? She's a *lovely* girl. If you find a way to make Keila love you, you'll be a happy man. And I will be a happy father-in-law. You have to think about other people when you marry, Rax. This is what manhood means."

Rax rolled his eyes and picked up one of the crabs. It

eyed him, ready to duel. He didn't want Keila; he wanted Sula. He growled at the crab like a hungry dog and made as if to bite it. Then he threw it back into the water. "I pardon you," he said grandly, and reached for another slimy rope.

Rax and Sula lay by the riverbank, their legs dangling in the water. Sula tickled Rax's earlobe between her thumb and forefinger. Rax didn't pull away. Instead he turned on his side to gaze at her, wishing she would lean closer. He liked the way she smelled on summer afternoons – like dry grass. "My father says I should marry Keila," Rax said suddenly.

Sula laughed, her mouth wide, showing off all her teeth. "You should. She's very clever and I hear she plans to become a doctor, so when you're old and can't reach the bathroom in time, she won't even flinch wiping up after you."

"That's disgusting!" Rax kicked out and splashed them both with water.

"As is the idea of marrying Keila. Why don't your parents like *me*?" Sula said with another laugh.

Rax rolled on top of her and she gave a playful scream. He kissed her lips and she didn't resist. After a few seconds she pushed him away.

"You *should* marry Keila. She'd cook all the meals and keep the bathroom clean," Sula continued. But she didn't laugh this time. She looked away and kept her mouth straight.

Rax sat up and felt for a stone with his fingers. He rubbed it idly against his shirt, but it still felt wet. He looked down at it.

Sula sat up too. She took the stone from Rax's hand and threw it into the water. "I'm going to start a rumour about Keila so that your family won't think she's the moon and stars. What should I tell people? Let's think of something." Sula's voice was serious. She took Rax's hand and rested her head on his shoulder.

He breathed her in, but something other than Sula came to his nose. With his free hand he felt for another stone and looked down at it. It was covered in black slime. Rax sniffed the stone. "Burning," he said.

"Burn her? How?" Sula asked. Her voice didn't betray any shock or resistance.

"No. *Burning*. Smell it." Rax put the stone under Sula's nose.

"Petrol," she said. "Maybe a motorbike was here." She looked for track marks in the clay but saw nothing. Then she stood up. "I have to go home. Papa will be waiting. He will be pacing and fuming if I'm not home before sunset."

"Please stay a few minutes more," Rax begged. He stood up behind her and put his arms around her shoulders like a blanket. "I miss you," he said.

"That doesn't make sense. I'm here. We're together."

"I know. But I do. Even when I'm with you, I miss you." He paused. "Don't you miss me? Tell me you do."

"You need to write poetry." Sula grinned and bit his hand softly. "You're too sensitive. I need a boyfriend who wouldn't be afraid to wrestle a bear."

"When would I ever need to wrestle a bear?" Rax asked.

"Use that big imagination of yours, Mr Poet." She turned and kissed the tip of his nose. "I'm going." And she was gone, dashing across the hard, dry earth, a silhouette against the orange sky.

"I miss you," Rax said again aloud. He sniffed the oily stone. "Who the hell owns a motorbike?"

Rax's mother was stirring a pot. Fish sizzled in a pan. His little sister, Mishla, was sitting at the table, a notebook in front of her, a stubby pencil in her hand. "Your hair has grass in it," Mishla said, looking up.

Rax's father came into the kitchen, wiping his hands on a threadbare towel. "Sula's father will beat you with a stick if any trouble comes to his daughter's door," he grumbled.

Rax's mother looked up from her cooking. "What does that mean? What have you been doing?"

"Nothing." Rax sighed and slumped in a chair next to Mishla. "Sula and I were skimming stones and reciting poetry. We don't do anything. Actually, that's not true. Sometimes she beats me up. She'd make a first-class boxer."

Mishla giggled and made kissing sounds with her lips.

"Oh, Sula. I *love* you." Rax thumped her in the arm and she swallowed down a squeal.

"I don't want to hear any more about that girl from either of you. Get the table ready for dinner," their mother snapped.

Mishla tidied away her notebook and Rax retrieved four bowls and four small plates from the shelf over the sink. The family sat, and Rax's father ladled creamy soup peppered with herbs into the bowls. His mother slid blackened fish onto the plates. The salty smell filled the whole kitchen and they ate quickly.

Rax's father smiled. "You make the best meals, my prize," he said to his wife. He finished his portion of fish and reached across the table to help himself to more.

"Some day soon I will stop cooking and watch you all starve," Rax's mother said. She laughed.

"As long as you keep coming to bed at night, I think I'll survive," his father said and winked.

Mishla groaned. Rax shook his head. He didn't know whether his parents said these things in front of him and his sister to annoy them or from genuine feeling. But they had been doing it for as long as he could remember.

"Can I go out and see Gloria and Maglee now?" Mishla asked, pushing away her empty plate and bowl. "I've finished my homework."

"Yes, you go out and have fun. I suppose I *should* do all the cleaning as well as the cooking." Rax's mother sighed.

"I'm just a servant in this house, after all."

"I'll do it," Rax offered. "Mishla can go. As long as she really is meeting up with Gloria and Maglee and not Roddy." He made his own kissing sounds. Mishla kicked him under the table and Rax laughed. His father and mother did not.

Rax and his father walked along the dusty road. The village was far behind them, the riverbank and a full day's work lay only a little way ahead. The morning was cool and Rax was thinking about Sula again. He wondered whether there was a boy at school who liked her. He guessed so. He guessed a hundred boys liked her and wanted her and had probably tried to tease her away from him. But he didn't feel jealous. It made him smile to know that she spent her evenings with him when she could have been with anyone, when she could have been with any of those clever boys who wore glasses and polished shoes and had stayed in school so they could leave the village to become bankers and lawyers and businessmen.

He was still thinking about Sula, not looking where he was going, when his father stopped suddenly and Rax slammed into his back.

Rax stepped out from behind his father's large frame. He could see fishermen standing on the riverbank ahead, waving their arms violently. They seemed to be shouting at one another. Rax ran towards the river and the men and found Sebi, a boy his own age with skinny limbs.

"Why aren't you out in your boat?" Rax asked him.

Sebi shook his head and pointed to the water. Rax blinked. Was he imagining things, or…? No. His eyes were not deceiving him. The water was silvery black. It didn't move at all and seemed less like a river and more like a pool of still, thick tar. And worse were the fish: hundreds maybe thousands of fish lay on the surface of the tar, motionless and open-mouthed as if they were sleeping. "All dead," Sebi said, as though Rax couldn't figure that bit out for himself.

Rax thought about the devil, how he didn't believe in him, or even in God, and wondered whether this was a punishment for that – whether this was a way for super-natural forces to make their presence known. He'd heard about plagues from his mother – locusts and flies. Was this what was happening? He couldn't think of anything else that would bring about such a scene.

Rax's father had reached the riverbank and was stand-ing a little upstream from him, looking at the black gloss on the surface of the water and talking to the other men. They shook their heads. Some began to shout again. His father rubbed his eyes and kicked the bow of his rowboat. Rax rushed over and stood next to his father.

"What is it?" he asked. "Is it a plague? Can a person have done it?"

"I have no idea," his father said quietly. "They're all full of theories." He pointed to the men near by.

A shout came from far off. Rax and his father turned to see someone running along the road towards the river. "It's Naro," Rax said. "Naro!" he shouted. "Naro, have you seen the river?"

Naro, a man in his early twenties with lines on his face like those of a man in his forties, skidded to a stop beside the group. He leant forward with his hands on his knees to catch his breath. He coughed and Rax banged him on the back.

"Oil," Naro panted.

The group tightened around him. "What did he say?" someone asked.

"Oil," Naro repeated, standing up and resting his hands on his hips now. "From the Findori region."

Sula's father, Dineedi, stepped forward, his head in the air. He was a man who regarded himself as an authority on most things. "Findori is over one hundred miles away. That can't be it."

"My auntie heard it on the radio," Naro continued. "A pipe burst in Findori and the river brought it down to us and even the villages south of here. It's everywhere, that black stuff. And it's oil all right."

"When will they fix the pipe?" Rax asked, knowing Naro couldn't really answer this question, knowing it was a stupid thing to say.

Naro shrugged. "They say no one wants to take responsibility. They say…" He paused and lowered his voice.

"They say it's hopeless. All the fish are dead. Half the crops up there are gone too."

Dineedi stepped between Naro and the group. He sniffed and scuffed the clay with his sandals. His toenails were hard and yellow. His feet were calloused and the skin wrinkled and dry. "They'll come and clean it, whoever owns the pipes for the oil. They'll have to!" Dineedi exclaimed. "It's the law."

"Is it?" Rax asked.

Dineedi frowned. "Of course it is. What if I came and shat in your garden? I'd have to clean it up, wouldn't I?"

"But how do you take oil out of water?" Rax asked tentatively. It was a question he should really have asked his mother.

Dineedi turned to Rax and looked at him properly, then without warning took him by the shoulders and shook him violently. "Aren't you listening? It's the *law*. It's the law to keep the river clean."

Rax's father pushed Dineedi. "Take your hands off my son. Come on, Rax, we're going home." He led Rax through the mass of angry fishermen, back towards the village.

"I think we should try to catch some fish," Rax said weakly. "They can't all be dead."

"Not today we won't," his father said. "But the sludge will wash away soon. Everything will be OK. You'll see."

★　　★　　★

The sludge had not washed away by evening. When Rax took Sula to the riverbank, there was nowhere on the ground for them to sit without getting sticky and they eventually had to climb a tree.

"Micky says it will take years to clean the water," Sula said quietly.

"Micky?" Rax squinted.

"My science partner. I told you about him. His father is American."

Rax bit the insides of his cheeks. "You didn't tell me about him, and anyway, he's wrong. The river will wash it away."

Sula shook her head. "The oil is still coming out. Until they fix it the oil will get thicker and thicker. Micky said it will kill the fishing industry and maybe the whole region."

"What does *he* know?" Rax suddenly shouted. He jumped off the branch and fell on to the ground, gashing his knee on a stone and grazing his hands. Oil squelched beneath his fingers. He didn't want to admit it to Sula, but the riverbank probably wasn't the safest place for them to be at that moment. Not until the oil was gone. And as his father had said, it would be gone soon. It had better be gone, or they'd go hungry.

"Would you like me to kiss your injuries better?" Sula teased, swinging her legs above him.

"Please *do*," Rax said, and smiled. He opened his arms

to catch her and she jumped. Rax pressed his nose against her cheek and inhaled.

"What if Micky is right?" Sula asked gently.

Rax sighed. "If he's right, then maybe we can declare him king. I'll make him a crown myself."

"Don't be touchy." Sula stared at the ground. Black sludge was seeping between the eyelets of her shoes and making her feet wet. "I'm worried," she whispered. "That's all."

Rax awoke to the sound of screaming. He bolted up in bed and ran into the kitchen. The door was open, and through it he could see his mother in their garden. She was kneeling by the vegetable plot.

Then Mishla was at his side. "Mama?" His sister gasped and ran outside. Rax followed.

His mother stood up. The lower half of her pale blue dress plus her hands and forearms were covered in oil. In her hand she held a tiny root vegetable. It was too small to eat. "It's in the ground. It's everywhere. We have to dig out the vegetables that are ready to eat before it smothers them."

"It's not urgent, Mama," Rax said, putting a hand on her slippery arm.

She pulled away. "Not urgent today, maybe. But what about next week? Next month when the ground is dead and nothing will grow? Then what? Will you live on air? Will you eat oil? Maybe you and Sula will eat kisses for supper?"

Rax flinched. Why did his mother have to bring his love for Sula into this? What was happening was not the result of them loving each other.

Mishla put her arm around her mother. "I won't go to school today. I'll help you dig out the good ones. And it will be OK. The people who did this will come soon and help."

Their mother's eyes grew narrow. "How will they find the culprits?" she snapped. "Everyone's saying they live halfway across the world in marble palaces where they cannot even see what they've done. They are far too busy having servants wipe their arses for them."

"A solution will come. I'm sure of it," Rax said. But he wasn't sure. How could they suck sludge out of the ground? What equipment would they use? Did such equipment even exist? He thought about the time he had spilt a cupful of cooking oil on the kitchen floor. It had gone everywhere. The dark splashes had never come out of the walls.

Rax was lying staring at the cracked brown ceiling of his room, when Mishla tiptoed in. "Rax? You awake?" she murmured.

He sat up in bed and patted his blanket, inviting his sister to sit, which she did. Then she spoke again. "The teacher said today that the oil company still hasn't sent anyone to assess the damage to the pipe. Miss Plee said she spoke to her sister in England. It's on the news stations there."

Rax hadn't wanted to know the foolishness Micky had

been spilling into Sula's head, but Miss Plee was different. She was a smart woman. She wasn't prone to exaggeration. Rax knew this because she had been his teacher only two years before. "What else did she say?" he asked, keeping his voice low.

"She said it's happened before and it takes months for the oil companies to admit fault. It takes years for the oil to be cleaned up. And this didn't happen in America, so they care even less about it. She said..." Mishla paused to bite on her thumbnail. "She said she's leaving."

"*Leaving?* What will happen to the school?"

"I don't know."

Rax nodded. He didn't know what to say. He knew it was too late to try to reassure Mishla. "You should sleep," he whispered, and reached out to pat his sister's shoulder.

"Should I tell Papa?" she asked.

Rax shrugged. "I'm not sure. But you should go to bed now. You have to be up early to make use of the school while it's still open."

Without a word more, Mishla stood and headed to her own corner of the house.

"Shit," Rax said aloud, once she was gone. He stared at the ceiling again. *"Shit."*

Rax and Sula carried their shoes through shiny puddles of oil. Tar-like clay and dead bugs stuck to their feet. Usually they chatted and poked each other on their way to find a clean spot beyond the village where they could lie down and embrace, but today they were quiet, and after an hour, when they eventually found a clump of trees with a dry mound beneath their branches, they sat down, leaving a space between them. "You don't like me any more," Sula told him.

Rax sighed and kicked the dirt. "I'm hungry," he admitted, impatiently. "I've eaten nothing but a dry piece of bread today."

Sula searched in her pocket and pulled out a brown biscuit. "Here," she said mildly. "Take it."

Rax frowned and shook his head. "I'm not a beggar. I'm not asking you for food."

Sula shrugged and bit into the biscuit.

Rax sighed. "I want to go back to work, Sula. All I do is wait. I wait and watch my father and mother pacing the house. I watch Mishla getting skinny. I'm starting to think…"

He paused, and Sula took the opportunity to kiss him hard on the mouth. He let her lips press against his but he did not enjoy the sensation – Sula only ever made the first move when she felt sorry for him, and he didn't want anyone feeling sorry for him, especially not her.

"What are you starting to think?" Sula asked eventually.

Rax looked at his hands. Dirt and grime were embedded beneath his fingernails. His skin was wrinkled and dry like an old man's. He couldn't see his own face but he imagined how it looked – probably similarly withered and beaten. Like Naro's. "I am thinking it's been almost six weeks and no one has come to help us. I'm thinking no one ever will. I'm thinking our village is dying."

Sula sighed and took his hand. "I have to tell you something." She paused. "We are leaving in three days, Rax. Father is taking us to Bellgik. He has a cousin with a big house and there is a good school near by."

Rax stared at her. "Are you serious? This is how you tell me?" he fumed. "It's not true. I don't believe you!"

Sula bit her bottom lip. A silver frog appeared from behind a rock and blinked at them. "Soon there'll be no water to drink. It's a graveyard here. But Bellgik is a big place. You could find a job there. We could all go together if your father agreed. Your sister could come to the school. Her school will close soon. Everyone is leaving, Rax."

Rax nodded. Every day another of his friends came to say goodbye. At first they had been the ones without prospects – with nothing to lose – but yesterday Glenko left the village, Glenko who was the best fisherman he knew. Rax's father had not come to the door to say goodbye. He had hidden in the back room where he spent his days writing angry letters that no one would ever read.

Sula was watching him. "Will you come with us? Will you try?"

Rax squeezed her hand. "I don't think I have a choice."

On their way back to the village, Sula stopped walking

and held on to a tree for support. Rax pulled her to him,
but he didn't know what to say. He stroked her back and
breathed in her smell. He tried to get his memory working
in case he never smelled her again.

A car drove into the village. A man wearing a grey suit and
carrying a clipboard stepped out. A police officer with a
badge and a gun followed him. The man wrote things down
and took some photographs. He walked to the riverbank
and back again with the villagers following from a distance,
some shouting, "Clean the mess!" and "Stop poisoning our
children!" and "Get the crap out of our village!" The man
in the suit didn't approach any of them and the police officer
made it clear this was as it should be. Finally the man in the
grey suit smiled and they got back into the car. The two
men drove away leaving a trail of fumes behind them.

The black puddles in the village were getting deeper. Every
bird had flown away. Rax packed up the few things he
owned and told his mother and sister to do the same.

"Sula says there's a school in Bellgik for Mishla, and
I know there'll be jobs for me and Papa. Not fishing but
something else. Her father's cousin has a big house. They'll
help us find something. Something better than *this*," Rax
said, and pointed through the open window to his mother's
garden covered in an oily black paste.

"My whole life in a bag," his mother whimpered. She

cried until it was dark outside and she had filled her suitcase to brimming. Mishla did not cry. She bit the insides of her cheeks instead.

They all sat at the kitchen table, waiting for Rax's father to come home from the riverbank where he went every day to check on the oil, to see if any living fish had appeared. Today there was no soup bubbling on the stove.

As the door opened, Rax's mother inhaled quickly. His sister sat up straight.

"What's this?" his father asked, looking at their bags. He massaged the bridge of his nose and coughed.

"Papa, we have to leave," Rax told him. He made his voice as low as it would go so he would sound like a real man.

His father shook his head. "We're not leaving. My boat is here. Our livelihood is in this village."

"Not any more. Now our deaths are here, if we stay," Rax said evenly.

His father banged his fist against the table and Mishla yelped. "*I* am the head of this household. We will stay, if that's what I decide."

Rax's mother looked at her husband. "No, Jan. We can't stay. We're going to Swandisea. My sister will take care of us there."

Rax flinched. His mother must not have listened, Swandisea was in the opposite direction to Bellgik. If they went there, he might never see Sula again. But this wasn't the time to argue about the details.

Rax's father slumped in a chair and pressed his face down on the table. He murmured something no one could hear.

"What did you say, Papa?" Mishla asked.

"This is my home," Rax's father whispered. "I have lived here all my life. My father lived here too. And my grandfather. I cannot leave."

"Yes, you can," Mishla said bravely. "You must. We all must."

Rax was staring at his feet. He was thinking about Sula's neck, how smooth the skin was, how she would tilt her chin back so he could kiss it.

"I am not leaving," Rax's father whispered. "Go to Swandisea without me." He stood up and marched into the back room.

The sun was not yet up. Rax was feeding their mule putrefied fruit. Mishla and his mother were scavenging in the garden for any leftover vegetables they could take with them on their journey.

Soon they were ready to leave. Rax's father stood outside by the window and looked at the sky as though assessing whether or not today would be a good day for fishing. "We hope you'll follow us soon, Papa," Rax said. "It is three days' walk to Swandisea. Don't wait until you are starving to do it."

Rax's father ignored him. He turned his back and went into the house. On the path, Mishla and his mother began to cry. "Come on," Rax said. "We have to go before the day gets too hot."

Mishla walked next to Rax. "Did you say goodbye to Sula?" she asked him as they reached the edge of the village. Her eyes were red and her breath unsteady.

"No," Rax said.

"You should," Mishla told him. "We can wait here for five minutes. It's nothing. You should tell her goodbye."

Rax thought of Sula's long legs and her lips. He thought of her hair, spiky and thick when she didn't have her braids in. He thought of her feet, the second toes longer than the first. He thought of her laugh, which could be cruel when she chose. And the vessels of his heart pumped so hard he had to lean against the mule to stand up straight. "We haven't time for fussing," he told Mishla.

His sister nodded and walked ahead so she could take her mother's arm and prevent her from slipping in the oil.

Rax watched them and then, without knowing why, he turned around. He saw a figure in the distance waving. He knew it was Sula. He would always recognize her, even from far away. And he knew he ought to go to her and tell her that soon they would live six days apart. That he wasn't coming to Bellgik after all. But he couldn't bear to see her again. He especially wouldn't be able to bear it if she tried to touch him. He turned away and moved quickly until he caught up with his mother and Mishla.

"Do you really think your father will follow us soon?" his mother asked.

"Papa's a smart man," Rax said. "I wouldn't be surprised if he was packing up his things right now."

He turned again to look at Sula, but she was gone. He sighed and gripped his mother tightly, while overhead a dark cloud covered the sun.

"Money talks. Sadly. And this is the reason why so many people face injustices. I have been particularly appalled by oil companies' lack of responsibility when it has come to major spills, and their paltry commitment to the communities they have destroyed. This was the inspiration behind 'Sludge'; I wanted to write about an imagined place in the developing world where their way of life was entirely devastated by a major corporation's irresponsibility. I care about the environment not because I'm a tree-hugger but because it's in the interests of humanity to care about the planet. I just wish governments and big businesses cared too." Sarah Crossan

BYSTANDER

Frances Hardinge

Learning about the witch trials at school gave me nightmares, so of course I passed them straight on to Isobel.
That's what big sisters are for.

I told her all about the witch hunts in Salem and in
Britain – the lies, the crazy accusations and the torture of
the so-called "witches". I made her imagine being trapped
in a leg-crushing device and thrown into a pond with her
right thumb tied to her left toe so she couldn't swim.

So of course poor ten-year-old Isobel woke up screaming in the middle of the night, saying that the Witchfinder
General wanted to burn her.

"Hush now, Izz." Mum smoothed back Isobel's hair and

gave her a hug. "It was all a long time ago, and it can't get you. Nobody does that sort of thing any more."

Afterwards, out on the landing, Mum tore a strip off me.

"Kay – why do you torture your sister?"

I almost told Mum about my nightmares, but she would just have sighed and told me not to be a baby. If I came home with a broken leg, I bet she'd say I was trying to get attention.

Scaring Isobel was silly and cruel, I knew that. I was three years older than her – old enough to know better – and I suppose that was why I did it. Isobel was allowed to be a "baby" and somehow I never was.

In the worst nightmare I was sort of me, but sort of someone else, and I was on trial as a witch. Everyone was there – Mum, Dad, Isobel and all my friends – and none of them would look at me. That was the worst part. Terrible things were going to happen, and nobody would stop it or speak up for me. Nobody would save me.

I could feel the threat of the pins and crushing machines, like teeth that might close on my flesh. But instead the witchfinders took me away to a room and made me walk back and forth, back and forth.

It wasn't too bad at first, but hours went by and I started to get dizzy. And whenever I sat down, or fell down, men came in and hauled me to my feet again and made me keep walking. Then most of a day had gone, followed by most of a night, and my legs were shaking and I wanted to sleep, or cry, or throw up. Then the sun was coming up again and the sight of it through the window made me feel properly sick, and I tried to sleep in tiny bursts, just closing my eyes for an instant, but they wouldn't let me. The next day was so long, and my eyes felt dry, and then the sun was setting and my legs wouldn't hold me any more, and my head weighed a ton, but they kept hauling me to my feet, and slapping me awake, and forcing me to walk. And it went on and on, and I cried and cried, and I would have killed for sleep, died for sleep, done anything for sleep, and my brain became a mad fog, and I started to see things: shadows shaped like smiles, and rats in the corner of my eye, and writing on the backs of my hands.

Witch, the men said, over and over again. *Witch. Witch. Admit that you are a witch.*

In the last moment of the dream before waking, something cracked in my brain and I began to believe that they were right.

Even when I woke up, I felt sick as I lay in my bed. I ought to have felt relieved. I ought to have felt safe. But instead the scenes in the dream ran round and round in my head. I saw myself abandoned, broken.

If witchfinders had burst into the house and tried to drag off Isobel, I knew my parents would fight to the death to protect her. But lying there alone in the dark, I didn't quite believe that they would do the same for me. Instead

I saw their faces as they had looked in the dream trial. Closed and cold, refusing to meet my eye.

I meant to stop teasing Isobel about witch trials after that. But when she couldn't find her gym shoes the next morning, I accidentally suggested that maybe the ghost of a dead witch had stolen them. It was a joke, but Isobel went white and scared.

I forgot about it straight afterwards, of course. But Isobel didn't.

That evening at dinner, I noticed that she was a bit quiet. But I wasn't really paying attention, because we had the TV on while we were eating, and the newsreader was talking about torture. That word jolted me straight back to my night fears.

It was a piece about a place called Guantanamo, which is sort of a prison where they put terrorists, or people they think are probably terrorists. Some of the prisoners were saying that they had been tortured there to get information out of them.

"That's *grim*," I said aloud. I didn't know what "waterboarding" was, but it made me think of the "witch-ducking" we'd learnt about at school.

"We don't know if it's true," said Mum curtly. "I don't believe American troops would do that sort of thing." Her brother is a soldier.

I couldn't be so sure. Maybe normal soldiers wouldn't, but armies and navies are huge. How could you know that *nobody* in them was torturing anybody, unless you checked?

"And anyway," added Dad, "even if there's some truth in it, it's probably more complicated than that. The secret services need something to go on, don't they? Innocent lives at stake."

"Dad!" I couldn't believe my dad was sitting there with a bottle of ketchup in one hand, making excuses for torture.

"Just playing devil's advocate," he said. It's his universal cop-out. *Playing devil's advocate seems to mean saying things to upset people and then pretending you didn't mean it.* "Remember, those prisoners aren't fluffy bunnies. They're dangerous people. Sorry, love, but you can't go soft on terrorists."

"But…" I didn't want to sound like I was on the side of terrorists, but, "it's *torture*! And what if they got the wrong person? What if they tortured somebody innocent? What if it was me?"

I wanted them to say that they would never let that happen, that I was right – torture *was* wrong – and that they would fight tooth and nail to protect me.

"Don't be such a drama queen, Kay!" Mum said instead, impatiently. "It never *would* be you."

Wouldn't it? How could she be so sure? If it could be someone, it could be anyone.

I glowered at my food while Mum and Dad watched the weather forecast as if our conversation was over and settled. It was then I noticed that Isobel was gobbling her food, and hadn't said anything all meal.

"What's up with you?" I murmured.

She leant over and breathed a macaroni–cheese–scented whisper in my ear. "I think the dead witch ghost went to school with me today."

My heart sank.

"Izz..."

"But it's true! Everything was moved around in my desk. And my packed lunch was gone again!"

"Ghosts don't eat, Izz." My brief feeling of guilt gave way to a much more comfortable emotion: protective anger. "Sounds like somebody nicked your lunch. Has this happened before?" I may not always be nice to my little sister, but I reserve the right to bring the hurricane if anybody else picks on her. "Have you told Mum and Dad?"

"No!" hissed Isobel, looking horrified. "We mustn't, or the witch ghost will be angry!"

I decided to humour her and agreed not to tell our parents, but I had no intention of letting the lunch thief get away with it.

Isobel and I are at the same secondary school, in different years. Isobel should still be at primary school, but she was moved up a year. Clever but sensitive, Mum says. We have our own friends, and don't hang out together much.

At breaktime the next day, however, I slipped round the

side of the school near the bins. There was a window that would let me spy on Isobel's classroom.

I got pretty bored standing there, with the wasps and the stink from the sun-cooked bins. But then I saw a small, skinny black girl, not much older than my sister, slipping quickly and furtively into the classroom. The slender plaits lining her scalp bristled with stray hairs, and she wore a faded red T-shirt and tracksuit bottoms.

She went straight to the nearest desk, and pulled out a Frozen lunchbox. I recognized it at once – it belonged to Isobel. She took out the sandwich, cereal bar and apple, put them in her bag and quickly stuffed the box back in the desk. She looked wary but also oddly matter-of-fact.

It took me a while to find a teacher on duty, and when I did it was Mr Wilton. He's got scuffed trainers and big, dopey, hopeful eyes, like he thinks he's in a different school, one that doesn't have barbed wire along the tops of the walls. It's funny but a bit sad watching him trying to keep order. He's like a wet paper bag trying to hold a typhoon.

When I told him what I'd seen, he looked harassed.

"Are you sure? OK … wait here."

He crossed the playground to where the skinny girl was sitting cross-legged on one of the benches, picking at a crack in the sole of her trainer. Mr Wilton squatted beside her and asked her something gently, and without a word she emptied her bag on to the bench. Even at a distance, I could see that I'd been outwitted. Exercise books, a pencil case, some sort of green plastic mascot. No sign of Isobel's lunch.

Like an idiot, Mr Wilton walked straight back to me, making it obvious who the telltale was. The skinny girl met my gaze, but there was no smirk, just a hard, tired wariness, as if she was trying to work out how much of a threat I was.

"Kay," Mr Wilton said carefully, "do you think you could have made a mistake?"

"No! She must have hidden it somewhere!"

"Grasnie's a good quiet girl," he said doubtfully. "She's never been in any trouble."

"Just because she hasn't been caught!"

"Well, there's nothing I can do about— OWEN! OWEN, PLEASE STOP THAT RIGHT NOW!"

Mr Wilton was off at a run, towards a fight that he had no chance of breaking up. And somehow a girl had just robbed my sister and got away with it.

I tracked down Isobel, and told her about the lunch thief. I even gave her one of my sandwiches – but not half my cereal bar.

"So who's this Grasnie, then? Does she have something against you?"

"I haven't done anything to her," protested Isobel. "I hardly even know her. She hasn't been in our class long – she turned up in the middle of the year. I *used* to talk to her a bit when she was new, but it was really hard because she didn't know much English. She speaks French."

"Is she from France, then?"

"No, she said she came from the Congo, in Africa. But anyway, she's gone a bit weird, and now I don't really talk to her any more." Isobel shrugged.

"Weird? What kind of weird?"

"She sits by herself all the time. And her hair's all…" Isobel used her fingers to mime Grasnie's matted hair. "And she smells funny, and she has gross rashes, and she's just … weird."

I was only half-listening. A plan was forming in my head.

"Listen, Izz, when school is over, get on the bus without me. Tell Mum that I have to stay on a bit to finish my art project because it has to be in tomorrow – I'll catch the next bus home."

I would follow Grasnie after school, I decided. When she retrieved Isobel's lunch from its hiding place, I would take a picture of her doing so on my phone. And then I could go to the teachers with proof.

I felt so proud of myself, playing detective.

After school I hid in the corridor near Isobel's classroom. When most of the younger kids had gone, I saw Grasnie slip back, drop to all fours and reach under one of the big cupboards in the classroom. I had my phone ready, but I was too slow to take a photo when she sat up and stuffed Isobel's lunch back in her bag.

I looked for a teacher but couldn't see one. Instead I followed Grasnie out of the school, keeping my distance. She would have to stop and eat it somewhere on the way home. Her parents would surely be suspicious if she brought back an unfamiliar lunch.

Pretending that I was looking at my phone, I dawdled down the road after her, then followed her into the park. She came to a halt in the play area, sat down in a hanging tyre and took Isobel's lunch out of her bag.

Crouched behind a bench, I angled my phone and took a photo of Grasnie as she unwrapped the sandwich, the rest of the stolen lunch in her lap. I could have sneaked away then, but something about the nervous eagerness in Grasnie's face gave me a queasy, uncomfortable feeling. So instead I stayed where I was.

I watched as the skinny girl ate the sandwich with hasty intensity, cupping her hand so no crumbs would fall and finally licking them off the clingfilm. She gobbled the cereal bar the same way, and then ate the whole apple, even the core.

Not mean. Not greedy. Starving.

Eventually she jumped down from the tyre and carried on walking towards a housing estate on the far side of the park. Her steps slowed and slowed as she approached it, as though she wanted to make the journey last for ever.

While Grasnie was hesitating in front of a house, a woman came out, face set and hard. She grabbed Grasnie by the arm without a word and dragged her in through the door.

I stood there staring. There was something wrong with what I had just seen. I couldn't imagine my mother looking at me so coldly, or yanking my arm like that. I crept closer, until I was behind the hedge, not far from an open window.

There was a lot of adult yelling going on inside the house in a language I couldn't understand – a woman, and at least two men. And then a much shriller voice cut through, desperately squeaking the same thing over and over. Even though I didn't know the words, I could feel in my gut what the girl was shouting.

I'm sorry I'm sorry I'm sorry I'm sorry.

Then I heard a slap. A loud, hard slap. And then another one.

Everything went quiet after that, and I crept back to the park, unsure what to do. After a while, Grasnie came back out of the house and began walking back to her tyre in the play area, still wearing a tired, matter-of-fact look on her face. There were tears on her cheeks she hadn't bothered to wipe.

When she looked up and saw me, she froze.

"Wait, I just want to talk!"

She didn't believe me, and I saw her getting ready to run. She must have recognized me from the playground. So I went straight to Plan B. I held out my phone.

"I've got a picture of you eating my sister's lunch!"
I hissed. "Don't run away, or I'll show *everyone*. Got it?"

She was still tensed up, but she stayed where she was.

"What do you want?" she asked. She *did* sound a bit
French. As I got closer, I realized how small she was – even
smaller than Isobel. It took the wind out of my sails, and
made my revenge plans seem stupid and petty.

"Somebody hit you, didn't they?" I said, glancing
towards the house.

She dropped her gaze and shook her head. I could see
now that her skin was slightly greyish, and a bit dry and
flaky-looking round her mouth. Again I noticed her hair,
and all the little plaits which should have been glossy and
immaculate but were scruffy and matted as though they
had been slept on night after night.

Weird, Isobel had said. But the only reason Isobel's hair
was shiny and smooth was because Mum made sure it was
washed and brushed.

It was then I noticed an angry reddish blotch on Grasnie's forehead, half hidden by her hairline.

"Well, what's that then?" I demanded, pointing at it.
Grasnie flinched.

"I hit my head," she said, still not meeting my eye. "On
a kettle."

"A *kettle*?" I supposed that it could be a burn or scald
mark, now that I looked at it. There were other marks and
scabs on her arms as well. *Gross rashes*, Isobel had called

them. But they could also be grazes or burns. And they couldn't all be accidents.

"Don't be stupid," I said. "Nobody bangs their head on a kettle. I *heard* them hit you! What's going on? You've *got* to tell me, or ... or I'll show this to the police!"

I held up the phone in front of Grasnie, my hand shaking. I couldn't think of any other way to make her talk. Whatever was happening to her, somebody needed to report it.

When I said the word "police", she stiffened. Once again she was watching me with that steady, cautious, calculating look, as though I were a firework that might still explode, or a gap she had to jump.

"Delete the photo first." She pointed at the phone.

I pressed a couple of buttons on my phone to set up the delete, and hovered my thumb over the confirm button.

"Tell me," I said, "then I'll delete."

Grasnie chewed her lip.

"You can't ever tell anyone," she said at last. Then she started to talk, quietly and haltingly. Before long I wanted to say, *Stop, I've changed my mind — I don't want to know any more.*

It had been happening for months, ever since her mother found a new church in London. It was a very small church, made up of only a few Congolese families, and didn't have its own building. Most Sundays it met in a room over a phone repair shop. Bible study sessions were held in

Grasnie's mother's house during the week.

At church meetings the pastor hit Grasnie, and poured hot candlewax on her skin. Once he had swung her against the wall, making her knock her head and see stars. Grasnie's mother always thanked him afterwards, and gave him money for the church.

At home Grasnie slept on the floor, in a different room from all her brothers and sisters. Sometimes her mother burnt her with matches, poured stinging liquid in her eyes or splashed boiling water on her skin. Some days her family fed her, some days they didn't.

It made me feel cold inside. I had friends who went to church, and grumbled about it, but none of their churches sounded like *that*. And Grasnie's family…

"Why?" I blurted out at last. "Why are they doing this to you?"

Grasnie met my gaze with tired eyes.

"Because I am a witch," she said.

I felt as if a well of craziness had opened up underneath me. The stories of witch trials had scared me, but witches themselves … for me, those meant Halloween wigs, warty noses, black cats. They were nonsense – they were *fancy dress*. But here was Grasnie talking about being one with flat, hopeless certainty. For a moment she almost made me believe it.

"When we first came here, I walked in my sleep," she explained. "My mother took me to the pastor, and he said

that I had *kindoki*. They want to get rid of the evil spirit."
She gave a very small shrug.

She was not much older then Isobel.

"You're not a witch," I said, my voice stupid and wobbly.
"You're just a little girl. And you've got to tell somebody
about this!"

Grasnie shook her head hard, and I flinched before her
gaze.

"Don't tell anyone," she said fiercely, "or I'll say you're
lying." She reached out before I could react, and jabbed her
thumb down on mine, pressing the phone and deleting the
photo.

"Why are you protecting them?"

The answer hit me before I had finished the sentence.
If the truth came out, her torturers might end up in prison,
and one of them was her mum. I couldn't have sent my
mum to prison. Not ever.

Grasnie's gaze flicked to one side, and I realized that we
were not alone. There was a man watching us. He appeared
to have come from the direction of Grasnie's house. His
watch looked expensive, and there was a small Bible tucked
in the pocket of his suit.

"Grasnie, come away. Don't bother this nice girl." He
had the same accent as Grasnie. His mouth smiled and his
eyes did not.

"She's not bothering me," I said, voice tiny. He scared
me.

"Are you from Grasnie's school?"

I nodded, and a moment later wished that I hadn't.

"Perhaps you should go home now," he suggested. "Grasnie's mother needs her."

Grasnie got up without a word, head bowed, and headed towards her house.

"Thank you for being kind to Grasnie ... but be careful. She is having trouble adjusting to her new home, you see. So sometimes she lies and steals. Maybe you should keep away from her."

Right then, I was so frightened I thought I would throw up. My head wanted to nod, to agree with him so I would be safe, but I didn't let it.

Instead I turned and hurried away through the park, my legs wobbly. That man was one of the people hurting Grasnie, maybe even the pastor. He knew my face now. If I told anybody about what was happening to Grasnie, he would probably guess it was me. And he knew where I went to school, which meant he would know where to find me.

I ran the last part of the way home and went straight to my room. I heard Mum calling me, but I put my music on and pretended not to hear her.

At last she came up and knocked on my door. When I opened it, I saw her annoyed expression melt away, and I knew I must be looking white and shaky. She didn't roll her eyes, or tell me not to be a baby. She led me back to the kitchen and sat me down.

I told her all about it. I told her how scared I was. And I sobbed more than Isobel had after her dream.

"Kay!" She looked flabbergasted. "Kay, I can't believe you've got involved in something like this." She took me by the shoulders. "You must promise me that you'll stay away from that house, and that little girl. Promise!"

"But we have to do something!"

"Kay, we can't just... It sounds like it's a complicated situation. It's another culture. We can't get involved."

I stared at her. I couldn't believe what she was saying.

"Whatever is going on, it's probably not as bad as you think, Kay." Mum smoothed back my hair, the way she often did with Isobel. "If this girl was really being tortured, don't you think the teachers would have noticed? Look – I'll give the school a ring, but you must *promise* to stay out of it from now on."

I mumbled something, a promise, and went to my room.

I had done my bit. Hadn't I? I had told my mother. But I was starting to realize that adults didn't always solve things. She would phone the school, she'd said so. But I could almost hear how it would go.

Sorry to bother you, but a little girl called Grasnie upset my daughter with some stories... Yes, that's the one... Oh, she's having trouble adjusting, and tells lies sometimes? I thought as much...

I took out my own phone. I knew there was a non-emergency police number that I could use if I wanted to report something. But instead I just sat there, staring at my phone.

I tried, I told myself. *If I do anything else, I'll get into trouble. Mum will be angry with me. And if she won't believe me then the police probably won't. Besides, Grasnie will deny it all to protect her mum.*

And that man, he'll come after me. Maybe he'll come after all of us. Isobel too.

Plus it's none of my business. She's not my friend. She's not even in my year. And maybe she really does make things up.

It's not my fault.

It's complicated.

But it wasn't complicated, not really. I knew that these were just excuses. I wanted to forget that any of this had ever happened. Somehow I had blundered into a terrible world of cruelty and unfairness. I wanted to get out of it, so I could go back to normality and safety.

My eyes filled with cowardly tears and my vision blurred. All I could think of was my nightmare about the witch trial, but from a new perspective.

The dream had scared me, but now I realized that it had always been a fantasy. Me as the tortured heroine. Me as the innocent victim. Me as the centre of attention. Me, me, me.

At last I understood what I really was. I imagined the

dream trial again, but this time I wasn't in the dock. I was just another coward in the silent crowd. Hugging my safety. Letting the torture happen. Looking the other way.

"Torture still happens, sometimes in distant lands, sometimes in our own neighbourhood. Faced with something that terrible, it's easy to feel out of our depth, and as if there's nothing we can do. There's always something we can do. If Kay had called the police, they might have listened to her. They have a unit that looks into cases like Grasnie's, as do charities like AFRUCA. She could have also tried telling her teachers, or phoned the helpline of a charity like the NSPCC.

Even when powerful people or governments commit acts of torture, we can still talk about it, find out about petitions, ask questions or make a fuss. Torture can only happen if the rest of us look the other way and do nothing to stop it." Frances Hardinge

BLACK/WHITE

Amy Leon

Black boy born with	White boy born with
Loose noose round his neck	Halo round his head
Black man will die with one	White man will die with one
Black boy loves to read	White boy loves to read
Black boy likes sports	White boy likes sports
Black boy is told	White boy has options
Sports will be his only path	
To success	

Black boy is told	White boy is told
He will be incarcerated	He will get away with
In his lifetime	Everything
Black boy is told	White boy is told
To be quiet	To have fun
Keep hands at side	Remember his lunch
Keep voice low	Brush his teeth
Look "civilized"	Be home by nine
Black boy is threat	White boy is child
Black man is overqualified	White man is under-qualified
Black man doesn't get	White man starts Monday
interviewed	
Black man in suit	White man in suit
Is portrayed as	Is portrayed as
Black boy playing dress-up	White man in suit
Black boy	White man
Makes the news	Reports it
Black boy	White boy
Gets shot at 17	Learned to shoot at 15★

★ *This is legal in America.*

Black boy
May or may not live
To see university

White boy
May or may not
Take a gap year

Black man will not
Know how to talk about this
With his son.

White man will
Never have to.

"'Black/White' was written out of necessity. Children of colour simply grow up with different expectations, opportunities and access. If I have a child, I hope this world will have changed by then so that my child will not have to constantly question the validity of their existence. I believe this will be possible." Amy Leon

THE COLOUR OF HUMANITY
Bali Rai

If I could speak to you again, I would remind you about the park that we played in. Those multicoloured rubber tiles in the kids' play area, surrounded by bark chips that would get stuck in our shoes. The fence around the perimeter that kept danger away, and us feeling safe. I loved the swings but you were a roundabout fan. We still enjoyed it the same, though, didn't we? I can see your mum sharing gossip with mine, the two of them watching over us, proud and happy.

Remember the other kids from the neighbourhood? My cousins Michael and Joseph, Ruby Khan and Mia McCullough – and so many others whose names I've forgotten. The laughter and the fun, and the sun shining over the holidays. Going home tired and sweaty, our fingers sticky from melted ice lollies. It's like a different world now, isn't it? Just a dream that we once shared. Maybe you saw something else in those images, something that didn't include me. Or was it later that we stopped being the same? I guess I'll never know.

I'd offer you my food, if I could see you again, like I did every time you came for tea. Fish fingers and chips, and those tinned peas that my mum always kept in the cupboard. You loved putting tomato ketchup on yours – smothering everything in it until your food was floating in a bloody lake. You'd get your fork and smear a chip around the plate, making patterns in the sauce. Call it painting. Mum used to say you'd become one of them modern artists, like that man who cut the shark in half, or that Banksy fella. Something avant-garde, she said, and we didn't know what she meant – looked it up on my laptop.

You never took my food though, did you? I didn't like ketchup. I used to dollop mayonnaise on my plate, and you'd pull that face, like there was a really bad smell in the room. *Mayo*, you'd say, sounding just like your nan. *Ma-yo? How can you eat that muck?* you'd ask. *It looks like sick.* And I'd just grin, spear a chip and wave it at you. Ketchup and mayo – that's who we were. Only, underneath the sauce, our food was the same. *We* were different, too – came out of different bottles, your mum said – but it didn't mean anything at all. We were always the same. Always.

In Year Six I'd help you with your maths. Mrs Cooper's class — remember it? Every bit of every wall covered in paintings and stories, and maps and times tables. That big chart about grammar and punctuation, and *were* versus *we're*, and all that stuff. Gold and silver stars next to every pupil's name, and the timeline of major world events. The yellow and red chairs that we'd scrape across the floor just to annoy Mrs Cooper. The tiny tables, the bookshelves, and the corner where Jordan O'Connor puked after eating all those chocolates, after we egged him on. Mia started crying because Jordan was her dad's cousin on his mother's side. She didn't talk to us again, until you bought her a bag of sweets with your birthday money.

You'd say you didn't do maths, called it the devil's language once. Mrs Cooper touched her crucifix necklace and called you a wicked child. But you didn't care, because maths was useless. You'd tap your calculator and say, *I've got this, haven't I?* Then you'd look over at my answers, and I'd let you see. Just you and no one else. I was your brother from another mother, you said. And I never cared about you copying my work, because I wanted to help you. I *liked* helping you. You were my best mate, and that's what friends are supposed to do.

If we could meet up again, I'd take you back to Nando's, like that first time we went. You and me, and our mums, walking through town without a care in the world, even though it was cold and wet, and the football fans were going to the match. My mum ordering us to cover our ears, and your mum telling those lads off for swearing around us. It was a big treat, remember? We'd finished Year Six and were on our way to big school. Money was tight but our mums had saved up, and we had chicken and chips, and that coleslaw that we ate out of the boxes.

I dared you to try the hot sauce, and you just laughed and said yeah. But when you tried it, your face went red and you began to cough. You grabbed every drink on the table and downed them, one after the other. Our mums were nearly crying with laughter and you ran off to the toilet. And all the time I didn't even smile, because I felt so guilty, like I'd hurt you, and I wanted to say sorry but never did. When you came back, you were angry and wouldn't speak to me until your mum told you to grow up. I can't help thinking perhaps that was the moment – because you were never the same after that.

I would ask you about Year Seven, if I could, and those first few weeks, when you found new people to chill with. I'd point at Mia and Ruby, and Michael and Joseph, and even Jordan O'Connor, and say, what's the deal with that Brandon lad and his dodgy mates? At first you were fine, told me you had new friends, nothing special. Just natural to meet other people, you said. And we were together anyway, in the same form, the same classes – all of that.

So when your Uncle Tommy took us to the football, it still felt the same. Like we were still brothers. You had your blue shirt and I was wearing red, but that didn't matter. It was just football. We went to the chippy, and then stood outside the pub while your uncle and his mates had a few pints and talked about the game. Remember the banter that day? We felt like proper grown-up men, not the kids we were. Like we were part of something. And even though your side lost, you were still OK with it, and we had dodgy burgers on the way home – still the ketchup and mayo twins.

But that was the last time, I reckon. The last time we were brothers. The last time it didn't matter that we hadn't come from the same bottle. That we weren't the same on the outside.

See, if I could ask, I'd point to the books. You know, the ones that I borrowed from school, and the local library in the neighbourhood centre. I'd ask why reading made me a geek, because that's what you started calling me. Was it so bad that I wanted to be something, to make my life better? How come you couldn't understand that?

Then I'd ask why you stopped knocking at my door, and why, when I walked to the shops, you'd be sitting there with Brandon and the others, acting all hard, like some wannabe gangster. Sharing cigarettes, thinking you were rude boys, or blagging cans of lager from some older cousin or whoever. Those girls you had with you, too – all wearing more make-up than clothes, and swearing like old men at the football.

I remember you looking to Brandon every time you spoke to me, like the two of you shared some private joke. Brandon grinning on the sly, or one of his boys pulling a face.

The big change happened in Year Nine, didn't it? It was that night in McDonald's. Michael and me had asked Ruby and Mia to come with us. We were on the bench outside, drinking Cokes, remember? You came up with Brandon and two other lads, and started causing trouble. The Asian security guard told you to leave, and you called him a *paki*, and the four of us couldn't believe it. You just said it, right out loud, like it was a regular insult − just banter, nothing more. Even though Ruby's dad was from Pakistan, and you knew it would upset her. You looked right at her and grinned.

When I saw you the next day, you told me I was boring and that I should go out more, and forget about school. Said I couldn't take a joke, and that I couldn't be properly English if I hung around with Muslims. We were at war, you said, and people had to stand up for what was right. All I remember thinking was that Ruby was just like us, just fish fingers smothered in a different sauce. And that your voice sounded familiar but the words you spoke weren't yours. They belonged to someone else, someone vicious and nasty and full of hate.

I'd rave about the basketball court at school if you were with me now. I loved that place; it was like a second home.

I spent every spare second there, honing my game, shooting from every angle, over and over again. The ping of the ball as it bounced off the concrete, with Mia watching from the sidelines, eating those sour cherry sweets that she loved. That was where it happened, the first time – if you're interested. When she told me that she liked me, and we went over to the Spar and I got her more of those sweets. Walking home with my basketball in one hand and her hand in the other.

I remember you and that Brandon lad, standing by the railings, watching me practise. I remember wondering if you wanted a game – to maybe play some one-on-one. I remember you watching Mia, watching me. I didn't think it meant anything.

But you got worse, didn't you? Acted like I'd done something to let you down. As though Mia and I owed you an explanation because we were together. All that time, I thought it was envy. But you'd never once talked about Mia that way, or told me that you liked her. You used to talk about other girls, and those celebrity women off the Internet. I must have been blind or stupid, or a bit of both, to think it was jealousy that made you cut the bonds between us. I must have been so naive, so caught up in the lie that we'd be brothers for ever. That nothing could divide us.

So, I think about the bus stop most of all. It's natural, I guess, because that was where it all happened. I think about the warm evening sunshine on my face. I think about the glow that holding hands with Mia gave me, as my cousin Michael teased us for being loved-up. We were waiting for the number 27 bus to take us into town, and talking about the film we'd decided to watch. Just three friends having a laugh. Three regular English teenagers, loving life and living it. No pressures, no school, no problems other than deciding which screening to go to, and which snacks to buy when we got there.

I think about that scene as the trailer from a longer film, and it isn't supposed to end there. There were so many more scenes to play out over the years. So many more happy afternoons, and mild summer evenings...

You came out of the pub over the road, remember? You and Brandon, and that thug with the beige Stone Island jacket. I never knew his name, just knew the type – shaven head, tattoos and that snarl when he saw me holding Mia's hand. That word that every one of my ancestors has heard since they were taken from their homeland. Since they ended up in this country. That word that makes us something less than people, that belittles our humanity, our experiences, our hopes and our dreams, until all we are is a colour.

What were you thinking when it started, I wonder? Where did that hate take root? You looked right through us, and Mia and Michael fled. They ran back through the park, screaming at me to follow them. But I didn't move, because when I saw you coming I saw my friend, my brother, the lad I'd known since we'd both worn nappies.

Brandon had the first pop — two punches to my face. I had to kneel, to try and regain my thoughts, my breath. I didn't cry then — I was too shocked, too angry. Then I saw your boot; just for a split second but I knew it was yours. I fell on my side, remember? Lay there, looking up at that hazy blue sky through tears, wondering where it had all gone wrong. When I went from being your brother to being someone with less right to walk down the street than you.

The thug, he pulled that thing from his jacket — I don't even know what it was. I just felt the crack and then all that pain. My skull felt like it was on fire. I knew then that it was over, and I tried to turn my head towards you. I managed to catch your eyes, and I *know* you remember that. Your face was twisted, contorted in rage, but your eyes were the same, brother. The same as when we ate fish fingers as the ketchup and mayo twins, the same as when we shared jokes and kicked footballs, and ran around the streets together. When what I was on the outside meant nothing to you.

So, let me ask you something else. Sitting in that cell, breathing in your own stink and that of others, what do you reflect on? Do you remember the playground, and the friends we had, and all those simple, naive childhood days? Do you find yourself back at the football, singing the songs and enjoying the banter? Does your mind play tricks on you at night? Does it take you back to the times when nothing but love and laughter and having fun mattered?

I lost so much that day. I lost my girl, and my family. I lost my chance to live a life the way it should be lived. I lost my dreams, my hopes. I wanted to be a lawyer. I wanted to have children of my own, and watch my mum play with them as she once did with me. I had the right to those things, just like anyone else. I had the right to become what I should have become. But ignorance and hate took that away. You took that away.

Only, you threw away as much of your own life as mine. The two of us, we're still the same, aren't we? Me in this bed, looking at nothing, feeling nothing, just a shell of the human I once was. You in that cell, your freedom gone, your life thrown away.

Neither of us is free, neither of us has a life. Mine ended that evening. I'll never get up again, never move on. I'll never walk or talk, or be able to hug my mum and tell her things will be OK. But your life is over too. Your life is rotting slowly away in there – and even though you can walk, and you can talk, you aren't *free*, are you?

Tell me, when you sit and stare at those walls, do you ever ask yourself when it happened, exactly where the turning point was? What caused the change?

See, humanity has no colour, brother. It did not start with a colour; it will not end with one. Remember all those lessons we were taught – to share, to accept, to respect the other? Well, when did I change for you, my friend?

When did you negate almost every aspect of my humanity until all you had left was my skin tone?

When did I stop being human first and start being black?

"My story is inspired by the tragic death of Liverpool teenager Anthony Walker in 2005, at the hands of racists. It is a re-imagination of the facts, an attempt to explore the emotions of the victim. I believe that empathy is the first line of defence against hatred and I want to live in a world where race matters less than eye colour. We are a long way off, but every step we take towards that goal is precious and welcome. My story is designed to make you think about what makes us human. I hope that it does." Bali Rai

WHEN THE CORRIDORS ECHO
Sabrina Mahfouz

It is a baby. A girl. Which is a good thing, so the family say. They don't see how a single mother like her could ever control a boy. The baby is called Ayesha and she is bought many things, all pink. With bows and sequins and cute ironic phrases that aren't ironic in any way.

All of this prepares her for who she will need to be by the time she gets to nursery. At primary school, Ayesha has acorns thrown at her head by boys who she won't kiss. When the acorns hit the pink metal clips that grip back her wild pieces of hair, it hurts a little but she says nothing. She has learnt not to talk with too much voice, as that is something nobody likes.

Ayesha's teenage bedroom is papered with Blu-tacked poster versions of happiness. There are boys from bands, their teeth blinding white and their hair slick with gel. But there are posters of female singers, too. Women she hopes to grow into, with globed breasts and bronzed skin, posing in shapes that make no sense, which makes sense to Ayesha, as the world is full of things that don't make sense. Pink metal clips that gripped back wild pieces of hair now keep her sparkly headscarves in place.

Ayesha spends most hours she's not at school in this bedroom. Her mother doesn't trust that the outside holds anything but pain for this girl she raised alone, so it seems best that she stays there, in that bedroom full of faces.

The very same day that Ayesha meets the air, a baby boy called Zayd is pulled screaming into a hospital room, his mother crying tears of happiness that she has had a boy; now her husband will be happy with her, her mother will be happy with her. She is happy with Zayd and smothers him with a thousand kisses.

He grows up wearing a uniform of blue, being told how much he is loved, adored. How much is expected of him. He plays with rockets, guns, swords and trains and can't sleep at night with all the thoughts he has of his future life running through his mind.

During the winter of Zayd's first teenage year, the snow comes down in buckets. It has never set so well in the city.

He puts on thick, warm clothes and big black gloves and goes out into the streets, whooping with the excitement that comes when a usually grey universe transforms, for a short time, into a sparkling white field. Along with some friends, he throws snowballs. They're medium-sized balls. Zayd is small for his age and his hands can only hold so much snow. He mostly throws them at his friends, but it is much more fun when he throws them at passers-by. Some laugh, others swear. They don't hurt – he mainly gets them on the leg. One of the strangers unexpectedly takes great offence at being Zayd's snowball target. They tut, and phone the local police as soon as they turn the corner. A few months later, Zayd is the recipient of an Anti-Social Behaviour Order, with strict conditions that he must be supervised by an adult at all times when in public. For the next two years. His mother cries from one eye. She told him not to play in the snow – she hasn't yet bought his annual set of thermals.

Three days before the fifteenth birthday they share, Zayd pours water from a bottle on to Ayesha's shoulder in the canteen. The water trickles off the acrylic of her school jumper. It takes a while for her to notice the dampness as she stares blankly into the bleak selection of lunch dishes.

Zayd is not sure why he did such a thing. He's on his own and so is she. The people around them are busy getting their food so they can spend the rest of the lunch hour doing something more interesting than eating pizza.

There's nobody to laugh with at his action, or to impress with his audacity. They've never even spoken before. He has seen her some afternoons, when school is over and the corridors echo with silence, when they seem to be the only two people on a post-apocalyptic planet. She glides past him to her regular spot in the study room as he roams around aimlessly until he is found by an overworked teacher. Ayesha's eyes never meet his, why would they?

When she finally turns around, Zayd has gone; he won't have lunch today. Ayesha looks at her shoulder and frowns, no longer surprised at how mean people can be for no reason. Just one more thing that makes no sense in this world.

Later that day, when the damp patch on her shoulder has dried and Zayd's stomach rumbles with emptiness, Ayesha is walking to her after-school spot in the study room. Her mother works until 6 p.m. and picks her up afterwards. The teachers agreed Ayesha could remain at school until then, as her mother spun some story about worries for the child's safety, threats from the family. It was a cruel world – they understood. Ayesha is supposed to do her homework, cross some books off the reading list. But really she pores over comics. There's nobody there to know, so she re-reads her weekly purchase again and again, the pages becoming softer each day. On Fridays she gives some of her saved lunch money to one of her few friends, who brings her a new comic each week. Her preference is for the traditional storylines, the outsider who has superpowers and saves humanity from certain doom. She never gets bored of this simple set-up. She loves how the colours are so bold, but blocked in by thick black lines. How the men are so manly and the women so womanly. The characters never seem to have parents; they are free agents, lonely but powerful.

On this day she is sweeping her eyes over the last page of her comic, soaking in the climax of the story, a culmination of flirtations between the two main super-heroes, their lips touching finally, amidst the happy crowd of regular humans they've just saved from death and destruction. The door to the study room creaks open a fraction. She looks up. Occasionally the cleaner, Juliette, comes in to hoover whilst Ayesha reads. They chat briefly about the music they're listening to at the moment, the lives of the singers that sang the songs, then they have nothing more to say and get on with their tasks. But it isn't Juliette. Ayesha sees a boy-shaped shadow through the gap in the door, though it doesn't open any further. She sits still, her hand spread wide over the last page of the comic as if she can cover up what she's reading. She arches her back and the tips of her toes are on the floor, ready to jump up and run if she has to. She calls out, *Hello?* Her voice sounds high and scared, not what she intended. She decides to stay strong and silent, just like her mother constantly tells her she should. The door opens a bit more, the creak harmonizing with the soft buzzing sound emanating from the computers on standby around the room. Zayd strolls in confidently, as if he never stood outside the door as a shadow, as if he didn't hear Ayesha's high and scared *Hello?* He nods at Ayesha, sits down right next to her at the round table. Her hand doesn't move from the comic but her eyes are on his; she doesn't look down. He smiles at her and she realizes her head is upright. Surprised at herself, she quickly bends her neck and stares at the edge of the table, a piece of grey chewing gum escaping from the underside and peeping up at her. Zayd says nothing, just gets his phone out and starts making quick, erratic movements with his thumbs accompanied by spasmodic facial expressions and the occasional sigh or other non-verbal sound. Ayesha angles her eyes up slightly, watches him for a minute. He doesn't look at her. Slowly, she removes her hand from the comic and tentatively goes back to reading. They sit there like this until Ayesha's mother calls to say she's waiting for her outside. Ayesha packs up her things and leaves the study room, Zayd still twisting his face in time with his thumbs.

The two of them continue like this for a few days, neither knowing that one of the days was their shared birthday. It was the same as any other day for both of them. They told nobody and nobody asked. Ayesha received some new headphones from her mother and Zayd's parents gave him a voucher to buy some more games for his phone. They both had cake when they went home.

Ayesha puts her new headphones in as she sits with her comic. Zayd feels this is a silent snub. He decides to embrace the possibilities of being fifteen – only three months left of his ridiculous Anti-Social Behaviour Order, which keeps him imprisoned at school after-hours until an adult from home is free to "supervise" him in public and pick him up. He can almost taste the freedom and it tastes like, well, like Ayesha's lips, although he's shocked at himself for thinking this. They've still never spoken, but she seems to him the most perfect human in the world. The way her almond eyes stare so intently at the pages of her comics, as if she's study-ing a secret book that tells the true history of the world. The way her headscarf is always so neat at the back but the front is constantly ruffled, her hair poking out and the seams lopsided from where she rests her hand on her head whilst she reads. She never smiles at him, but she doesn't look at him like he's rubbish, either. He really, really likes her. He waves his fingers in front of her eyes and she turns to look at him as if they're already mid-conversation. He raises his eyebrows, unsure of what to say. She takes one headphone out and the tinny sound of a female singer becomes audible. The corners of her lips turn up slightly. *Yes?* she says. Her voice is lower than he expected, strong but with a tone of apology. *New headphones?* he says, uninspired. She nods. *I got them for my birthday.* He nods back. *Happy Birthday. It was mine the other day too.* He feels more confident now. *Oh? What day?* Ayesha seems genuinely interested and Zayd replies as if he's telling her the answer to a question that has haunted her for years. *It was last week, Thursday.* Ayesha takes her other headphone out from her ear and scrunches up her brows. *What the hell? That's my birthday too!* Her choice of words and the excitement in her voice surprise Zayd, but he keeps his expression as neutral as possible. *Play it cool, play it cool*, he says to himself. *No way, well, like, I guess that means we share some sort of fate, right?* He can't believe he said that. How cheesy. But Ayesha smiles. *Yeah, I reckon. That's proper amazing. We were born the actual same day. What time?* Zayd doesn't know what she means. *What time were you born?* He has no idea. He shakes his head, sorry that he can't answer every single question she could ever ask him. *Ask your mum tonight – what time and where? I was born at 8 p.m., Royal London. Imagine if we were in the same ward at the same time!* Zayd nods, shellshocked that they are finally having a conversation. He can't remember the last time somebody was excited to talk to him. Ayesha puts her headphones back in, signalling the end of their chat, but she's pleased. She feels safe with Zayd now, something about sharing a birthday makes him feel more familiar than he felt five minutes ago. He's like family. Yes, she thinks, like a cousin or something.

A few weeks later, when Zayd and Ayesha's friendship is noted by observant teachers and typed into the Ones to Watch box due to the strange hours they keep and their quiet, introverted personalities, Zayd gives Ayesha his carton of apple juice in the study room after school as he always does. His mum became obsessed with making sure he got his five-a-day following his snowballing ordeal. She was told by one of the advisors that children with healthy diets tend to display less anti-social behaviour. She stuffs his schoolbag with tangerines and cartons of fruit juice every day. He doesn't like apple juice: too sweet. He prefers water and eats salad at lunch, but his mum doesn't believe him. Ayesha loves apple juice but is only allowed water, as *her* mother believes it is the only drink that will keep her skin clean and clear – and in a few years, when her mother finds her a good man, she will have to have clean and clear skin. Ayesha doesn't mind, she knows her mother is just scared she will end up alone, like her. And besides, the thought of a good man is quite a nice one. This exchange of a water bottle for an apple juice carton amuses and pleases the two friends. It is secretive and disobedient, but it hurts nobody and once again shows how well matched they are, that they each have what the other needs. As Ayesha sips the juice through the straw, Zayd shows her the new game on his phone. It's a brain training one – they usually are – to do with guessing long words from only two letters. Ayesha isn't very interested but smiles when Zayd shows her that he is the top player in the region. Suddenly embarrassed at his boasting, Zayd quickly asks Ayesha to tell him about her comic. She begins to retell the story, becoming more animated as she goes along. Ayesha tells him how glad she is that for once it is a female superhero saving the day, that there isn't a love story, that there isn't even a main male character, which is rare. Ayesha hadn't thought about it until she began to say this, but she realizes what a nice change it makes. Zayd asks to see this female superhero. Ayesha passes the comic over and Zayd looks at the muscly blonde woman with pale skin whose breasts pour out of the neckline of her superhero suit, and he raises his eyebrows, hands the comic back. *Wouldn't you rather have a superhero who looked like you?* he asks her. Then he worries he's overstepped the mark. These comics are precious to Ayesha – he doesn't want to take away whatever magic she finds in them. But Ayesha nods. *I'd never thought of it before, but, yeah, I guess that would be cool. Wouldn't ever happen, though. You know that.* Zayd wants to prove her wrong. He gets up and goes over to one of the computers, gesturing for her to follow. Ayesha laughs as he types *female Muslim superhero* into Google. Articles come up about young Muslim girls who have left the country to go and fight in foreign lands for organizations that are not thought of kindly. They read some of these, intrigued by the stories, the thought of even leaving the school gates unaccompanied unimaginable for them.

Eventually Ayesha suggests clicking on images instead, and after scrolling through a few pages of heavily made-up eyes peeking out of a niqab, finally there it is: a leaked prototype of a new Marvel comics character, their first female Muslim superhero. Ayesha and Zayd high-five.

* * *

The head teacher's office seems so small with all these people standing around the sides. The head herself looks diminished beside these suited people who stare and never smile. Zayd and Ayesha sit in the middle, confused, unable to give the outsiders what they want. Nothing the two teenagers say changes the questions they're asked again and again. Ayesha's head spins with the words being fired at them – *extremism, family, war, terror.* And then they ask, *Does your mother know?* Ayesha begs them not to tell her mum about the comics. She won't like them one bit, nor the fact that Ayesha buys them with her lunch money. One of the questioners laughs unsmilingly as he gets out two pairs of handcuffs, which glint in the sun shining brightly through the window of the office, making the headteacher's face a blank circle of light. *That is the very least of your worries, young lady,* he says.

"Recently there's been a lot of talk from politicians and commentators about the importance of intrusive, presumptive policies such as the current Prevent strategy, obliging schools to report students who show any signs of being 'vulnerable to radicalization' to the police, without providing staff with proper training as to what these signs might be. Ayesha and Zayd are the loveable, inquisitive teenage characters who came to my mind when thinking about how these strategies negatively affect young people's everyday lives and freedom." Sabrina Mahfouz

I BELIEVE...

Neil Gaiman
Chris Riddell

CREDO.

I BELIEVE

THAT REPRESSING IDEAS SPREADS IDEAS.

I BELIEVE

THAT PEOPLE AND BOOKS AND NEWSPAPERS ARE CONTAINERS FOR IDEAS, BUT THAT BURNING THE PEOPLE WILL BE AS UNSUCCESSFUL AS FIREBOMBING THE NEWSPAPER ARCHIVES.

IT IS ALREADY TOO LATE.

IT IS ALWAYS TOO LATE.

THE IDEAS ARE OUT, HIDING BEHIND PEOPLE'S EYES, WAITING IN THEIR THOUGHTS.

THEY CAN BE WHISPERED.

THEY CAN BE WRITTEN ON WALLS IN THE DEAD OF NIGHT.

THEY. CAN BE DRAWN.

I BELIEVE THAT IN THE BATTLE BETWEEN GUNS AND IDEAS,

IDEAS WILL, EVENTUALLY, WIN.

BECAUSE THE IDEAS ARE INVISIBLE. AND THEY LINGER,

AND, SOMETIMES,

THEY ARE EVEN TRUE.

EPPUR SI MUOVE—

AND YET IT MOVES.

NEIL GAIMAN

"I wrote this after the Charlie Hebdo murders. Watching people killing other people because they were scared of and threatened by ideas seemed so wrong that I thought I would write what I thought and felt. I sent it to Chris, and he took my thoughts and made something beautiful."
Neil Gaiman

THE IMPORTANCE OF SCREAMS

Christie Watson

I've always loved airports. People's faces. The emotion as they meet the eyes of a loved one. I like to imagine the stories: the son returning from a gap year, the grandparents from Australia seeing their grandchildren for the first time, a couple in love reunited after a work trip. I like watching the hugs, the kisses, the tears.

My husband, Labi, and I wait at the back of a crowd, peeking through gaps. I hold his arm. Our eyes search for her, but she is nowhere to be seen. Heathrow arrivals hall. The August heat is visible. In front of us is a layer of men in suits with cardboard handwritten signs, followed by families huddled together; all looking expectantly at the doorway, where people mill out, tired-eyed, pulling cases or small children behind them. The airport is filled with chatter and shouting and babies crying. A stag party bellow out past us, all wearing black T-shirts with *Magaloof 2016* printed on the front, and on the back a different name for each of them: *Big Dog, Nobby, Bat Crazy*. Everything rotates in and out, from the people to the smells: mustiness followed by sweat then bleach returning to mustiness. A toddler in a bright orange jacket weaves his way through his family's legs, making patterns in the air. I watch him until his mum grabs his arm and pulls him towards her. Another child squeals loudly and chases his sister.

When I first hear "Eeeeeeee, eeeeeeeeee!" I don't recognize her voice, but Labi rolls his eyes – *Here we go* – and then we see a short old-woman version of him appearing through the doors. His mum is wearing a red curly wig that I've not seen before, and a thick winter coat. She clutches a plastic bag to her chest. A security guard is walking next to her pulling two large clacking cases that are wrapped in plastic.

"Remind me, how long's she staying this time?" I ask. Labi's face is expressionless, then the corner of his mouth twitches into a half-smile. "I'm serious. Last year you said ten days and she was here most of August." I press my fingertips on to his damp arm. My feet are hot in my flip-flops and sweat trickles down the centre of my back.

Labi's mum finally reaches us, the security guard in tow.

"Hello, Mum." Labi pulls her towards him and almost lifts her off the ground. He hugs everyone he sees but reserves his best hugs for me and his mum.

"This man," she shouts. "He is taking me!" She turns to the security guard. "My passport is valid and my son is my sponsor. He is a lawyer, you know!"

"Hello, Mum," I say. She stops waving her arms around for a few seconds. It is always difficult for her to see me. I try to understand how hard that must be, for her only son to marry someone so outside their culture.

"Eeeeeeee!" she shouts, grabbing my arm. She smells of nutmeg and something else I can never place. "Eeeeeeee. My daughter. They think I am illegal. Illegal! Checking my passbook as if I have no sponsor, no visa. All those people looking at me."

"They were probably simply checking it," I whisper, but my voice is too quiet in the airport noise.

"They will send me to that place," she continues. "Brother Kayode saw it on CNN. Detention. They treat you like rats. Rats!" She sweeps her eyes back to the security guard, who is now talking quietly with Labi. Eventually the security guard shakes his head, bends slightly and shrugs before walking away.

"No courage! Now my son is here. Look at his courage fading like the colour in cheap fabric." She looks up at Labi and squeezes his cheek between her thumb and forefinger. "My son is a big man."

I laugh. I'd forgotten how easily she makes me laugh. "How are you, Mum – apart from your airport security ordeal?" I step forwards but she narrows her eyes.

"You see this?" she shouts, pointing to the shops. "So many shops." She looks at me and narrows her eyes even more. Soon they will be completely closed. "As if women have time to shop all day!"

Labi pulls my hand towards him. His skin is warm-wet, and softer than ever.

"What is this?" she continues, pointing at the toilets. "Is that the *facilities*!"

Labi's mum has been to England many times. Every year, at some point over the summer, she comes to visit, to see us and the children. And every year the airport routine is the same.

"Look at the shortness of that woman's skirt. Look how it sticks to the side." I follow Labi's mum's eyes to the female toilet sign.

"I will not be pissing in there," she says.

When we arrive home, our ten-year-old twins, Tife and Toni, are splashing around in the giant paddling pool that my friend Kat, who has been watching them, has inflated and filled. She has added some washing-up liquid, a trick I remember my mum doing, and the garden is patchy with foam. Labi's mum runs immediately over to them and gets in the paddling pool. She is still wearing her thick winter coat. They squeal with laughter. "Nanny! Nanny!"

"Don't wet my hair," she shouts. She lifts her legs up on to the edge, and half the water slides out. She is covered in foam and the girls stick to her too, despite being nearly as tall as she is.

"Two girls," she says. "Twin girls. May God bless you with a son. Pray to Jesus. You are blessed." She begins to sing, loudly.

I pour some wine into a glass, add ice, say goodbye to Kat. Labi disappears into his office. I can't taste the wine, my mouth feels numb. Outside, I can hear an ice-cream van in the distance and smell a barbecue. I try to ignore our retired neighbour, who is pretending to paint his fence and keeps looking at Labi's mum. I think of last summer and how she knocked on his door one day while I was at work and went into his house, sat down on his sofa and spent hours talking about Jesus.

That night I serve fried chicken for dinner, and Labi's mum covers hers in ketchup and salt.

"Can *we* have tomato sauce, please, Mum, please? Like Grandma?" Tife looks up at me with her moon-eyes and Toni flicks her head between us.

I smile, open the bottle and squirt a tiny amount on each plate. "Sure."

"Aunty Bunmi has a new business," Labi's mum tells us. "Making bricks. She makes so many bricks the labour-ers can't build fast enough. She is building faster than they are! Ha! If she wasn't so fat she'd be better off building the houses herself."

The twins laugh. "Do you have a job, Nanny?" Toni asks.

"I have fourteen jobs."

Labi looks at me. A stare with one eyebrow lifted.

"Fourteen?" Tife puts her fork down. "That's a lot."

"Exactly. I do the Sunday school, the choir costumes, the snacks for the congregation, organize the floor sweepers, test the microphone, go to market, buy the fish, make the pepper soup – so many, many jobs. And I've joined a theatre group. We go to the villages to teach those village girls about cutting."

Labi looks up. "Er, Mum, let's not go into too many details about all of your jobs. OK?"

I find my head spinning. What is she teaching those girls?

She looks at Labi, then the girls. She is drinking shots of peach-flavoured schnapps, a shot between each mouthful of food. Half a bottle is gone already. Tife's eyes are wide.

"They should know. Plenty of girls their age know first-hand."

I stop chewing. My fork cracks against my teeth. More thoughts enter my head, one particularly nasty, but I push it away and swallow.

"Hmph. We have to work hard in Nigeria but it is a much better country. This country," she says, adding more sauce and gravy and so much salt I can see a layer of it on top of her food. "England. No taste to the food."

"About that," I say, and Labi flashes me a look. "I know you mean well, but please don't put extra pepper and seasoning in the cooking this year. Last summer the twins had a layer of skin come off their tongues." I laugh. "They're not used to spicy food. Especially Scotch bonnet peppers."

"Send them to me in Nigeria. They would get used to it. They could come for the school holidays."

"I couldn't be without them," I say quickly, and I laugh again, quietly, then there are a few moments of silence before she stands suddenly.

"I'm going for a rest," she says. The schnapps bottle rolls to the edge of the table. No one tries to stop it falling off.

"I hope I didn't offend you? I didn't mean to − it's just…"

"No, no," says Labi's mum. "I'm tired, that's all."

Labi says nothing.

I can feel my stomach churning. I look at the girls.

Their mouths are so far open I can see the gums where their teeth end. Toni begins to eat, quickly, focusing on her food, eyes down.

"Mum," I say, "I did not mean to upset you. Of course I'd love the girls to visit Nigeria. I'll bring them one day. *We* will." I look up at Labi. I can't even talk to him about my fears. Girls are cut in Nigeria. His mum told me herself. Many girls, too many. Would she let that happen to our girls? Would she condone it? I will never, ever let them visit without me there.

"Upset?" she repeats, sitting down again. "Upset? You give me this flavourless food on my arrival day and you disrespect me?" Toni stops eating, and moves closer to her arm. Tife puts her thin hand on her shoulder. Both girls look at me as if I'm a monster.

I look to Labi. "Do something," I say. But he just sits, eyes down, shoulders rounded.

"And you never visit!" she screams. "I never see these, my granddaughters – you do not want to see my face! No wonder they do not like spice. Their tongues would be strong if you brought them to Nigeria! They have weak English tongues. My own grandchildren. English-tongued grandchildren."

In bed later, I punch Labi's arm. "What the hell were you thinking? Your mum has some kind of episode and you say nothing? I didn't mean to offend her but now she's upset. It's hard work when she stays, Labi. Hard work. She nearly set the kitchen on fire last year! And the year before she flooded the entire house trying to wash all her shoes in the washing machine. You need to be with her. Take some time off."

"You know I can't take two entire weeks off right now. You know that, Tan."

I watch the tiny scar on the back of his arm.

Eventually he turns over and sighs, looking at the ceiling, pulling me towards him. He kisses the top of my head. "Try to understand her," he whispers.

I push him away and sit up. "You want me to say nothing when she does these things? Nothing?"

He shakes his head. "Of course not. It's hard for me too, you know."

Suddenly a knocking on our bedroom door. I pull the covers over me.

"Hello, hello, you young people always fighting like children." She walks in wearing a pair of Labi's pyjamas and my new sequined flip-flops.

"Mum, can you give us a minute, we're talking." Labi smiles too widely.

"We are all talking, *abi*. I am head of the family in Daddy's absence. I will help to solve you both. All us family talking together." She sits down on the bed on my side, on top of my foot. I cry out.

The girls run in seconds later. They are not used to talking, knocking, in the night. Soon there are five of us in the bed. I hold them close, Tife and Toni, their skin warm and smelling of sleep.

Labi's mum farts, loudly. "Sorry," she says. "I have terrible gas from the bad food. In Nigeria I never produce a fart like this." The girls laugh so hard I worry they may never be able to stop. They roll about until Toni falls off the bed, then Tife joins her in a giggling heap on the carpet.

They behave much younger when Labi's mum is here. They become children once more.

Labi's mum looks at me. "We can learn from children," she says. "They don't keep anger for long."

I smile at her despite myself and feel Labi gently stroking my arm. Before she returns to bed she gives me a hug so tight I can't breathe.

"Let us not fight any more, my daughter."

She leaves and ushers the girls back to bed. She is not holding me but I can still feel her. I move towards Labi, rest my head on his chest.

Before leaving for work the next morning, I give Labi's mum strict instructions not to cook anything, visit the neighbours or touch the washing machine, but still I am nervous when I approach the house at lunchtime, walking along the street to the sound of lawnmowers. It was only a few hours, and an unmissable meeting, but still I felt sick leaving her. And then I see it. All my underwear in perfect women shapes laid out on the front lawn. A couple walks past and points and laughs. I feel the redness in my face and neck and for a few moments I want to run away, back to the office, with my tidy desk and order and routine and normality.

There are seven invisible women. Seven sets of my finest underwear. I see the curtains opposite my house move suddenly. The redness reaches my ears.

Labi's mum is in the front garden cutting all the heads off the roses. "You have to cut these back or you will attract wasps."

I want to scream. Instead I scoop up every piece of bone-dry, stiff underwear and try not to imagine what she has washed it in.

"Taneeeeya, are you well? You have a look of illness. Shall I make you pepper soup? I could add lemon to reduce the heat for you."

I stomp into the house, up the stairs and into our bedroom before dialling Labi's work number. My hand is shaking.

"I'm going to kill her."

Labi sighs down the phone.

"She's put all my underwear out at the front of the house. All our neighbours have seen it. God knows how long it's been out there!" I am crying now. Big, fat, child-like tears. "And she's cut all the roses off."

Labi sighs again. "Hang in there. Don't lose it."

"How can I not?"

"Look, we don't want a repeat performance of last night. Please don't upset her."

"Upset her?"

"I know it's hard, but it's good of her to look after the kids while we're at work. Go out for the afternoon. It's lovely out. Please, Tan. I'll talk to her tonight, I promise."

The girls burst into the room and hug me either side. I push my tears back. "OK, we'll go out. I'll see you later."

"We're going out? Can we go to the park? Cinema? Please, Mum, please. Can Nanny come?" Labi is right: they really do love their grandma.

"Of course." I scoop them up onto the bed and kiss their heads, ignore the underwear in a heap next to us. "Let's have some fun."

Liverpool Street Market is exactly the same as last year. Labi's mum wants to look at every stall, buy the same material she can get in Lagos. She chats to the stallholders, asks of their family and regularly holds up material or clothing, or a new wig, and shouts, "Taneeeeya, Taneeeeya, is this worth ten pounds? Am I too fat for such a colour? Is this woman stealing from me? Is this market full of thieves?"

I smile and nod and focus on the market sounds. The fruit seller: *"Pound a tub o' strawberries!"*

Labi's mum insists on buying me a traditional Nigerian costume with matching shoes. The shoes are far too shiny and have *Gucchi* written across the front in diamanté lettering. The girls laugh so hard they pretend to fall over. I stand in the shop watching them curled around each other shaking with laughter, tears shining their cheeks.

On Friday we decide to go to the park for a picnic. We arrive at Valley Lake and spread out on top of two blankets. Labi's mum is staring at a squirrel and hissing when it gets too close. "Vermin," she says.

She is wearing her winter coat.

The girls weave patterns on the grass, kicking a ball between them. "Don't go near the water," I say, taking out my newspaper.

"Girls! Girls!" They run over and sit by her feet. "This lake," she says, "reminds me of Miracle Lake."

I put salad and couscous on two plates and push them at the girls. Mum produces two packets of Monster Munch crisps from her plastic bag and hands them one each.

"Miracle Lake in Nigeria cures everything," she tells them. "Any disease." She undoes her coat slightly to her neckline.

"Can it cure verrucas?"

"Of course!" She looks at Toni's feet. "If you took off your socks and washed your feet in Miracle Lake the verruca would be gone."

I focus on the line of sweat pooling on her top lip. "Go and play now, girls," she says. "Off you go. Find a tree to climb. I need to take a small rest."

I watch the girls running backwards and forwards on the grass, then open my newspaper, my eyes glancing up every now and then when their shrieks diminish. Labi's mum asks me to read aloud to her. She always says she's forgotten her glasses but I've never seen her wear any. I read an article about house prices in London; she tuts and tuts. "Come live in Nigeria. You would live like kings."

The next headline is about female genital mutilation.

I stop myself. My mouth closes over the words.

"Go on," she says.

She is sitting up now and looking straight at the newspaper. "The next article is a bit sensitive," I murmur.

"Ha!" she laughs. "Everything is sensitive to you English. Read it. My ears are tough as toenails."

"It's about cutting. Female genital cutting." I close my eyes. My midwife friend told me all about it last summer. I told her to stop. Put my hands over my ears. But I could still hear odd words: *genitals*; *barbaric*; *death...*

"Read it then," says Labi's mum.

I open my eyes, read: *"Teachers are being told to be vigilant as the school holidays approach, as concern is growing about the number of teenage girls undergoing female mutilation during the summer. It is estimated that female genital cutting is becoming more prevalent within the UK, with twenty thousand girls under the age of fifteen at risk..."*

I look up. Labi's mum is shaking her head. I try to focus on our surroundings, anything but the thoughts in my head. The girls visiting Nigeria in summer. *The park, the park,* I think. The park is full of families in slow-motion, technicolour August sunshine. The trees are almost unnaturally green. The grass is soft and dry, a ladybird lands on my arm, walks slowly towards my hand, then flies off. A cat chases squirrels and the geese bellow and run in short bursts. I breathe.

Labi's mum lies on her back. "It is better now in Nigeria.

This thing is no good for women. Terrible for girls. Britain needs to catch up. Talk openly. Tell girls to shout. Like my theatre group. Progressive."

I look at her face. It is pulled together tightly, and her eyes are wet. Whenever she's spoken of it before she has seemed less emotional than this. Not for it, but not against, as if she had some kind of understanding that I never could.

I shouldn't ask her. I've never asked before. It's never *occurred* to me before. But the words leak out of my mouth. "Did it happen to you?"

She taps the grass between us. "It needs to stop happening. It is no good."

Her face cracks as she talks. How could I imagine she'd expose our girls to such a thing? How could I have thought that of her? I feel the redness on my chest, rising up to my face, threatening to burn me with heat.

"These young girls in Britain. Suffering for what? Because people don't like to talk? You English need to learn how to talk. Silence is dangerous."

I look at her for a long time. She is totally against cutting. Of course she is. I am an idiot. A racist idiot.

"Can we have bubblegum ice cream, please, please, please." The girls run towards us. I focus on Labi's mum, her legs crossed in front of her near my feet, her toenails painted in blue and white stripes. She is right. It's happening right here in England. In London. Thousands of girls at risk. Girls like my girls.

"Can we take off our socks and shoes?"

I give Toni five pounds. "OK. But straight back." Before I finish, they are barefoot, running towards the ice-cream van at the edge of the lake, disappearing behind it. I listen to the geese, a dog barking in the distance, children's laughter.

My eyes read a few more lines. I turn the page of the newspaper. Read half a page. A page.

A scream. Tife. Tife's scream. A scream that is other-worldly, the one that she reserves for serious injury, or terrible loss. Her broken arm from falling out of a tree, the death of her grandfather.

I'm not aware of my body but somehow I'm running and Labi's mum is beside me, shouting, "Eeeeeeeeeeeee. Eeeeeeeeeee. Eeeeeeeeeeee. Is she hurt? Is someone hurt?"

I see her in the water and my body suddenly slips and my knee cracks and I'm on the ground. An upside-down girl in a lake, her head bobbing up to suck in air, then falling beneath the surface again. My girl. Toni. I try and get up, but the grass is slippery near the water and I fall again.

Labi's mum has thrown off her coat and waded into the water in the seconds it's taken me to stand and scream and grab Tife, who is shouting enough that a crowd has gathered, and run towards the lake.

"Call an ambulance!" I shout. "Call an ambulance!"

As we reach the water, Labi's mum emerges covered in thick green pond slime, minus her wig, her giant breasts clinging in wet clothes. Toni has changed colour. She is dusky, grey at the edges, the colour of moonlight. Labi's mum sets her on the ground and hits her chest. I can't move. I can't breathe. I can't even cry.

"Eeeeeeeeeeee," Labi's mum shouts. "Naughty girl! Eeeeeeeeeee!" She shouts and smacks her hard again and again. Toni coughs. Suddenly and violently. Labi's mum rolls her to her side, hits her back repeatedly until she is coughing and vomiting and breathing and her edges become daylight once more. Then she cries.

I let go of Tife and drop to the ground, let the tears come.

"Good girl," Labi's mum says. "Good, good."

The day of Labi's mum's flight home, the girls cry until their pillowcases need changing. They do not want to go to the airport. Last time Labi's mum left they found it so hard.

"Let us say goodbye here," she says.

As they tell her goodbye before Kat arrives to watch them, I tip the leftover schnapps down the sink, clean the mess that Labi's mum has left in the spare room. I find sweet wrappers, magazines, four empty jars of marmalade, a dummy, seven Ikea catalogues, three pairs of Labi's pyjamas, my electric toothbrush. I find a handkerchief that smells exactly like her and put it in my jeans pocket.

Heathrow is not as busy as it was a few weeks ago.

There is room for us to spread out, but we don't. Labi's mum holds me close. "Taneeeeya," she says, "I will miss you so much."

"Me too." I feel tears on my cheeks and I don't know if they are mine or hers. "Thank you," I say again. I've said it hundreds of times but I could never say it enough. The worst moment. "You saved her life."

"Of course I did. She is my heart. They both are. And Tife's scream saved her. It is good that when one child is in danger a person will scream. When one girl is in danger, another girl will scream loudly."

Labi puts his arms around us and gently pulls her towards the departure gate. "You need to go, Mum. Have you got any toiletries? They have to go in a clear bag."

"I know what to do," she says. "You came from my body."

My head swims with what her body might have suffered. What I thought she agreed with. How wrong I was. The dangers of fearing offence. Of assuming. The dangers of silence. The importance of screams.

Labi laughs. "Have a safe flight. We love you. And we will see you next summer."

"We'd like to visit you before then," I add. "Maybe in the Christmas holidays."

Labi nods and nods. His mum begins to dance. She stops after a few minutes and looks at us both without talking, then begins to walk away.

She turns, smiles, waves at us, looks around and then disappears into the crowd.

We stand in silence amid the noise of the airport for the longest time, looking at the air where she stood. I reach for Labi's hand, and with my other hand reach into my jeans pocket for her handkerchief. I bring it to my face and close my eyes.

"In writing this story I wanted to highlight a reality that so many girls in Britain are facing. I believe in a future world where female genital mutilation is eradicated and young girls never have to suffer this most extreme form of gender-based violence. We must all shout." Christie Watson

WHAT I REMEMBER ABOUT HER

A. L. Kennedy

There was just something weird about her – not right. She was not right. You could watch her – not watch her, exactly, because you weren't that interested, but you could see her going along the corridors and up and down stairs and that, and you could see that she wasn't right. I mean, you noticed her, because people who aren't right stand out. You didn't have to be trying to notice – it was just something about her.

It's not that you would hate her, or anything like that, it was just this way she had of moving which made you notice her. We're in a big school, massive, but she was always *there*. Too much. In amongst everyone else, you could see her too much. She stood out. And she joined Year Seven in January so her uniform still looked like she just got it out of a shop when nobody else's did. Tina said it looked like someone sent it in some kind of aid package – refugee aid package. It was too neat.

And it stayed too neat right until practically now – which is June, almost the end of the year. Her in her refugee ironed-up clothes.

She wasn't a refugee, though.

I said that.

We'd have known if she was a refugee.

I did say that.

And now we're sure she wasn't. We're like sure we're sure.

Not that it's bad to be a refugee – I didn't say that then and I'm not saying it now – she just wasn't one. That's the truth.

Tina said it would be a food bank, then, who gave out the blazer and the rest of the uniform. They give you clothes in a food bank as well as food. Or your social worker gets stuff for you.

Her blazer was like it was meant for her big brother. Which she didn't have. Or not round here anyway.

She did seem like she wouldn't have a big brother, or any brothers or sisters. And there was no one but her at our school and when you saw her you could tell she was an only child. I think that's a fact – her being by herself.

She didn't look like she'd understand how to be with other kids in a family. She would walk about in this kind of a sliding way. She'd be on the stairs and she would slide along the wall, slide with her shoulder against the wall, like she was cleaning it, or as if she was showing us how we were all too much for her – which we were not. We've never been too much for somebody. When she did that, it was like she was being a demonstration for us of how she was really sensitive, and shouldn't we be paying her lots of attention, or caring, or stuff?

You couldn't try that in a family – they'd tell you to quit it. When she was sliding, she looked like she really did have a social worker.

Or else like she lived somewhere weird.

Sonja said that was probably true. Tina and Sonja and Sinead and Elshaday made up this whole story about some orphanage place with metal beds and stuff and eating at a big, long table and we were all laughing. I did laugh, because it was so stupid, it was funny. Then it ended up that we were imagining this horrible kids' home so it was more and more like Hogwarts and we added in a Harry Potter and hundreds of Weasleys.

Then Sinead practically screamed, "Dobby!" Right in the street.

We were out near the back of the mall on lunch break and we'd got sandwiches and Sinead had a salad and we were going to spot the ugly shoes in that crap tiny shoe shop next to the crap tiny card shop on Arlington Drive and the shoe assistant was practically standing there in the doorway as if he wasn't going to let us inside – when there would be no point stealing his get-them-free-with-a-Burger-King-burger-shoes and when we're not thieves.

If you're a kid, people assume you're a thief and it's crap and not true.

And Sinead just yelled.

And we didn't know what was wrong for about a second and the assistant jumped right back, but then we realized – she meant Dobby in the Harry Potter movies. Dobby, with his sad little elf refugee face and his sad little elf I-need-you-to-help-me shirt thing he wears, and how he's so pathetic the whole time and you're supposed to feel sorry for him when he dies – *that* Dobby. Dobby was just exactly like the girl.

That was just the truth.

She was Dobby.

And she couldn't help it and we couldn't help it. That's what she was like is all we were saying.

Or I wasn't the one to say it, but I was there. Sinead said it. I did agree. I probably nodded.

So after that we called the girl Dobby.

I mean, we didn't call her Dobby when we talked to her, we didn't really talk to her, why would we? But when we were talking about her, we called her Dobby.

Somebody, though, somebody a few weeks after that

humped into her, coming down the corridor from double chemistry and said out loud, "Sorry, Dobby."

People thought that was hilarious. It was loads of LOLs.

I heard it was Nikki who bumped the girl, or if it wasn't Nikki it was Steve who's like Nikki's boyfriend, or this kind of stupid thing that's not a boyfriend so he gets to do what he wants, but Nikki only wants to hang about with him, so they break up a lot, even though they're not together. It was either Nikki or Steve who did it. I wasn't there.

The girl got bumped into and didn't say anything herself, but she looked at either Nikki or Steve – is what I was told – and it was like she was going to answer as if Dobby really was her name.

That cracked people up.

When I first heard about it, I did think it was funny.

And I told Sinead, only she'd already heard and said it happened on the way to citizenship and not on the way from double chemistry. She corrected me – which is what she does. She always wants to make you feel like you're an idiot and that she knows best. That's why she eats salad. One day she'll be someone's mum and then she'll get to be that way in her own house all the time. Her husband will have to eat salad – everyone will – and they'll all have to keep on being wrong, so that she can stay happy. In the end, her kids'll run away from home, or get married to just anyone, or be terrorists, or go crazy.

Dobby might have been a bit crazy – if you looked at

her it seemed that way – which wouldn't have been any-one's fault. Being crazy is an illness, like breaking your leg. I'm just saying that she looked a bit crazy in her eyes. She mostly didn't face where she was going and just checked out the floor, probably so that you wouldn't catch her eye. Or because she was hiding, trying to hide.

She looked like a person in a prison or in a mental hos-pital. It was pretty much her face I described when I had to write an essay about paying a visit to a relative in prison. I think the essay was in case any of us had relatives in prison, so the whole class could join in and be sympathetic, only Carl actually does have a cousin in prison and he said he could do without writing essays about it as well as having to hear about the cousin whenever his dad had a go at Carl about being rubbish at maths. This cousin is supposed to be a warning about terrible shit that will happen in the future if you don't know about maths. Even though nobody is sure if the cousin could do maths or not – and it's not like he's in prison because he can't do linear equations, or that stuff they keep asking us. One of our maths tests had this ques-tion about plastic bottles being made into fleece jackets and how many bottles would make how many fleeces, which was a total waste of time. That doesn't teach you anything. All it does is prove that fleece jackets are shit, which you already know.

And Mrs Martin – who teaches English, so the essay was her idea – didn't know that some of us were in John's

Road Infants together and knew this boy called Graeme whose dad committed suicide because he owed this monster amount of money to a gang and couldn't pay it back. He killed himself to stop them killing him. And he probably didn't want the gang to hurt Graeme, or Graeme's mum. That's what Graeme said. It was sort of a kind of type of suicide. There can be that type. There's lots of types, but they're all stupid. They all make other people feel bad.

Having been in the same class as Graeme means we know, or some of us do, about prison. Or people that ought to be in prison.

They never caught whoever Graeme's dad owed the money to, and it isn't a crime to lend money, plus it was Graeme's dad who killed Graeme's dad, so really there was no way anyone was going to prison, but they should have. People who are guilty should go to prison.

Anyway, that's why I didn't write about a man in a cell. I wrote about a woman, but she had Dobby's face, pretty much, the way I described it.

I don't know where Graeme went after primary. He took a month off after his dad died and then he came back and said he was better off without him, but didn't act like he believed it. After John's Road I don't think anyone saw him again, so maybe he moved away.

He didn't kill himself or we'd have heard.

Carl in Mrs Martin's English class has never visited the

cousin in prison. He says the cousin is a wanker and should stay locked up.

Dobby wouldn't have been in prison, but I wondered if maybe she'd been in some hospital somewhere. No one has said. She seemed a bit hospital – more than a bit hospital – because of that way she would slide around. She made it look like it took some big effort when she needed to go through a doorway, or walk all the way across a floor without something propping her up. She never went to the lunch hall, maybe because of that.

And she could seem like she was waiting for someone to bring her something, or tell her what to do.

I did sometimes think that I would say something so she could relax a bit.

Not threaten her – just tell her when it was the last lesson before going home, or something like that. Not because she wouldn't have known, but maybe it would have been relaxing for her to hear it. And she might have been glad it was nearly home time.

I know she went home to a flat and that she lived there with her mum.

I know that now. I didn't know then. It's been explained.

Dobby didn't do PE.

I suppose you can't do PE if you have to slide along walls. You can't be any use to anyone like that.

And she would be no use anyway. That was something

we thought. I'd have told her not to try in case she hurt herself. That wouldn't have been ganging up on her.

I'd like to have been allowed to skip games. She did well with that.

She didn't even sit out on the side with whoever was having bad periods, or pretending they were having bad periods – which is the only useful thing about periods, they can get you out of gymnastics, or circuit training, all that rubbish.

She just never went anywhere near PE.

She didn't do games, either. No running up and down pretending to be interested in hockey, or running round and round and round the track in the summer. (That's not even a sport – that's just running, like you do for a bus. And pervs hang about along the back fence because we're in shorts and they can't get enough of us.)

I mean, you're lucky if you don't have to do games.

So she just did the things she did – the sliding and the being quiet – and we really didn't pay that much attention to her.

You can't be friends with someone just because you get told you have to.

You shouldn't be horrible to people, but you don't have to be their friend – it's not fair, otherwise, if you don't like them, or know them, or want to spend time with them, then you've got nothing to talk about or do if you are with them. You'll make each other bored.

I've already got friends.

I already had friends then.

People have asked since if I'd have done things differently with her, as if it's my fault, or anybody's fault.

It's not someone's fault. There's no need to feel bad.

Or perhaps it was Sinead's fault, because she made up Dobby's name. If that was a problem. The girl might not have known about being called Dobby, though.

Besides, people love Harry Potter. There's a theme park and people keep on being fans, even though it's been around for a while now, and they buy Gryffindor scarves and keep reading the books. So Dobby could have been a good name to have.

We could have turned out to have given her a good name.

It's not fair that all this ended how it did, because we didn't mean anything. We were making a joke.

And probably whatever else happened to her was what was wrong and she didn't even notice us. She never seemed to notice us.

If we'd known about what had happened at the other schools then I would have spoken to her more, or smiled at her if it looked like that wouldn't scare her. I would have said it was time to go home soon, or if it was really hot, or if somebody was being a dick I would have made some kind of comment. I would have just had some chat with her, maybe.

Which would be what I would have done differently, I suppose. I don't think that would have changed anything. I don't think she would have enjoyed it, in fact.

The first I knew that something was wrong was when we were heading home one Thursday and it was going to thunder – it felt that way, really stuffy – and I wanted to get away and have a shower and be online in my PJs and have a chilled evening.

I suppose online stuff could have been easier for Dobby, for the girl, because then she wouldn't have had to be in the room with people, or been looked at, but then there's lots of shit online and crazy and horrible people. I'm not part of anything like that. I wasn't part of anything like that. She probably had a computer, but I don't know.

When I'm surfing, I look at fake movie trailers and those Indian singers with subtitles, and stuff that makes me laugh. I just use it for stuff that makes me laugh. I'm not even allowed to be online for that long. I get limited hours in the week. I'm not a person who does bad things anywhere – not even online, which is where everybody thinks they'll get away with it.

Nothing that happened can change that.

And I don't feel bad when I think about the Thursday when we were all heading home. It was this Thursday when there was this woman over on the other side of the street – opposite the main entrance to the school – and she could have been anybody, anybody's mum, until she started screaming.

I think I guessed then that she had something to do with Dobby. I don't know why. Maybe it was because she was weird, or because the screaming made her look like her daughter.

After a while Mr Carlyle and Mr Porteous came out because of the noise and they didn't quite touch her, but they got very close on either side of her.

Then the woman – Dobby's mum – hit them. She hit Mr Porteous and then he held her arm and she started crying. They walked with her towards some man, just some guy from in the street, and they all got her in their arms and she was fighting them – all these people trying to help, I suppose. After that I didn't see anything else, because we were all told to go away.

I wasn't staring.

I wasn't enjoying it.

I didn't know for sure that the woman was Dobby's mum.

It was nothing to do with us.

She only said it was – yelled at us and said it was our fault. She was blaming us for something, because she was upset and there wasn't anything else that she could do.

That's the truth.

She was blaming us for stuff we didn't mean to do.

We wouldn't have wanted a bad thing to happen to Dobby. Anything bad was Dobby's choice.

People said that.

I agree with them.

And it's all finished now, but it still upsets me.

"I have long been an admirer of the human rights legislation and declarations that arose after the terrible events of World War II. They represent some of the finest and most generous products of human imagination. I was delighted when I heard that Amnesty was putting together an anthology based on enshrined and essential human rights – rights which are now under threat for us all as they may never have been since WWII. I based my story on Article 39 of the UN Convention on the Rights of the Child. It is easy for children to be victims and to find no support, or even to be blamed for the effects of their own suffering and victimized again for seeming strange."
A.L. Kennedy

BARLEY WINE

Kevin Brooks

Imagine a reflection in the silver convexity of a convenience-store mirror. That's me – or something of me – in a long black coat and rain-darkened hair, making it winter in Victoria a lifetime ago.

Imagine it's late.

The pubs have closed. Late-night cars ride the puddled street. A tired breeze sighs across the rooftops scattering rainwater in the gutters, and the starless sky is low and dull. The chemical glow of streetlights has reduced the night to little more than a second-rate day.

Inside the convenience store, Day-Glo stars advertise lonesome goods – Beans! Bread! Milk! Pies! Beer! – and the cramped aisles are stacked with things you might not even know you need: firelighters, salt, pens, playing cards, toilet rolls, combs, laces, shoe polish. There's a perspex rack for car magazines and girly magazines, cardboard boxes of crisps on the floor, sweet potatoes loose in trays. Sitting on a high stool by the stockroom door is a white-haired old man mumbling through the Koran, while at the front of the store his daughter works the till. If you watch her carefully you'll see how she pilots the counter with a natural indifference, as if the cigarettes and alcohol that surround her don't actually exist. And even if they do exist, they're nothing more to her than packets and bottles and cans. Although she's a fair distance away, you can see her quite clearly. You can see the delicate lines of her face, her unblemished skin, the gloss of her long dark hair shining soberly in the fluorescent light. And on the wall behind her you can see a pink bikini girl pouting from a salted-peanut display.

There is no god but God.

That's me, though, in the mirror, looking down at the cheese and cold pies. The curve of the glass has given my figure the distended look of a nightmare – shoulders hunched, hands in pockets, face loomed in back-of-spoon distortion – like something from the underworld. What I know – my wisdom – is that the big refrigerator is the place to look when you're drunk and hungry, when you need some cheese or a cold pie.

It's a question of faith.

What I'm thinking is, I could ask the old man about it. I could turn to him and say, "Excuse me, mister ... hey, mister..." but I doubt if he'd want to talk to me. Why the hell should he? He has his own concerns. You can tell that by the way he's sitting. And, anyway, what am I to him? An Englishman at the refrigerator, a customer, a potential thief. A profit or a loss. Good or bad. Right or wrong. Whatever it says in his book, it's got nothing to do with me. So let's forget about him and take a look in the refrigerator.

What have we got? Sausage rolls, pasties, pies, Scotch eggs, packs of meat, all kinds of things. And just along from the pies and stuff there's a tray full of cheeses. Most of them don't have much appeal, they're just pale yellow slabs wrapped in clingfilm, but the piece of Edam is different. It stands out. Look at it, it's like a red-rimmed wedge of golden sun in a frosty winter sky. Now you might think that's rather fanciful — and you might be right — but don't forget it's late at night and I'm drunk-hungry. No doubt it would all look different in the cold light of day. But for now the sun's made of cheese and I'm shuffling over to get a better look at it, pretending to check the price, and I'm simultaneously picturing myself walking back through the rain, peeling back the waxy skin and taking a good fat bite...

A gust of wind rattles the shop window and brings me back to now.

There are things to consider. Things to do.

Take another look in the mirror. The aisles are empty. Wet bootprints track the linoleum floor and a smell of heat hums from a vent on the wall. Over by the door the old man is still holding the Koran in his white-smocked lap, his head bowed as he reads with an arthritic finger. His hands are dark and moley, his lips fluttering silently in search of Paradise. At the till his daughter is swiping a debit card and wrapping a bottle of Thunderbird in a sheet of green tissue paper.

Zina.

I think she might be called Zina.

You can see by the way she wraps the bottle that she knows it's a waste of time. She might as well just screw the tissue paper into a ball and throw it into the gutter herself, cut out the middle man.

The middle man in this case is a sad-eyed drunk in a rain-sodden cheap beige suit.

The shop door tings when he leaves.

And Zina looks up and catches my eye in the mirror. I know she can read my thoughts. Her eyes are blank to hide her desires, but I know it. She can read my thoughts. And I think to myself, wait a minute. Just wait a minute. Listen, Zina. Listen to me. Let's say we're somewhere else, like a nice quiet room somewhere, just you and me. A room that smells of flowers and spices. You wouldn't have to say anything, just listen to me. All I want to do is to tell you what it's like. You see, I'm not a bad person, just a little drunk right now. I don't know what you think about that, you know, what with your religion and everything, but listen, let me tell you what it's like for me.

And then I tell her.

I tell her how I arrived in London about a month ago, with my battered blue suitcase, my coat, my fur gloves and my anxious hat. How the short walk from Victoria station to the hostel was never going to be long enough, no matter how many times I stopped to rearrange things. How the weight of the suitcase ached in my arm as I shuffled up the broad length of Buckingham Palace Road towards the address that was written on the back of a folded envelope in my pocket. It was a hostel, that's all I knew about it. A place for civil young men with reasonably good jobs but nowhere to live. I got a letter telling me I could stay there. I didn't even think about it. I just went.

And then I tell her how I stopped by Elizabeth Bridge to rest my arms and smoke a cigarette. London raced and hummed its big city blues all around me and I knew already that I was nothing to it. Do you know what I mean? I was invisible. I watched the cars and buses and black taxis and thought it was like something in a film.

Meanwhile a pavement artist was kneeling on the ground near by, scraping coloured chalks into a concrete myth of curly-maned lions and magic trees. With his dirty old coat and his long hair flapping in the wind, he looked something like a maddened king. Every now and then a passer-by would lob a small coin into an upturned cloth cap, but he didn't seem to notice. He didn't say thanks or anything, just carried on drawing. I watched him for a while then finished my cigarette and moved on.

In the weeks to come I'd pass him every day, and it didn't take long to realize that curly-maned lions and magic trees was all he could do. The same picture every day, meticulously chalked into the pavement only to be scuffed out by pedestrians or washed away in the rain of night. He didn't care, though, that was his job.

As I'm telling her all this, I'm checking in the mirror to gauge Zina's reaction, and what she's doing right now is reading a magazine. She looks bored. Scanning a page, licking a finger, turning the page ... scanning a page, licking a finger, turning the page...

But I know she can hear me. And I'm thinking to myself, this is OK, don't stop now – tell her about the hostel.

And I tell her it's a big old four-storey town house just off Belgrave Road, near Victoria Coach Station. A world of broad streets, pillars and railings, plane trees and gated squares. A world that's out of place and out of time, where bearded gentlemen in top hats should be hailing horse-drawn carriages or shooing away street urchins with a swish of their brass-topped canes. And there I am, look, standing on the front steps of this big old house, sweating in the cold city wind, gazing up at the high walls of whitewashed brick and black windows, scared to death. It never struck me then that I had a choice, and I don't suppose I did. You see, I always knew I'd get there in the end.

Then I take Zina inside with me on that very first day and I show her the miles of polished wood staircases and halls and hard floors that echo to the sound of footsteps and voices. And I let her smell the viscid stink of disinfectant and homesickness that clings indelibly to everything. Put your hand there, I tell her, placing her hand on my chest. Feel that? That dull wooden thump is the beat of my heart.

Do you want to know what I'm thinking? I ask her. All I'm thinking is, I don't want to be here. I don't want to be doing this – going up to a partitioned window in the hallway, telling the stern grey woman behind the sliding glass panel my name. The badge on her nylon dress says: *Supervisor*. I sign some papers and she passes me a key.

"Four-oh-seven," she says. "Fourth floor, end of the corridor. There's four to a room, no food, no drink, no visitors in your room. Breakfast between seven and eight, evening meal at six. Laundry in the basement, TV room down the corridor."

At the end of each corridor there's a toilet and a place for washing and shaving, a row of chipped sinks and mirrors. That's where we stand in line in the mornings, farting, laughing, shaving with cold razors, defining ourselves through the degradation of shared ablutions.

It steels me. Do you understand what I'm saying? It steels me.

Up the stairs to Room 407, take a look inside. This is where I live. It smells bad. Imagine how it was on the day I arrived. Opening the door, not knowing who or what was inside … opening the door to the most spiritless room in the world. There was no one there, the room was empty, just four beds and four cupboards and a window. Three bedside cabinets showed signs of occupation so I guessed the fourth must be mine, the bed nearest the door. One cream pillow and a slate-grey blanket. Imagine that. I sat on the bed and stared at the wall. It was early evening, around five or six o'clock. Every few minutes the silence of the room was punctuated by footsteps on the stairs outside. Voices, laughter, jostling. Residents coming in from work, residents going out. Each time the sounds approached, my heart raced in anticipation. What were my roommates like? What would they think of me? What should I say? What should I do? I felt empty and numb. I hadn't eaten all day, but the thought of food made me feel sick. I didn't know what to do. So I just sat there studying the sparse belongings of my unknown roommates. Alarm clocks, a tie, an erotic paperback thriller, a copper bracelet, a packet of mints, cotton wool, a pair of boots, a tube of something … other people's things.

After a while I went downstairs and found the communal TV room on the ground floor. It was dark inside, lit only by the flicker of a large TV screen at the far end. Chairs were ranged across the room, but the dozen or so occupants were concentrated down at the front, right up close to the TV. Their heads turned to look me over as I opened the door. I nodded – all right? – then found a chair at the back and sat down. The TV boys watched me settle then turned their attention back to the screen. I don't remember what was on, probably *London Tonight*, or a quiz or something. Nothing remarkable. The colours were all wrong, too much red; it was like watching TV in a Chinese takeaway. I pretended to watch for about twenty minutes, then left and went back to my room.

Sometime later I was kneeling on the floor, unpacking my suitcase, when the door opened and a flabby fellow came in.

"Oh," he said, surprised.

"Sorry," I said, moving the suitcase to let him pass.

He was wearing pyjamas and a green cardigan and he had a towel draped over his shoulder. The way he walked reminded me of a sick old man – a kind of flat-footed, weary shuffle. He lay on his bed and watched me with idle indifference. He seemed harmless enough.

"When did you get here?" he asked eventually.

"About an hour ago."

He nodded but didn't say anything else. From the corner of my eye I could see that he was cleaning his fingernails with a small penknife. I finished unpacking, closed the cupboard doors and slid the empty suitcase under the bed.

"What's it like here?" I asked.

He smiled blankly and shrugged. "It's all right."

I found out later that he bathes every day because he has something wrong with his glands. Apparently it's a rare hereditary defect that makes his skin smell of uncooked meat. Not that it matters, given the overall stink of the place. The reason it smells so bad in this room is a man called Jackson, a squat young Scot with a stone-cold face. What he does, when he gets in from work, he strips half-naked and stands in front of the mirror lifting dirty great weights, grunting and straining and stinking the place full of sweat. And when he's done, he doesn't wash. He just peels off his jockstrap and drops it on the floor then pulls on a pair of jeans and a sweatshirt and goes out drinking until two in the morning when he lurches back into the room, drunk as a pig, and pisses in the wastepaper bin in the corner of the room. It's a terrible wet metallic sound. I lie there, pretending I'm asleep, listening to him emptying his bladder and cursing at the dark – "Fookin bassa whassa fook up w'yse ya fooka…"

And I think to myself, then and now – is this how it's meant to be?

I look up at the mirror and see that Zina is serving a customer. As she reaches behind her for a packet of cigarettes, her pale-blue T-shirt rides up, revealing a two-inch film of bare skin. The man buying the cigarettes stares, then looks away as she turns and puts the packet on the counter. I wait for Zina to give him his change, watch him go, then tell her some more.

I tell her I work in a tall building in Horseferry Road about fifteen minutes' walk away. That I sit all day at a desk in an L-shaped office not knowing what the hell I'm supposed to be doing. That in my desk drawers are a mug, a box of tea bags and a tin of powdered milk. I hate powdered milk. I have a telephone, too, but whenever it rings it's always for someone else. Every hour or so I go down to the hot-water urn at the end of the corridor to make another cup of tea. The tea tastes sick and dusty. At lunchtime I buy a thin cheese roll from the cafe across the road and sit on a wall watching the winos beg for wine money. Sometimes, when I can't avoid it, I'll go for a drink with the boys from the office, Dave or Sham, or Dave *and* Sham. They don't often talk to me at work, but once in a while they'll invite me out for a drink, and it's hard to say no. Dave has long curly hair like a prog rock star and he wears a denim jacket over his suit. Music is his thing. He likes to talk about music – groups, concerts, records.

"Yeah," I say to him. "Yeah, uh-huh, right, yeah…"

It does the trick.

Sham, I think, is a family man. He has nice white, even teeth, wears a navy-blue double-breasted blazer with gold buttons, and drinks very slowly. A pint will last him an hour.

In the afternoons I go to meetings. There'll be a handful of people sitting at a long table looking at reports and tables and graphs and computer printouts, and they'll all be talking, offering opinions, suggestions, ideas. I can never work it out. I have no idea what any of it means. I look out of the window and watch the birds.

After work, when I'm walking back to the hostel through the greyed height and breadth of Victoria, I feel so small that it frightens me. I could walk for ever and never get anywhere. I'm afraid to stop in case I disappear. When I get back, I eat alone in the hostel canteen. Some kind of meal – soup, a main course, a bowl of sponge pudding or something – and then more bloody tea from another bloody urn, surrounded by the clatter of plates and cutlery and the chatter of communal dining. After eating, and after scraping the plate scraps into a bin and self-consciously exiting the canteen, I go up to the pub near the coach station. It's a long, narrow place with lots of tables so there's always plenty of room. Most of the other drinkers are bone-tired travellers who've spent all day on a National Express coach from Leeds or Newcastle or wherever, and all they want to do is sit somewhere warm and get drunk. There are no regulars hogging the bar stools, no one I feel obliged to nod to when I go in. No one knows me. I can just sit there on my own, drinking, smoking, watching people, thinking. I think about the same things every night – I'm not staying in this place. I can do what I want. I'm young. I can choose. There are other places, other things, other lives. There's got to be more than this. You only live once. I'm all there is. I know it. I know things. I'm not stupid. I could go home. If I wanted to. I could go home. Couldn't I?

What do you think?

Tell me.

Please tell me something, Zina.

Anything.

Tell me about your faith. What's it like to commit yourself to the power and virtue of God? What's it like to believe that your fate is in his hands? How does it feel to give praise, to live in accordance with the commandments, to obey the Word of God? Is it comforting? Does it make things easier? Do you *really* believe you'll attain eternal reward and dwell for ever in Paradise?

No offence, but I find that hard to imagine. Paradise, I mean. What the hell must *that* be like? Pretty damn good, I suppose. But, you see, the thing is, it's not that I'm faithless. Oh, no. I have faith. I have faith in the magic of intoxicated blood. I sink into its promise. I drink barley wine, I tell her I always have, ever since I was a child. And to prove it I show her that shaky old ciné film that constantly plays in the darkened rooms of my mind. I set up the projector, aim it at the wall, turn out the lights, and there we all are...

See? That's my mother and father sitting at home drinking barley wine from crystal tumblers. Mother with a cigarette, Father with a small cigar. Both of them watching the television. And that's me, cross-legged on the floor, glancing up at them every so often. See? That's me. I'd be about eleven then, eleven or twelve, something like that.

Now if you listen carefully you can hear what I'm saying.

"Dad?"

"Hmmm?"

"Can I try some of your beer?"

"You're not old enough," he says, or, "You won't like it."

"Just a sip, Dad. Go on, please. Just a sip. Please?"

He smiles at me, smiles across at Mother.

"You won't like it," he warns me again, passing me the glass of nut-brown beer.

I grin and take a mouthful and – *bleaah!* – I've never tasted anything so foul in my life. How can you *drink* that? How *can* you? It's dis*gus*ting.

And Father smiles knowingly. "I told you you wouldn't like it."

And the ciné film cuts back to the start, with Mother and Father sitting at home drinking barley wine from crystal tumblers. Mother with a cigarette, Father with a small cigar. Both of them watching the television. And that's me, cross-legged on the floor, glancing up at them every so often. See? That's me. I'd be about eleven then, eleven or twelve, something like that.

Now if you listen carefully you can hear what I'm saying.

"Dad?"

"Hmmm?"

"Can I try some of your beer?"

"You're not old enough," he says, or, "You won't like it."

"Just a sip, Dad. Go on, please. Just a sip. Please?"

He smiles at me, smiles across at Mother.

"You won't like it," he warns me again, passing me the glass of nut-brown beer.

I grin and take a mouthful and – *bleaah!* – you've never tasted anything so foul in your life. How can you *drink* that? How *can* you? It's dis*gus*ting.

And Father smiles knowingly. "I told you you wouldn't like it."

And the ciné film cuts back to the start again … and here I am, Zina, one hundred thousand sips of barley wine later, standing stooped and drunk in your convenience store staring down at the cheese and pies in the big refrigerator. Drunk and homesick and hungry. I've been soaking up the Word, you see, just like your father there. I've been soaking up the elements of my faith in the chapel up the road. I've surrendered to the will of my god and now I'm broke, and I can feel the spirit within me telling me to take that cheese, that tasty-looking wedge of Edam. Take it, it's saying, go on, stick it in your pocket and go. It's a question of faith, you see. A matter of understanding. I understand that it's a sin to steal, and that if I sin and don't repent I'll be condemned eternally to the fires of hell. But you have to understand that I have no choice. I have to obey the Word of *my* god, and my god says, "Take it, take the cheese." Listen to me, Zina. Let me explain. You see, faith wouldn't be faith if it wasn't blind, and the only thing… Zina? Are you listening to me, Zina?

She's not listening.

A slim dark man in a white shirt has entered the store and is standing at the till, talking to her. Although he's a fair distance away you can see him quite clearly. You can see that he's tall, with a pencil-thin moustache and slick black hair and fingers ringed with gold. And you can see him leaning on the counter jangling his keys and grinning like a dog, and you can see that Zina's smiling ... she's smiling at him. Now he's nodding his head to indicate a bright red car parked on the street outside, and Zina is leaning across the counter to take a look. She says something to him, he laughs, and then she leans back smiling with her arms stretched behind her head, arching her back. That gets him staring, which she doesn't seem to mind. And then he's moving closer and whispering something and Zina's raising a hand to her mouth to stifle a giggle, and I can't stand it any more. So I turn to her father to see if he's watching, but he's not – he's still lost in the murmur of his book, lost in another world. What's the matter with him? Hey, mister, what's the matter with you? Look. Can't you see what's going on over there? That's your daughter. Look at her. See what she's doing? See the kind of man she's with? See the way she's taking a stick of gum from him, curling it under her tongue while he lights a cigarette and flicks the gum-wrapper to the floor? See that? Don't you care? Hey, mister! Listen to me, don't you *care*? Hey. Wait a minute. No. Just wait a minute, Zina. Hey, Zina. What about us?

Me and you in a nice quiet place, talking together. I only want you to listen to me. I could make you laugh if that's what you want. I can be funny. I'm funny. All that stuff about faith and surrender, it doesn't matter – we don't have to talk about that if you don't want to. It doesn't matter. We could talk about anything. Hey, I'm funny, I can make you smile...

Zina?

Hey, Zina...

But she's not there any more. My Zina has gone. There's just a girl at the till chewing gum, open-mouthed, like a cow.

So I bow to my god and grab the cheese and slip it inside my coat.

When I leave the shop the girl at the till is too busy laughing and joking with the slim dark man to notice anything else. I could have the whole damn refrigerator stuffed under my coat for all she cares.

I walk on by, open the door, and step out into the rain.

DEEDS NOT WORDS
Mary and Bryan Talbot
Kate Charlesworth

DEEDS NOT WORDS!

The suffragettes were campaigning for women's right to be treated as men's equals; for the right to participate in the public world of decision- and law-making. They could hardly achieve this objective without even being able to speak in public. It was a source of infinite surprise to the campaigners that a woman's voice raised in a public meeting excited such hysteria.

The *Liberals* will keep the light of freedom shining!

What about freedom for *women* then?

The hussy!

Chuck her out!

How *dare* she? She's just a *woman!*

Give her the boot!

Green Lady Hostel, Littlehaven
September 1908

Oh!

And *that's* why I'm covered in cuts and bruises!

Oh, *sis!* You poor love!

Lady Constance Lytton first encountered suffragettes at a seaside holiday house. She really didn't approve of them at first.

Poor dear Annie!

Annie's sister here has just been released from *Holloway*, haven't you, Jessie? Why don't you tell Lady Constance about it?

You- you mean to say, you're *suffragettes?*

I have to say that, while I share your desire for votes for women, I do not at all *approve* of your *methods!*

So, you are sufficiently *interested* in our policy to criticize it. *That* is abundantly *clear.*

Will you be *sufficiently* interested to study its *cause* and read up our case?

Well, I... *Yes*, of course.

I ask you this: *How* can we *improve* working conditions for women and children in this country without any *say* in who runs it and writes its laws?

By the end of the month Con was sympathetic. She became a member of the **Women's Social and Political Union.**

4 Clement's Inn
13th October 1908

Then three of the leaders were arrested...

We must *march* on Parliament Square!

Oh, I'm *sorry.* I can't do *that* sort of thing!

Are there any *lesser* services I can render?

Well, could you ask the Home Secretary if he'll give them *political prisoner status?*

It was the contemptuous treatment Con received that day that finally converted her.

Away with you!

Parliament Square
24th February 1909

Her first demonstration was a rough one.

And she was convicted, along with others.

But Constance wasn't just any suffragette. She was **Lady Constance Georgina Bulwer-Lytton,** daughter of a former **Viceroy of India,** with a brother in the House of Lords. The Government didn't want her in prison. It was an **embarrassment.**

When she started to notice that she was receiving privileges because of her status, she protested.

She started to write "Votes for Women" on **herself,** with a sharpened hairpin.

What are you doing? Stop that!

But the doctor "checkmated" her.

If you carry on like this, I'll have to *release* you!

Newcastle Police Station
9th October 1909

The second time she was arrested, she was with Emily Wilding Davison. Emily was let off, but Con went to prison.

We want to make it known that we shall carry on our protest in our prison cells. We shall put before the Government, by means of the hunger-strike, four alternatives: To release us in a few days; to inflict violence upon our bodies; to add death to the champions of our cause by leaving us to starve; or, and this is the best and only wise alternative, to give women the vote.

TO DEFEND THE OPPRESSED, TO FIGHT FOR THE DEFENCELESS, NOT COUNTING THE COST.

Newcastle Prison
14th October 1909

Once she was in prison and on hunger strike, she was expecting the force-feeding that was inflicted on her fellow suffragettes.

Instead they called for expert opinion from a London doctor, in concern about her heart. To her consternation, she was released immediately.

She didn't breathe a word about what she planned to do next...

Manchester
13th January 1910

She took out a new membership of the WSPU, this time under the name of Jane Warton, seamstress.

Do you have any that are less *strong?* They are for *stage* purposes, you see.

Lime Street Station, Liverpool
14th January 1910

Walton Gaol, Liverpool

Do you know what *torture* is being done to women behind these walls? Will—

When force-feeding of suffragettes was threatened in Dundee, 2,000 men assembled to protest against it.

Hunger strikers were released and *no* force-feeding has been inflicted in Scotland. Can't *Englishmen* do the *same?*

Let the men of Liverpool be the first to wipe out the *stain* that has been tolerated up till now!

We are outside the gaol where these *barbarities* are actually going on!

I call on you all! Follow me to the Governor's house!

What was that you was sayin'?

Bridewell Police Station, Liverpool
15th January, 4 a.m.

Don't stop now. Empty all your pockets.

Walton Gaol, Liverpool
18th January

Absolutely *not!*
I cease to resist taking food in prison when our legislators cease to resist enfranchising women.

Then I must feed you at once.

In sharp **contrast** with the care over *Lady Constance's* health in Newcastle, *Jane Warton's* heart was proclaimed to be "splendid".

The tube-feeding continued twice daily.

This was ordinary **Jane Warton** and the doctor had nothing but contempt for her.

The Home Office signed her release on grounds of weight loss. **After** her aristocratic identity had been revealed.

23rd January 1910

That year Constance suffered heart seizure and partial paralysis. Her health never recovered. But that didn't stop her from protesting.

Bow Street
24th November 1910

Votes and riot are the *only* form of appeal to which this Government will respond.

They refuse us votes; we fall back on riot.

Constance died prematurely in 1923 as a result of her injuries. She was one of numerous women who died fighting to win for women the same democratic rights as men.

This Edwardian case study is drawn from the autobiographies of two prominent British suffragettes: Constance Lytton and Emmeline Pethick-Lawrence. It happened only 100 years ago, yet it seems a world away. Unfortunately, it's not. At all. In our world right now, people are in prison for calling for free speech; detainees are still being tortured.

"The three of us worked together on Sally Heathcote, Suffragette, *a detailed account in graphic novel form of the Edwardian struggle over civil liberties. It's a reminder of how hard-won, and how precious, our civil liberties are. There are people today going through ordeals very much like those endured by the suffragettes, so for this anthology we decided to focus on one courageous woman whose story isn't told in the book."* Mary and Bryan Talbot/Kate Charlesworth

HARMLESS JOE

Tony Birch

I want to tell you bout this man. Harmless Joe. I'm not saying that was his *true* name, but it was the name others used for him. *There goes Harmless Joe,* people round the town would say. He walked the streets in the daytime, and at night he slept in the best place he could find, long as it was in the shadows where no one watched over him. He was always keeping to himself, minding his own business. *Harmless.*

But them wild boys from the town who hung out on the street, kicking off when they was drinking, they done real harm to old Joe. Smacked him and belted him when they felt they needed some fun. Police did nothing bout it.

Town people did no more than look the other way. Joe, he got hurt by them boys.

Joe was an Aboriginal man, though most called him *abo* or *boong*. He had more than a stomach full of trouble in the end and took off out of town. Joe walked along the railway track, by the big silo, crossed the bridge over the creek and went away into the bush to an old cutter's shack, overgrown and out of sight. Nobody knew he was up there. Any time he went into town to scratch for some food, he doubled and tripled back and no one seen where he was hiding out. I seen him, though, cause I followed him.

I have me an old push bike and I ride it through the canals and drains along the edge of town, picking up this and that what people throw away. Like Joe, I don't have no one to talk to. But I'm different than him. He's an old man and I'm just a boy. First time I seen him on the railway track he was sneaking home to the shack, carrying a bag of potatoes. I was underneath the bridge listening to different sounds. Echoes. I seen Joe up above me, crossing the bridge. Then he left the bridge behind and was on to a dirt track and gone. I followed him, way behind, walking soft as I could, breath quiet as a sparrow. Joe got to the shack and I hid in the bushes and watched him looking round for any strangers. He opened the door and he closed it behind him. I waited and soon I seen smoke coming out of the chimney and I reckoned Joe was warming himself in there and cooking up his dinner.

Next time I seen him, he was heading cross the bridge to town. I waited till he was a long way off, then took off to the cutter's shack. The bolt on the door was broke. I opened it and stepped inside. Quiet. The room had a mattress on the floor and blankets, folded neat as a handkerchief, sitting on top. I seen a kettle, a tin mug and plates, a fork and different spoons. Odd shapes and sizes. It wasn't no house most people would live in, but it was clean and tidy and homely as the best house could be. Pages from magazines were stuck on the walls, mostly pictures of famous people. The Queen, she was up there, right alongside Mr John Lennon and a football player kicking a ball. I sat down on the mattress for some rest and looked round the room and could hear the wind rattling the sheets of tin on the roof, and then the rain beating a tune. I lay down for a time, listening to the rain and thinking that Harmless Joe had a good life.

It was close on dark when I woke, sitting up with fear, knowing nothing bout where I was until I looked up and seen the Queen, tiara on her head, looking down on me. I jumped up, left the shack and ran for home. But I seen Joe on the bridge, making his way back with a bag swinging at his side. I sprinted off and lay down in the dirt and held my breath until Joe had passed by, then ran all the way home and had explaining to do bout why I was late. My gran, who looks after me, she knew much more than I did bout Joe. I even seen her talking to him on the street. Only person in town who ever done so. When she asked where

I been and why I was late, I could have spoke the truth and told her I been up at Joe's shack, sitting on his bed and smiling up at the Queen. But I knew better. She don't like me out late, no matter where I been or who I'm with. And she got no time for the Queen, telling me once, *that girl is in the wrong country.*

In the wet season we get more rain here in one day than some people have in a year. Builds up in the west and charges at the town like a runaway train. The streets flood, and the drains and hollows too. Land goes under and everywhere looks like a lake. One time my gran took me into the bush and showed me waterfalls running red long the valleys, into the rivers and creeks. She said to me, pointing her old bony finger, *that there is the Earth, Tyrone, and she's bleeding for you. She's bleeding for all of us, cause sometimes we're no good.* You can believe her or not. It don't worry me, cause I know every word she speaks is true. The story stuck to me, and next time it rained I headed for the water and sat and watched the rush, and just like my gran said, the Earth bled for me.

After the last big rain I was resting on the bank watching the creek run crazy when I seen Charlie Hooten's van scream along the dirt track by the creek. He was with the wild boys at one time, way back. Now he's a man. The whole town knows Charlie and his van. He rides through the main street calling out to the girls, getting drunk and picking a fight any place he can find one. Charlie has always been *plain stupid*, my gran says. *Don't you forget it.* That don't stop him being cruel and a bully. I call him out – *stupid* – whenever I see him. But I keep the words well under my breath so he don't hear me.

Charlie come to a stop next to the wire fence keeping the town dump from the roadway. I didn't want him finding me by the creek so I crawled behind an old gum tree and spied on him. He got out of his van, walked round to the other side of the car and opened the door. I seen a woman sitting in the car and Charlie swearing and screaming at her. She screamed right back and he dragged her out of the van. That's when I seen her long red hair and knew straight off who she was. Rita Collins. She was no woman after all. Rita was a girl, no older than me, who was taken out of school by her ma before the new school year started. No one seen her round the town after that. As she stood by the van I seen she had a big belly. Not like she was fat or something, but like she was gonna have a baby. They yelled some more at each other, and Charlie pushed her and she pushed back. And then he hit her. Not like two kids going at it on a street corner. Not a bit like that. Charlie, a man, hit Rita like she was a man too. She fell to the ground, kneeling in the red dirt, bleeding with the Earth. He stood over her, laughing like there was something funny bout what was going on. But there wasn't. Nothing funny in hitting a woman. He looked down at Rita, smiled, swore at her again and got into his van and drove away. Left her alone in the dirt.

I stood behind the tree, watching her. She lay down and I could hear her crying and, a little while after, moaning. She sat up, lifted her dress and looked between her legs like her own body was a mystery. Rita didn't notice me at all till I was standing near her. Maybe she thought I was Charlie come back for her? She ducked and covered her face with her hands until I called her name. Soft, so as not to frighten her. *Rita.* She looked up at me like I was a stranger. She didn't know who I was, except that I wasn't Charlie.

I'm gonna have a baby, she cried. I told her I knew so cause I seen her belly, and I seen pregnant bellies before. *Now! Now!* Rita screamed. *A baby is coming now!*

The rain come again. Out of nowhere. Rita's skin turned grey and the rain belted her round the body. I looked long the track and said, *come with me*, and held out my hand. She put her hand in mine and I helped her to stand up and we walked long the bush track away from the creek. She looked at me, turned away and looked at me again. *You're Tyrone*, she said, *the slow kid from school.* Pulled her hand away from mine and held the other over her guts, moaning more and more. *Where you taking me, you creep?* I never been no creep and would have left her be, to find her own way, if she hadn't been in pain that way. She screamed out and looked between her legs again. I seen liquid running down, the colour of weak milk. *You gotta come*, was all I could say.

You gotta come. She looked at me like I made no sense in the world, but took hold of my hand again just the same.

I seen the smoke coming from Joe's chimney and felt good that he was in. I knocked at his door. Not too loud. When he didn't come I knocked harder and called out to him, *Joe, Harmless Joe, I need you to help.* I put my ear to the door and heard some rustling round, and then I heard the latch and the door swung open so quick I nearly fell into the room. Joe was standing there, squinting at me, white hair, white beard and skin like burnt leather. He said nothing. Looked me up and down, looked at Rita out of the corner of his eye and went to close the door again till I said, *Joe, a baby. She says a baby's coming.* If Joe had turned us away right then, if Joe had shut the door on his shack, I can tell you for certain, that girl, Rita, she might be dead. He looked at her, down to her belly, and hauled her into the room, where she fell onto Joe's old mattress. I'd felt a ton of fear without knowing why, but inside the shack, warmed by the fire, with Joe throwing a blanket over the girl, talking to her in a voice both soft and strong, my heart stopped jumping. Rita was screaming loud enough to lift the roof, and Joe sat next to her and told her, *you got to work, girl. You got to work.*

I would be dishonest if I told you I seen the baby come out. I'd like to say I did, as that would be a better story. But I seen nothing. Rita screamed and swore and slapped her own legs and kicked out and even spat at Joe one time she was so crazy. I ran to the corner and closed my eyes and covered my ears. Then I heard some crying and knew it was too high a pitch to be Rita. I looked up at the Queen, and was sure I could only be going crazy cause she was smiling and she wasn't smiling at all the last time I looked at her. Then I looked cross the room and saw Harmless Joe holding something in his dark arms. It was wriggling and squirming and was pink and bloodied and covered in some paste. It was a newborn.

Get up! Joe barked at me. *Run and get help, boy!* I stood up and walked over to where Joe was sitting, at the bare feet of Rita. She was staring up at the baby like she been witness to the greatest miracle of all time. Joe had the baby resting in his arms and I could see the tears in the eyes of that old man.

I ran harder than I thought I could that day, through the red dirt and into town, straight to the hospital. My lungs were afire and I couldn't speak a word, and in the Emergency Department I heard a voice behind me say, *it's that imbecile, Tyrone,* but I didn't listen and I didn't care cause all I could think bout was Rita and the baby lying in Joe's shack. Took an effort for the ambulance to get cross the bridge and onto the track, and then they could go no further, except on foot, carrying a stretcher and blankets and medicine. Joe was waiting, holding the baby in a blanket. Rita was lying back on the mattress stained with her own blood. They carried her out and let Joe walk with the baby in his arms and me falling in behind. At the hospital they took Rita and the baby away and some nurse told me and Joe to sit and wait on a bench until the police come. I sat longside Joe, looking at him and at me in a mirror cross the hall. I could look straight at him that way, without him knowing. He was small and tight and strong. The nurse, she come back and told us, *police be here in five minutes.* And soon as she was gone Joe stood up, looked down at me and patted me on the top of my head. Soft as a feather. He lifted my chin so I was looking him straight in the eye and said to me, *my name is Goruk – the magpie.* I looked down at the wooden floor and mouthed his name, trying to speak it right. I knew the story of Goruk, a special bird from another time who takes care of the land, and takes care of all of us, together.

When I looked up again he was gone, though I was sure he never walked away.

Day after day from the time he disappeared, I went to Harmless Joe's shack looking for him. And I seen Rita on the street one time with the baby in a pusher. She said to me, *thank you, Tyrone,* and asked if I knew where Joe was, as she wanted to thank him too. But he never come back. Joe was too smart for such attention.

One day, in the winter, I took the bloodied mattress from the shack and set it afire with petrol. Then I took

Joe's old broom and swept up the shack and put some wood in his stove and lit the fire and sat on the floor feeling the room warm. I thought bout him and where he had got to. *Goruk – the magpie.*

"I wrote this story as a way of focusing on those among us who we push to the margins of society – and, in doing so, strip of their humanity. The concept of community has no tangible value unless it is inclusive in the fullest sense of the word. Without community we cannot survive."
Tony Birch

PUSH THE WEEK
Jackie Kay

If I had cash, I could get some *cassava gari*
Down Great Western Road, shop in Solly's
And make some *sukuma wiki*; stretch the week.
But this card don't buy me African food
Or let me shop in *Marie Curie*
(although they have nice things in there).
Only in the Salvation Army store.
(Where the clothes are a bit of a bore.)
You think just because you're an asylum seeker
You don't care what you wear?
And from eating the wrong food, my stomach's sore.
If I didn't just have this card to use

I would buy some maize meal flour, avocado, yam.
If my mother were here she would say:
That woman is not my daughter.
Even I don't know who I am.
If I had cash I could buy some *corn pones*,
dried fish, beef … curried mung beans…
Kachumbari, my God, how I wish!
Expand the chest. My spirits would lift, *eh?*
Not so worthless, not so angry.
Ugali would make me less depressed!
Not so homesick. *Nyama choma.*
But the Home Office never consider
How it feels to be dispersed to Glasgow.
No cash for cane row, no money for Makimo.
No dosh for monthlies. No pounds for sweet potato.
The week repeats. We are scattered families.
Now it's HIV. No TV. Just CCTV – watching me.
Non-stop scrutiny. Anyone shouts, *Asylum seeker,*
Bash them with your saucepan. *Man stealer!*
(I have yet to see one to write home about!) *Cassava!*
In your imagination, you have new friends to dinner.
You picture a cooker. A table. You light a candle.
You shine some cutlery. You see your face in it.
And you say, *Stick in till you stick oot*, and you say,
Help yourself. Go ahead. Have some chapati, mbazi, gari.
Here's what we eat in my country. You see.

ROBOT KILLERS

Tim Wynne-Jones

So Val says, "How about Robot Killers?"

Costa nods, vaguely, and stares into the middle distance, thinking of some drawing, a logo, maybe. Ahmed frowns. Estelle glares one of her if-looks-could-kill best.

"It's sort of like Drone," says Val.

"But it's *not* Drone," says Estelle. "*We're* Drone – or we *were* Drone." She turns up the glare until it is definitely an eleven.

"It's not my fault," says Val. "I told you! Crying Out Loud blew it. They invited two bands named Drone to the festival, and because the other one's way bigger, we've got to come up with another name."

"Robot Killer*s*, plural?" says Ahmed. "With or without *the*?"

Val shrugs. "Whatever," he says, but his eyes go all shifty.

Estelle never misses a sudden shiftiness in a guy's eyes. "Val?"

He swallows, can't meet her eyes.

"Val, you didn't!" She hits the roof. (Well, Costa, actually, cos he's sitting on the floor next to her.)

Costa says, "Ow!" and rubs his arm, right where he has the blue bird of happiness tattoo. Such irony.

"You already gave them the name change," says Estelle, in full-bore, pitch-perfect accusation mode.

Val visibly diminishes in stature.

"This whole 'let's-try-to-think-of-a-new-band-name' thing was a total waste of time," she adds. "Admit it." She makes quote marks in the air around her stupendously long adjective, but the quote marks turn to fists as they land like dead birds in her lap. Although they obviously don't look quite dead enough, because Costa skitters his butt out of reach and leans against the wall.

Val finishes flinching. "Sorry," he says, looking at Estelle pleadingly. "They needed a name right away, OK?"

"Not OK."

"They're making posters, putting together press kits! I just thought it was, you know, a reasonable substitute."

Estelle growls. It's something she does sometimes when

she's singing, and it sounds cool … onstage.

Costa, still rubbing his arm, says, "Posters, Stelle. Somebody's actually paying for a poster."

"And it *is* kind of like Drone," says Val, again.

"Technically, no," says Ahmed. "A drone is an unmanned aerial vehicle under real-time human control, whereas a killer robot identifies, tracks and destroys a moving target without human intervention."

Costa claps. Ahmed bows. It'd be pretty impressive but for the fuzzy Ewok hat he happens to be wearing.

Estelle crosses her arms and throws herself back against her amp.

Mood swing: irritation and defeat, nicely accentuated by her Littlest Mermaid T-shirt. Except she's wearing it with camo pants and spiky blue Docs.

"Sorry," says Val. Again.

"There shouldn't be a *the*," says Ahmed. "Because there are lots of killer robots."

"Robot Killers," says Val.

"Sweet," says Costa.

The band *Robot Killers*, formerly known as *Drone*:

> *Val Rydell* – drummer and guy with a large shed, decoratively but only somewhat effectively insulated with egg cartons. Guy with a van. Guy who gets the gigs and does the paperwork. Destined to be a local politician.

Costa de Leon – bass player, back-up vocalist and artist extraordinaire, as can be witnessed on many bridges, railway carriages, toilet cubicles and fire-escape doors in the vicinity. Destined for art school and/or jail.

Ahmed Tahan – keyboard player and human search engine. Destined to beat Deep Blue at chess.

Estelle Seymour – singer/songwriter and lead guitarist. Destined to truss Val Rydell up like a chicken in chains, shove him in a sack and throw him off a very high bridge. Very soon.

The Crying Out Loud Summer Rock Festival draws some pretty big names but they always leave a couple of spots for up-and-comers. Estelle, at home in her room, glares at her computer screen, aiming a death ray at the festival's home page. It doesn't burst into flames. She has looked up Drone – the *other* Drone, who are actually *The Drones*. For a minute she thinks this could be a loophole, but she can't see herself fighting it out with the festival organizers over a definite article and an *s*.

She throws herself back on her bed. Why is she so angry? It's not just Val. Val works his tail off for the band. Not only that – he puts up with *her*! Her father once asked Val if he offered seminars. But this… This…

She pulls out her phone.

"Hey," he says. He sounds wary if not exactly frightened. He's safe at home three streets away.

"I'm not phoning to apologize," she says.

"Good," he says. "Because I'd drop dead from surprise."

"I never even liked Drone," she says.

There's a pause while he regroups. "What do you mean?"

"What I said."

"It was your name."

"No, it wasn't. Ahmed was going on and on about how we should call the band something to do with black holes or—"

"The Schwarzschild radius."

"Right, and I said, *drone, drone, drone,* and everybody said, *that's it!*"

"Yeah, because it's totally cool."

"And kills people."

"But it's not like we were advertising. *Hey, everybody, go out and buy yourself a drone and kill people.* Anyway, there are useful drones. One day soon they'll be delivering the mail."

"And killing people."

"Anyway," he tries again, "we're not called that any more."

"So now we're something even more deadly. A robotic death squad."

"Stelle," he says. "They don't even exist yet. It's sci-fi. After you left—"

"You mean stormed off in high dudgeon."

"Eh? What's *high dudgeon*?"

"Apart from a way better name for our band?"

"Stop, already."

"OK, outrage… That's what high dudgeon is. Maybe I'll change *my* name to High Dudgeon, or did you already give them the names of the musicians, too."

Val swears, colourfully. "After you skipped out," he says patiently, "Ahmed gave us one of his patented hour-long lectures on lethal autonomous weapons systems and artificial intelligence and blah, blah, blah, and he said it was still, like, years before anyone would be deploying anything like that."

"So not *entirely* sci-fi. Come on, Val. *Killer Robots?*"

"No," says Val, exasperated. "Robot Killers. Why don't you listen to me?"

"Whatever."

"No, there's a…" Estelle hears a voice at Val's end. Corinne arriving. Distracting Corinne. "Listen," Val says, "I've got, you know, homework."

"Never heard it called that before," says Estelle and clicks off.

Her sleep is disturbed by dreams. Of rifle-waving terrorists and refugee camps. Wastelands. TV newscapes of fallen places, bent metal skeletons and smoke. And because she did her own research on killer robots, which people *are* making, no matter what Ahmed the human search engine says, she sees them emerge from the smoke, prowling on tractor treads across no man's land. Little R2-D2s with machine-gun turrets instead of cute heads.

"Stop!" cries her nightmare robot. Then fires anyway.

She wakes into semi-darkness, angry and frightened.

Mood swing: rage dissipates to helplessness. Angst. The sense of waking up somewhere she never intended to be. Nowhereville. It's not yet three, but words are lining up in her head, hurling themselves into one configuration after another. It's like an injection – an intravenous feed of Red Bull. She phones Ahmed at six.

"Call me in England," he says groggily.

"What do you mean?"

"In England it is eleven o'clock in the morning. If you phone me there I will answer you." He hangs up.

She phones him at eleven. "I had this terrible nightmare," she says.

"No, you didn't," he says. "I was the one who had the nightmare."

★   ★   ★

Planet Wrong

It was the wrong house on the wrong block.
Inserted my key into the wrong lock.
Kicked off my shoes in the wrong vestibule.
Turned on the tube in the wrong living room –

I'm a girl in shock,
Since you gave me the news.
I can hardly breathe the toxic air
I'm so confused.
You were so short,
When you said so long.
And left me here stranded on Planet Wrong.

Woke up this morning on the wrong side of the bed.
Buttered my toast on the wrong side of the bread.
Cop flagged me down, said, "Girl, can't you read?
You're goin' the wrong way down a one-way street."

I'm a total wreck,
Since you lowered the boom.
Bumping around like some blind fool
In a darkened room.
It had been so clear,
Our love was so strong.
But now we're at war here on Planet Wrong.

Band practice. Working on the song that got her out of bed. "Needs a chorus," she says.

"Needs a B-3 solo," says Ahmed, doing an arpeggio on the yellowing keys of his chipped and stained old Hammond. The sound comes out of the Leslie speakers as a tremulant squeal.

"What makes it do that?" says Costa. "Sounds like an ambulance streaking past."

"Doppler effect," says Ahmed, chopping out some kind of a break.

"*There's* a good name for a band," says Estelle. She glares at Val, who makes a sour face but with just enough eyebrow to it to let her know he's only going to suck this lemon for so long.

"Good song, Stelle," says Costa.

"Yeah, whatever," says Estelle, taking off her beat-up Fireglo Rickenbacker and hanging it on its guitar stand.

"Time for a break," says Val.

Estelle ups and leaves.

She walks down to K Street. Wishes there was an O Avenue that crossed it so she could stand at the corner of OK, just to see what that would feel like.

Planet Wrong. Alienation.

That's what this has been about – this feeling – but she only finds the word now. She wonders why other people can find the right word for something so easily and she has to write a whole song to find it.

She looks around and scowls. People out on a mild summer evening. Then she unscowls. They're not the enemy. Val's not the enemy. Even the folks at Crying Out Loud aren't the enemy. It's this thing that happens. Somebody takes your name. Just like that! Gone. And it's not necessarily that you even *liked* your name, but it was yours and now it's not. It's about … what?

Expedience.

This time the word *does* come. She's not even fully sure what it means. She leans against a lamppost, pulls out her phone, looks it up. *The situation in which something is helpful or useful, but sometimes not morally acceptable.*

Ka-ching!

As in, *it would be expedient for you to change your band name because there's a bigger Drone out there already.* Or as in, *it would be expedient for our country to attack your country since you've got all those oil reserves and we want them.* Or, *it would be expedient for us to eradicate your people because they're not the same as us.*

People in the world are really suffering – it never stops. And is it always about expedience?

"Get over yourself," she mutters.

A guy passing says, "Wha…?"

And she shakes her head. "Not you," she laughs.

He looks like he might make something out of it but then just walks away, looking back in case she's a killer robot or something. Yeah, well…

It gets to her. She lets it get to her. But it's not like she wants it to.

Mood swing: I can't do anything about this. What's the point? So, stay in your room. Try to write words. No words come. And words are all you've got. Basically, you've got sweet boo all. So…

1. Blow off Mum.
2. Blow off Dad.
3. Blow off Val.
4. Stop answering the phone.
5. Repeat.

Saturday. Two weeks until Crying Out Loud. She has blown off three rehearsals. Where has all this come from? Had it always been there? This sense of indignation. High dudgeon. Whatever.

"Yeah, but a bad time for it to surface," says Ahmed. He's been phoning so often, finally she has to answer.

"When would be a good time?" she asks.

Ahmed cannot think of a reply. Imagine that?

"Estelle," her mother calls. "Costa's here."

"Is this a concerted attack?" she asks Ahmed.

"Yes," he says. "Check your window. A drone from Val should arrive any moment."

Estelle growls and hears Ahmed *tut, tut, tut* as she hangs up.

Costa stands in the hallway, resplendent in a new T-shirt. One he has clearly designed himself. It's black, except for a white circle in the middle. There's a killer robot in the circle – something silvery from some fifties B-movie. But

Costa has put the red circle-backslash "No" sign over it. He smiles and turns around. Estelle approaches him to read what is written on his back.

Asimov's Laws

1. A robot may not injure a human being or, through inaction, allow a human being to come to harm.
2. A robot must obey the orders given it by human beings except where such orders would conflict with the First Law.
3. A robot must protect its own existence as long as such protection does not conflict with the First or Second Laws.

Estelle turns him back around to face her. "Asimov, the science fiction dude?"

"Who wrote *I, Robot*," says Costa. He looks down at his chest, holds the shirt out so he can see it better. "He wrote the laws in 1942. Can you believe that? And the UN is sort of adopting it as a code of conduct or something."

"Where'd you hear that?"

He shrugs. "Did some googling. There's this thing called Killer Robots and the Rule of Law written by a woman at the UN." He looks up. "This is OK, right?"

"Right, except…" She frowns. "So how can we be killer robots and wear T-shirts that say we're against them?"

Costa throws his hands up in the air. "We're *not* killer robots, Stelle. You weren't listening. We're *Robot Killers*."

Estelle sits on the bottom stair. "Oh," she says.

"Val kept saying he'd renamed us Robot Killers. The thing is, he didn't really even notice it himself – the difference, I mean. So I figured a visual might help."

Estelle nods. "Right," she says. "How'd I miss that?"

Costa smiles. "There's this cool thing in the article about the tortoise and the hare. You know, the old fable?" She nods. "So, the woman from the UN –" he clicks his fingers – "Angela Kane, that's her name. Anyway, she says the new arms race is between the tortoise of international law and the hare of changing technology."

Estelle nods. "And she thinks the tortoise has a hope in hell?"

"He wins in the fable, right? Come on, Stelle. Lighten up."

She growls. Costa growls right back at her, then hands her a T-shirt. He turns to go, then turns back again. "Practice tonight. Be there."

She's there, breathless and kind of hyper. She straps on her Rick. Starts chording something.

Val rolls his eyes. "Nice to see you and all, but we don't have time to learn something new."

"We don't have time *not* to," she says. Meanwhile, Ahmed is following the chords and starting to riff. Then he abandons the keyboard and picks up his Strat. He never thinks of himself as a guitarist, but for some songs keyboards just don't cut it. Estelle nods, encouraged.

"We've got exactly four more practices before Crying Out Loud," says Val, raising his voice over the music. "There's an agent coming, guys. Club dudes. We've gotta sound like we know what we're doing." But Ahmed's already calling out the changes and Costa is thumping on his Fender. Val accepts defeat ungraciously, which is great because he pounds out his frustration on the drums.

Estelle sings and Costa throws in a raw-edged harmony. Then Ahmed stops them and suggests a guitar setting. Total grunge. Robot Killer grunge.

The big day arrives. The weather holds. There are goodly crowds in party mode even for the early acts. Robot Killers set up and look out over the crowd. Val's got that shifty look on his face.

"What?" says Estelle, worried.

"You'll see," he says and drowns out her next words by counting in the reggae beat of the first tune, "Banker Pod Man", a little ditty about alien spawn taking over the international banking scene.

And on it goes. The band rocking, the crowd growing in numbers, dancers in colourful rags under blazing blue skies while sunburns blossom on an acre of exposed skin. Estelle is in her element, playing her heart out, eating the mic, sending out all those words that were so hard to find and which these wonderful boys of hers – whatever they're called – help to shape into missiles of sound. These words are missiles filled with impressions of a world she doesn't get so well but passionately believes in and wants to understand – demands to understand – and is willing to work at. This is why she does it, she thinks, and she turns to Val, whose grin reflects her own, but with something else. A glint in his eye. What?

Way too soon their set is almost up: time for one last song. The new one. The one that proclaims the words on their T-shirts. Says it loud and proud.

Val strikes his drumsticks together to catch the pulse of it, but then it's all Estelle, pounding out the grunge on her trusty Rick, a petite giant killer channelling Neil Young through Foo Fighters through some seismic event in the Pacific, where the new mountains force their way up from the sea to be taken notice of.

Plate tectonics. Reshaping the world.

Now Ahmed appears out of his nest of keyboards with his Strat stuck on and he's playing the riff with her. And Costa steps up to the front to give it some bottom end and, finally, Val brings in the heavy machinery. It's like he's pounding the skins with baseball bats. The crowd goes ballistic.

Robot Killers

Kill it.
Kill the cancer.
Cos a killer robot don't
Take no for an answer.

Kill it.
Don't let it grow.
Cos the fool thing cannot tell
If you're friend or foe.

Kill it,
before it starts to kill.
You gotta sign a petition
And make your politicians
put their names on a bill.

Cos it don't matter
If it's day or night,
When a killer robot's
Got you in its sights.
It's a bot on a mission,
Lookin' for a fight.
And it don't know squat
'Bout human rights.

And so it goes, with the audience jolting and jiving and joining in on the chorus:

Find, fix, track, engage – attack!
Find, fix, track, engage – attack!

Which is when the robots come.

First one, then another, then two more near the back of the bopping, weaving crowd. Then more, half a dozen, a dozen. Little silver bots with clumsy hands and big cute eyes, rolling into the arena so that for one horrible, electrifying moment Estelle thinks it's here: World War R.

So she sings harder as if it's the last thing she might ever do and rock and roll is the only thing left.

Except…

People are laughing. They're dancing their hearts out and punching the air with their fists and singing along and digging it! And laughing. Laughing at the cute robots and… *What is this?*

They're taking pamphlets from the robots' mouths, patting them on their cute shiny heads. And now, instead of seeing what has been thrown up into her vision by her darkest fears, she sees what's in front of her eyes. The robots are wearing Robot Killer T-shirts. They're aluminium activists. Some fan girl in a yellow bikini top and faded blue jeans that match her hair comes up to the stage, waving pamphlets at Estelle. She's yelling something and Estelle falls to her knees at the edge of the stage to hear her.

"Your words!" Blue-hair shouts, her face an enormous sun-filled smile. That's what the robots have come to deliver, with their appealing metal faces and their tech allure.

Estelle turns to Val, who's laughing his head off, clobbering the drums like an out-of-control heart. "We are Killer Robot Killers!" he shouts at her and the words are caught up in his mic and echo out over the music and the crowd. "Killer Robot Killers unite!

"I'm so glad to be a part of this important collection and to raise my voice along with Estelle Seymour's against killer robots. It seems that the further we remove ourselves, physically, from the grieved acts of warfare, the easier it is to turn our backs on the suffering. As a rock 'n' roll singer, I know how loud a song can be when the amp is cranked up high. But drowning out the noisy business of killing people isn't the point; one has to hope that songs and stories of protest find their way into the ears of those who can stop the violence." Tim Wynne-Jones

SPEAKING OUT FOR FREEDOM
Chelsea Manning

Chelsea Manning grew up in a conservative community in the Midwest of the USA. As a teenager, then known as Bradley, she moved with her UK-born mother to Wales. She joined the US Army in 2007. She realized she was transgender – outwardly male but inwardly feeling she was female – but felt she had to hide this identity in the military. In 2009 she was sent to serve in Iraq, where the US Army was in the sixth year of war against insurgents after the overthrow of dictator Saddam Hussein. As an intelligence analyst, Chelsea gained a shocking insight into the secret reality of the way the Iraq War was being fought. In 2010 she exposed what she had learned to the world. She is now serving a 35-year prison sentence but believes strongly that she acted for her country and her duty to others – and was true to the spirit of the American tradition of freedom.

Chelsea E. Manning 89289
1300 North Warehouse Road
Leavenworth, Kansas
**Statement through Amnesty International
for Public Release**
Subject: Interview for Amnesty International

Why did you become a soldier?

I enlisted as an intelligence analyst in the United States Army in summer 2007. At the time I had a job as a barista at Starbucks and was struggling with my gender identity. Each night I came home to news reports on the television of more soldiers and civilians dying in Iraq during the troop "surge". I felt a strong sense of duty to people, and felt that maybe I could help out my country. I also thought that if I went into a war zone I might not have to deal with my feelings of wanting to be female any more.

Were you proud to be a soldier?

Absolutely! I was proud then, and I still am today. I am very proud to have served with my comrades to my left and right. I am also very proud to have sometimes succeeded in protecting the people of Iraq.

That's what I think instils pride in most soldiers – the sense of duty and commitment to those around us.

What led you to the job that gave you access to all this information?

I was highly skilled at collecting and sorting through pages and pages of raw information and breaking it down into something that could be more easily understood. I have always worked a lot with computers, even when I was much younger. The military recognized that potential and placed me in a job where I had access to a lot of information going back several years.

I went to college to learn to be an analyst, and they taught me some of the tools and methods that can be used to sort through all this information. But I think you need to have a natural talent to be able to do this kind of job successfully.

I also had to get a government security clearance. This required a lot of paperwork, and I had to submit to a thorough background investigation. The government even sent investigators to interview my family and friends.

Did you gradually realize the implications of what you were reading, or did you realize it all at once?

It was a very gradual process. All this information seemed overwhelming at first. It didn't make sense to me because I hadn't put all the pieces together in my mind yet. But as I got used to it and became more familiar with how it worked, it slowly made more and more sense. The moment I realized that the information in these documents was attached to real people, from real places in the real world, was a powerful moment – and emotionally quite overwhelming.

For example, while in Iraq I came to figure out the details of a national crackdown on people who disagreed with the Iraqi prime minister at the time. The government sent police to arrest, torture and even kill people who were merely expressing a different opinion.

Describe how you felt as you came to decide what you had to do.

I felt afraid. I felt completely overwhelmed. It was a lot for me to try and figure out. It was a very lonely place to be. There was a lot at stake, for me personally and for everyone around me. When it comes to hard situations, sometimes there isn't anyone there to tell you the right or wrong answer. You might not have a lot of time to make a decision. In situations like this you have to follow your instinct. I felt I had to make a decision within a couple of months. It's a very humbling feeling – I felt very small and powerless for a lot of this time. But I still had a decision to make, and I wondered how I might feel ten or twenty years from that time if I didn't do anything. I made my decisions based on that feeling.

What did you hope would be the outcome of making this information public?

I was hoping there could be a more informed public debate on America's foreign policy. The public in America did not understand what was actually happening in the world around it, and without information they couldn't contribute to how its government and military were operating.

I was hoping that such a debate could lead to reforms on government secrecy, and on the conduct of the American government abroad. But mostly I was hoping to promote more of an understanding about the kind of wars we were having in Iraq and Afghanistan. Wars between militaries and insurgencies are very, very messy. A lot of innocent people get detained, threatened, displaced or killed – by both sides. The portrayal of this kind of war in America was becoming glorified and heroic – which was very, very far from the reality.

Why do governments keep information secret? Why is the fact that they do so regarded as an even more dangerous secret?

Governments are supposed to keep information secret to protect people – most often their citizens. But often governments use secrecy as a means of protecting themselves.

Using government secrecy policies to cover *anything* and *everything* is a common habit for governments, and it is important for the public to counter and combat this whenever they can. I believe it's the job of normal citizens to stay vigilant, because governments often hide things – and won't come clean unless they believe it benefits them.

Tell us how the words of former US president James Madison resonate with your experiences.

When I was a teenager, I read *The Federalist Papers*. James Madison wrote most of these articles, back in the late 1700s when the USA was just starting out as a nation. He talked a lot about checks and balances in government and outside of it. He talked about the separation of powers between the courts, the lawmakers and the policy-makers, as well as the role of the public and of the press. I thought about this a lot while I was in Iraq. I saw the failure of their government to provide for their citizens and it reminded me a lot of James Madison's powerful logic. The level of secrecy by the military and the government in America also became clear to me. Madison talked about how the accumulation of these powers – legislative, executive and judiciary – in the same hands or in the hands of a few can be dangerous for society. My experience of government has been of this danger becoming a reality.

You are one person, and the military and the government are so powerful. Through all this, have you ever felt afraid?

I am always afraid. I am still afraid of the power of government. A government can arrest you. It can imprison you. It can put out information about you that won't get questioned by the public – everyone will just assume that what they are saying is true. Sometimes, a government can even kill you – with or without the benefit of a trial.

Governments have so much power, and a single person often does not. It is very terrifying to face the government alone.

Can you describe a moment when you have particularly felt this way?

It's a very difficult feeling to describe. Not long after I was first detained by the military, I was taken to a prison camp in Kuwait, where I essentially lived in a cage inside of a tent. I didn't have any access to the outside world. I couldn't make phone calls. I didn't get any mail. I had very limited access to my lawyers. There was no television or radio or newspapers. I lost the sense of where in the world I was. The military had total control over every aspect of my life. They controlled what information I had access to. They controlled when

I ate and slept. They even controlled when I went to the bathroom. After several weeks, I didn't know how long I had been there or how much longer I was going to be staying. It's an overwhelmingly terrifying feeling. I became very, very sad. At one point, I even gave up on trying to live any more.

Do you hope good will still come from your actions? What might this look like?

This is a very difficult question to answer. I don't know. I don't even want to try and work it out. I am hopeful that people can gain more of an understanding of how the world operates. Across the world, governments can easily become centred on themselves and their interests, at the expense of their people.

I am also hopeful that, perhaps, the next time a democratic government thinks about committing military forces to the occupation of a country which is likely to lead to an insurgency, we can try and look back, and learn from the last time. War is a terrible thing, and this type of warfare is one of the worst. I hope that we can avoid getting excited about this kind of thing in the future.

You had some bad times in detention, particularly before your case went to trial. What is it like for you in prison now?

I try to stay as active and productive as possible. I don't have access to the internet, but I read books and newspapers a lot. I work hard at the job that I have in prison – work with wood. I am also always trying to learn more, working on my education. I also exercise a lot. I run all the time! I do cardio exercises to stay in shape. I write a lot, too.

What helps you to stay positive in prison?

I love reading the mail that I get from all over the world. I love talking on the phone with people I care about. I always feel so much better when people send me their warm love and strong words of support. I love staying active and engaged with the world. It is an amazing feeling!

Thank you so very much for taking the time to interview me. I appreciate you offering to hear my answers.

Why This Book Is Important

Amnesty International is the world's largest human rights organization, and together with eight million supporters worldwide, we stand up for human rights, believing that everyone has the power to change the world for the better. We seek to protect people wherever justice, fairness, freedom and truth are denied. Human rights belong to all of us, no matter who we are or where we live.

This book is inspired by the fact that human rights can be denied or abused even in countries like the UK or the USA, and we need to defend them constantly. Stories and poetry are a wonderful way of making us think, helping us understand the world and other people. More than that, they can inspire our empathy — which we need if we're to overcome prejudice.

In the Western world many of us take our human rights for granted. But our rights are as much part of our proud heritage as our books, music, art and ancient monuments, and they need defending. They are part of our ever-evolving culture and have been crucial to our development beyond the violence and oppression of the Middle Ages.

At the end of WWII, the European Declaration of Human Rights set out a list of basic protections to prevent the horrors of that war from happening again. They were meant to be enduring and timeless, but even now some politicians threaten to take them away.

Human rights come about only through long, hard battles (e.g. "Deeds not Words", on page 263, shows the struggle of the suffragettes to gain equal rights for women). There are always individuals, corporations and governments who think they would be better off if we enjoyed fewer rights. Discrimination and bullying happens at home, in schools and in the workplace and it's all too easy for some rights to be cast aside. Writers and artists are often the first to be thrown into prison by dictatorial regimes, probably because those leaders are afraid of the power of stories and pictures to provoke new ideas and inspire action.

Most of the content of *Here I Stand* is fiction, but it is rooted in truth. Frances Hardinge's story about the child accused of being a witch is inspired by the case of Kevani Kanda, who was similarly tortured by her family and church minister and grew up to become a campaigner for children suffering abuse of this kind. Ryan Gattis's story, "Redemption", came about after his real-life correspondence with a man on death row. Jackie Kay wrote her three poems after talking to refugees in Scotland.

We hope that at least one of the contributions to this anthology talks directly to you. We hope you'll feel inspired to stand up and make a difference in your community, school or the wider world. Peaceful protest is, after all, your right.

Nicky Parker, Amnesty International UK

Take Action for Chelsea Manning and Others at Risk

Every day, Amnesty supporters send messages of hope to individuals at risk, as well as appeals to authorities. It works. All these actions can help free a prisoner, stop an execution or help a bereaved family receive justice.

Since Amnesty was founded, in 1961, it has sent millions of letters, emails and faxes. Chelsea Manning is just one of the recipients. This simple action gives people hope and inspiration, letting them know that they have not been forgotten. It also sends a message to the authorities that people around the world are watching what they do.

You can take action on behalf of individuals whose human rights are being violated. Your support really can change someone's life. Your solidarity can help make the world a better place. For more information, go to:

www.amnesty.org.uk/actions

And do remember that situations change – please check our website for up-to-date information before you take action.

Acknowledgements

Enormous thanks are due to Bindmans LLC in London, especially to Jules Carey and Saimo Chahal, also Tamsin Allen, Gwendolen Morgan, Jamie Potter and Mike Schwarz, who entered into planning this book with such enthusiasm and have been exceptionally generous with their time and advice.

Many of the authors who contributed to this anthology undertook research and sought advice in writing their pieces, and we are very grateful to all who helped them. We thank Daniel Phelps at Carers Trust for his insights into the experience of child carers and also Farhana Yamin Yule for help with the Urdu references in Sita Brahmachari's story; for generously sharing their knowledge of child sex trafficking we thank Rebecca Clarke, Gareth Russell and Philippa Roberts at Hope for Justice; for their invaluable insights about children accused of being witches we are extremely grateful to Kevani Kanda and Ronke Phillips.

We are, as ever, grateful to our wonderful publisher Walker Books, especially Gill Evans and Emma Lidbury for editorial expertise and for caring about human rights.

Finally, our immense gratitude to all the writers and artists who are part of *Here I Stand* and have collectively created such an important book. We at Amnesty cannot thank you enough.

Tony Birch was born in Australia into a large family of Aboriginal, West Indian and Irish descent. His upbringing was challenging, and much of this is captured in his adult debut, the semi-autobiographical *Shadowboxing*. His other novels for adults are *Father's Day*, *Blood*, *The Promise* and *Ghost River*. He is currently a Research Fellow in the Moondani Balluk Academic Unit at Victoria University, Melbourne.

John Boyne is the author of fourteen novels and a collection of short stories. His novel *The Boy in the Striped Pyjamas* has sold more than six million copies worldwide and been made into a feature film. He has won three Irish Book Awards and numerous international literary prizes, and is published in over 45 languages. His most recent book is *The Boy at the Top of the Mountain*.

Sita Brahmachari's creative projects with diverse communities are at the heart of her writing. She has been Writer in Residence for Book Trust and Islington Centre for Refugees and Migrants. Her books for young people include *Artichoke Hearts*, winner of the Waterstone's Children's Book Prize, *Jasmine Skies*, *Red Leaves* and *Kite Spirit*, which was selected by Reading Agency as a Book on Prescription.

Kevin Brooks' first novel, *Martyn Pig*, was published in 2002, and since then he has gone on to publish a further nineteen novels for children and young adults, and a crime fiction trilogy for adults. His books are published worldwide and have won numerous literary prizes, including the Branford Boase Award and the CILIP Carnegie Medal. A feature film is currently being made of his YA novel *iBoy*.

Photo by Nadja Meister

Kate Charlesworth has drawn cartoons, strips and illustrations for many publications, including the *Guardian*, *Independent* and *New Scientist*, and more recently has contributed to graphic novels and collections that include *Nelson: To End All Wars* and *IDP: 2043*. She co-collaborated with Bryan and Mary Talbot on *Sally Heathcote, Suffragette* and is currently working on her own graphic memoir.

Sarah Crossan was an English and drama teacher before writing her first novel, *The Weight of Water*, which was shortlisted for the Carnegie Medal and won the Eilís Dillon and UKLA book awards. Her novel *Apple and Rain* was shortlisted for the Carnegie Medal and the FCBG Children's Book Award and her latest novel, *One*, won the YA Book Prize and is currently shortlisted for the Carnegie Medal.

Neil Gaiman writes books. Some of them are for adults, like *American Gods*, and some of them are comics, like the Sandman series, and some of them have pictures, like *Fortunately, the Milk* or the Chu series. He was awarded the Newbery Medal and the Carnegie Medal for *The Graveyard Book*, the first novel to ever receive both. Most recently, Neil has written *The View from the Cheap Seats*, a collection of non-fiction.

Photo by Kimberly Butler

Jack Gantos is the author of 49 books for children, ranging from picture books to young adult novels, which include *The Love Curse of the Rumbaughs*, *Desire Lines* and *Dead End in Norvelt*. His works have received a Newbery Medal, a Scott O'Dell Award, a Newbery Honor, a Printz Honor and a Sibert Honor, and he has been a US National Book Award Finalist.

Photo by Cheryl Richards

Ryan Gattis is a writer and educator whose most recent book, *All Involved*, is grounded in two and a half years of research with former Latino gang members, firefighters, nurses and other LA citizens who lived through the 1992 LA riots. Translated into eleven languages, it has been called "a high-octane speedball of a read" by the *New York Times* and its film rights have been acquired by HBO.

Photo by Sam Tenney

Matt Haig has written novels for adults and children, including *The Humans* and *A Boy Called Christmas*, as well as the number one bestselling memoir *Reasons to Stay Alive*.

Photo by Clive Doyle

Frances Hardinge started writing her first children's novel, *Fly by Night*, while working for a software company, and it went on to win the Branford Boase Award. She has now written seven books for children and young adults. *Cuckoo Song* won the Robert Holdstock Award and was shortlisted for the Carnegie Medal; *The Lie Tree* won Costa Book of the Year and is currently shortlisted for the Carnegie Medal.

Jackie Kay's critically acclaimed poems and novels for adults have won a variety of awards, and her children's book, *Red, Cherry Red*, won the CLPE Poetry Award. She was awarded an MBE in 2006 for services to literature. She is Chancellor of the University of Salford and Professor of Creative Writing at Newcastle University, and has recently been named Scots Makar – National Poet for Scotland.

A.L. Kennedy is the author of three works of non-fiction and five short story collections, including *All the Rage*. She won Costa Book of the Year for her novel *Day*, has twice been selected as one of Granta's Best of Young British Novelists and is a Fellow of the Royal Society of Literature. She is also a dramatist and broadcaster and has a regular blog with *Guardian* online.

Liz Kessler worked as a teacher and journalist before writing full time, and has since written sixteen novels for children and young adults. Her Emily Windsnap books have sold over four million copies worldwide, appeared on the *New York Times* Bestsellers list and been translated into 25 languages. Her first young adult novel, *Read Me Like a Book*, features a teenage girl coming out as gay.

Elizabeth Laird was born in New Zealand to Scottish parents. She has since lived in Ethiopia, Malaysia, Iraq, Lebanon and Austria, and is now resident in Britain. Elizabeth's work has been widely translated and won many awards, and she been shortlisted six times for the Carnegie Medal. Some of her children's novels are set in Britain, while others tackle modern issues in the Middle East and Africa.

Amy Leon is an actor, poet, singer and Harlem native. She fuses music and poetry through powerfully transparent performances, focusing on social inequalities while simultaneously celebrating love, blackness and what it is to be a woman.

Sabrina Mahfouz has been a Sky Academy Arts Scholar for poetry and a poet in residence for Cape Farewell and is currently writing plays, librettos and for TV. Her creative work has attracted a number of awards, including an Old Vic New Voices Underbelly Edinburgh Award and a Westminster Prize for New Playwrights. Sabrina has published a book of poems and plays entitled *The Clean Collection*.

Photo by Naomi Woddis

Chelsea Manning is an American soldier and whistleblower. She is serving a 35-year sentence in military prison for leaking classified US government documents to the WikiLeaks website, publicly revealing that the US Army, the CIA and Iraqi and Afghan forces committed human rights violations. Amnesty International is campaigning for her release.

Image by Billie Jean/agencyrush.com

Born in 1991 in Lagos, Nigeria, **Chibundu Onuzo** started writing novels and short stories at the age of ten, and less than a decade later became the youngest woman ever to be signed by Faber and Faber. Her debut novel, *The Spider King's Daughter*, won a Betty Trask Award and was shortlisted for the Commonwealth Prize. Her second novel, *Welcome to Lagos*, will be out in 2017.

Photo by stylingmile

Bali Rai is the multi-award-winning author of over 30 young adult, teen and children's books. His writing pushes boundaries and has made him extremely popular on the school events circuit across the world, and two of his books are recommended reads for KS3 and GCSE. He wrote his first novel, *(un)arranged marriage*, while managing a city centre bar in his native Leicester.

Chris Riddell has collaborated with a number of authors, including Paul Stewart, Neil Gaiman and Michael Rosen, and won many illustration awards, including the Kate Greenaway Medal (twice). He wrote and illustrated the highly acclaimed Ottoline titles and the award-winning *Goth Girl*, and in 2015 he was appointed Children's Laureate in recognition of his outstanding achievements in children's books.

Dr Mary Talbot is an internationally acclaimed scholar of gender and language who now writes graphic novels. Her first, *Dotter of Her Father's Eyes* (with Bryan Talbot), won the 2012 Costa Biography Award. Her second, *Sally Heathcote, Suffragette*, came out in 2014 and her third, *The Red Virgin and the Vision of Utopia*, was published in 2016.

Bryan Talbot has written and drawn comics and graphic novels for over 30 years, including *Judge Dredd, Batman, Sandman, The Adventures of Luther Arkwright, The Tale of One Bad Rat, Heart of Empire, Alice in Sunderland, Dotter of Her Father's Eyes* (written by Mary Talbot) and his current series of steampunk detective thrillers, *Grandville*.

Christie Watson won the Costa First Novel Award for *Tiny Sunbirds Far Away*, which, along with her second novel, *Where Women Are Kings*, was widely translated and received international critical acclaim. She is currently working on a novel for young adults about a future with no NHS.

Tim Wynne-Jones is the author of numerous YA novels, most recently *The Emperor of Any Place*. He also wrote *Blink & Caution*, winner of a Boston Globe–Horn Book Award and the Arthur Ellis Award; and *The Uninvited*, shortlisted for the Arthur Ellis Award. In 2012 he was named an Officer of the Order of Canada for his services to literature.

Stand Up for Human Rights

Every one of us can make a difference by standing up for ourselves and others. If you're under 18, live in the UK and are keen to take action on human rights, you can find out how to join our network of Amnesty youth groups — or how to start a youth group — at www.amnesty.org.uk/youth

If you are a teacher, take a look at Amnesty's many free resources for schools, including our "Using Fiction to Teach About Human Rights" classroom notes on *Here I Stand* and other novels, at www.amnesty.org.uk/education

Amnesty International UK, The Human Rights Action Centre, 17–15 New Inn Yard, London EC2A 3EA
Tel: 020 7033 1500; Email: hre@amnesty.org.uk
www.amnesty.org.uk

Wherever you are in the world, you can stand up for human rights:

Amnesty International Australia (www.amnesty.org.au)
Amnesty International New Zealand (www.amnesty.org.nz)

BELIEFS

EQUALITY

FGM   REFUGEES

VOTING

CRIMINALIZATION

ABUSE

CHILDHOOD

SLAVERY

SURVEILLANCE